SEPARATED AT DEATH

Berkley Prime Crime Titles by Sheldon Rusch

FOR EDGAR

THE BOY WITH PERFECT HANDS

SEPARATED AT DEATH

SEPARATED AT
DEATH

SHELDON RUSCH

BERKLEY PRIME CRIME, NEW YORK

THE BERKLEY PUBLISHING GROUP
Published by the Penguin Group
Penguin Group (USA) Inc.
375 Hudson Street, New York, New York 10014, USA
Penguin Group (Canada), 90 Eglinton Avenue East, Suite 700, Toronto, Ontario M4P 2Y3, Canada
(a division of Pearson Penguin Canada Inc.)
Penguin Books Ltd., 80 Strand, London WC2R 0RL, England
Penguin Group Ireland, 25 St. Stephen's Green, Dublin 2, Ireland (a division of Penguin Books Ltd.)
Penguin Group (Australia), 250 Camberwell Road, Camberwell, Victoria 3124, Australia
(a division of Pearson Australia Group Pty. Ltd.)
Penguin Books India Pvt. Ltd., 11 Community Centre, Panchsheel Park, New Delhi—110 017, India
Penguin Group (NZ), 67 Apollo Drive, Rosedale, North Shore 0632, New Zealand
(a division of Pearson New Zealand Ltd.)
Penguin Books (South Africa) (Pty.) Ltd., 24 Sturdee Avenue, Rosebank, Johannesburg 2196, South Africa

Penguin Books Ltd., Registered Offices: 80 Strand, London WC2R 0RL, England

This book is an original publication of The Berkley Publishing Group.

First edition: April 2008

Library of Congress Cataloging-in-Publication Data

Rusch, Sheldon.
    Separated at death / Sheldon Rusch.—1st. ed.
      p. cm.
    ISBN 978-0-425-21948-5 (alk. paper)
  1. Hewitt, Elizabeth Taylor (Fictitious character)—Fiction. 2. Policewomen—Illinois—Fiction. 3. Separated people—Crimes against—Fiction. 4. Beheading—Fiction. 5. Serial murder investigation—Fiction. 6. Job shadowing—Fiction.
I. Title.
    PS3618.U74S47 2008
      813'.6—dc22   2007047255

PRINTED IN THE UNITED STATES OF AMERICA

10 9 8 7 6 5 4 3 2 1

ACKNOWLEDGMENTS

In writing this novel and others, I have had the wonderful support, understanding and love of my wife, Katie, and our three children, Shannon, Michaela and Jackson. Writers are not the easiest people in the world to live with, especially when they're writing. Thank you for sharing your worlds and your dreams with me, and for helping me to find mine. My great respect and appreciation to my agent, Paula Balzer; my editor, Tom Colgan; the keeper of the flame, Sandra Harding; and my many teachers, benefactors, saints and gurus. At the top of that sublime list are my mother and father; my sister, Jodi; and my brother, Todd, without whose love and encouragement I would never have had the vision and courage to do some of my best dreaming while wide awake. Deepest thanks also to Catherine Ross, Ashok Bedi, Diane Rusch, and John and Jean Schloegel for your generous guidance and support.

SEPARATED AT DEATH

1

IT was funny how such a small change to one of your hands could keep waking you up at night. She knew, of course, that her physical body wasn't the only part of her that had been altered. Her mind and her soul had also come along for the ride. Which meant pretty much every aspect of Elizabeth Taylor Hewitt's being was focused on the massive presence of an object that was, in reality, ridiculously small.

It wasn't ridiculously small to Brady Stephen Richter. Two months of a detective's income—probably more, judging from the physical evidence— were a big hairy deal on the side of the gender fence where Brady's palomino played.

It was all quiet in the corral now. Except for the horse's deep, secure, happily-ever-after snoring. It was a hell of a lot easier for him, though. His hand wasn't the one trying to find a way to assimilate the Rock of Gibraltar.

Hewitt was lying on her back, in textbook ceiling-stare mode. From shoulders down, the rest of her body remained corpse-still as her neck and head rolled to the clock-radio.

Three o'clock. On the freaking nose. She could hear the little town crier inside her head making the announcement to the village of Hewitt-Richter.

"Three o'clock and all's well."

Well, all was well if you were lying on your belly, dead to the world.

If you were on your back with a picture-perfect view of the middle-of-the-night ceiling, maybe the assessment wasn't quite so simple.

He snored less on his belly. Fifty, sixty percent less. That was one good thing. At three o'clock in the morning, you looked for affirmations wherever you could find them.

Hewitt's hand was looking for one now. Crawling spider-like up the side of Brady's naked hip. She was in the small of his back now, where she paused. Her mind paused too. Rewinding to her first-ever visual encounter with his new back. The lower part. The sections of skin beneath his kidneys that hosted the exit wound scars. The skin was healed. Or as healed as it was going to get. But the nerves that served the skin were still numb, confused, wondering what the hell they had done to deserve that.

This wouldn't be the first time her fingers deliberately visited the scar tissue, to touch it, to stimulate it, to see what would happen.

The first encounter had been purely incidental. An old habit. More involuntary than learned. Although once she assessed the degree to which his reaction would make her world a more interesting place, she was all over it. Discretely, delicately, all over it.

She discovered it the first time they had sex after the healing process. The phenomenon that if she gently touched the widest swath of the scar tissue while they were in full boink mode, it would stimulate a nervous system chain reaction that would cause his pelvis, his low back, his hips to do a quick little something between a shiver and shimmy. The kinetic effect of it went all the way to the lead singer in her psychosexual opera, the end result of which was a pushed-up volume, a higher pitch from the temperamental soprano.

Her left index finger was right at the edge of the scars now. But instead of touching it with the tip of that finger, she let her ring finger lift over the area and lower itself slowly, stopping short of allowing her skin to make contact, but coming close enough that the coolness of the underside of the ring touched down in the *Sea of Healing*. Instant shiver. Instant shimmy.

"Cut it out, Hewitt."

His voice rubbery with sleep. A sleep that resumed immediately.

She smiled her own rubbery, outskirts-of-sleep smile. Her little adventure in alchemy had yielded one very important finding. And she knew she would have to conduct the experiment again—multiple times—to confirm the results.

As her investigational hand left him and slithered down the side of him to rest against the fitted sheet, she wondered if, as her husband, he might finally get around to calling her, at least once in a while, by her first name.

2

SHE is wearing a chastity belt. She has never worn such a ridiculous thing before. But in this setting, in this place, the experience has come to her. As if she is meant to wear it. As if she deserves to wear it.

She is alone in this place, surrounded by flowing curtains. Maybe ten feet away. Maybe twenty. The white light of the space seems to be oscillating between reaching, touching the curtains and falling back into darkness. A darkness incomplete, as if it holds a pocket of light from which some being, some entity will emerge. Maybe to explain to her the chastity belt. Maybe to remove it.

There is no waver in the illumination now. And she looks down, sees the bizarre contraption that houses her private self. Especially, she sees the keyhole on the front locking piece. And seeing it, she feels, instantly, the key in her right hand.

The key, warm in her palm. As if she has been holding it for some time. As if she has been holding it all along.

And she understands now. It is not someone else who will be coming to free her from the chastity belt. It is her decision whether or not to free herself. But not simply that. Because it is also a decision of how she will present herself to the being that will come from the other side of the curtain to learn what decision she has made.

*   *   *

THE sound of the key entering the lock startles her. Not enough to deliver her fully from the bonds of sleep. But her mind begins to disengage from the dream. She feels her right hand resting against the soft pad of her pubic hair, feels the wetness of the tips of her middle and index fingers.

Awake. All of her now. Sitting up at the sound of movement in the house. Movement in the front hallway.

"Shit."

She hears the word flutter desperately around the room, like a moth caught between a window and a screen. She should have changed the locks. But she never thought he would actually show up in the middle of the damn night. Either drunk. Or lost. Or hopeless. Or all of it.

He had never been a *honey, I'm home* kind of person. He was more the slip inside the house unannounced. Then slip inside a tumbler with his Jameson's and crushed ice. The smell of that—of the double-digit hours since his last shower and the double Irish whiskeys on his breath—wasn't something she missed.

He was in the hall, approaching the bedroom now. She dried the tips of her fingers against the sheet.

Even though her only child was in her first year of college at Iowa State—and traveling in Europe with a couple of girlfriends at the end of summer—she was still in the habit of leaving the bedroom door mostly closed, but cracked just enough to say: *Honey, if you really can't sleep, come on in and we'll whisper about it in the dark like we used to.*

It was in this crack of mother-daughter compromise that her husband manifested. Stopping there. Standing there. As if he was either finally realizing he wasn't in the right house, or if he was aware of where he was, maybe it wasn't such a good idea now that he was here.

"If you come in, I'm going to report it to the court," she heard her nighttime voice say.

God, she sounded bitchy. But bitch, queen-sized, was the only thing he understood anymore.

She waited.

For once—for one freaking once—there was no argument. And at that, she almost felt like sticking her fingers back down there to celebrate. But *touch* wasn't the sense that had gone on full alert. Strange as it was that her estranged husband hadn't spit out a profanity-spiced argument, odder still was the fact he wasn't giving off his usual late-night potpourri.

Because even if he had found it within himself to shower within the last few hours, by now the Irish whiskey should have made its way to the bed.

3

SPANGLER'S call sucked Hewitt's brain from sleep, slowly and not without some serious resistance.

Somewhere around four o'clock, she had finally let go of the *till death do you part* clause and had proceeded to die a little herself, her tumble into sleep having been that bottomless.

Her eyes caught the clock as she picked up the phone. 8:14. Which meant she was fourteen minutes late for work. But being a Friday with nothing terribly pressing on her calendar, and her spanking new fiancé lying in bed next to her, she was merely fourteen minutes late in cashing in one of her official State of Illinois sick days.

"Where are you?"

No salutation. Just the question. In his serious business tone.

"Under the covers with the man I just agreed to marry."

In a perfect world, the perfect comeback. But it was too early to tell if the world was anywhere close to perfect that morning. Or if it was ready for that outrageous news.

"I'm using a sick day," Hewitt offered. "Sorry I'm late calling it in."

"I'm sorry too," Spangler said. "Because you're going to have one very disappointed person sitting in your office."

It hit Hewitt with the instant regret and guilt of a forgotten anniversary.

"I have to admire your quick recovery," Spangler said after she informed him she would be coming in after all.

"I've always been a fast healer," Hewitt countered, her recognition of the bullshit of that, on the psychological side, as instant as the breakfast she would be making. Now the guy lying next to her, still half asleep, *that* was healing. A willingness not only to take one in the gut for her all those months ago but to leave his back exposed now.

She signed off with Spangler.

"You're not going in, are you?" Brady managed in his weekend sleep-in voice—which was what it was, with Friday being his Sunday, schedule-wise.

"When Ed Spangler came back from his heart surgery and managed to slow-dance Ritchie Lattimore into the Division of Administration, I made a deal with myself to pretty much do anything the man ever asked of me again. Today he's cashing in a few of his chips."

JEN Spangler looked less like someone who was there to job-shadow a member of the department than to replace them. That was Hewitt's take as she paused at her own office door to observe the young woman who had come to observe *her*.

She was used to seeing Jen in jeans and hoody sweatshirts, looking generally frazzled as she tried to balance life as a single mom and life as an undergrad in Criminal Justice at UIC. This look today, the black pantsuit with crème-colored top and a pair of absolutely ass-kicking heels—black with a piss and vinegar veneer—this was going to take some getting used to. And the messenger bag—the Louis Vuitton knockoff—that really sealed the deal. Assuming it was a knockoff. It had to be. Unless, in addition to raising her kid, living with her dad and going to crime school, Jen was turning tricks on the side. She wouldn't have been the first former choir girl to make the transition. And with those heels, you could almost make the leap.

"I'm sorry I'm late," Hewitt offered as she did her best breeze-in, imparting her first lesson—that for a woman in this business, it was okay to apologize with your words but never with your body.

"Not a problem," Jen Spangler responded, telling her also, nonverbally, that she had already learned one important piece of protocol from her father. That it was okay to accept a half-assed apology with your words but not your eyes.

Jen stood up as Hewitt circled the desk, waited until Hewitt sat down before she reclaimed the visitor's chair.

"Well, is there anything you'd like to ask me up front?"

Jen was wearing her game face. She'd spent considerable time in front of the mirror putting it on.

"I'm just here to be here. To observe what I can. To do my best not to get in your way. And unless requested otherwise, to keep quiet."

Hewitt saw that Jen's eyes had made their initial sighting of the new topography of her left hand. She gave Jen a muted smile.

"I don't expect you to keep quiet about that."

"Holy shit."

"Those weren't my first words," Hewitt said. "But that was pretty much my first thought too."

"The detective?"

Hewitt nodded, a little uneasy with it.

"The one from Wilmette?"

Hewitt nodded again, read the way her observer was eyeing the stone.

"Did you pick it out together?"

"No. He had the honor himself."

"Wow. He did great then," Jen said, a sparkle of envy in her eyes. "I mean he did his homework. Or did you coach him in the four Cs and all that?"

"The four Cs?"

By getting tripped up on this thing she had some vague recollection of but couldn't quite pull up on the radar screen, Hewitt knew she'd given away some power.

"You really are an antibride," Jen said, confirming the drainage. She then offered a helpful but not totally sweet tutorial on the four Cs.

Carat, clarity, color, cut—the alliterative evaluation system the diamond industry had fostered for the edification of apparently every potential bride on the planet but Elizabeth Taylor Hewitt.

"So what's your assessment?" Hewitt asked when Jen took a breath. "Money-wise?"

"No. Just based on the aesthetics of the four Cs."

Jen pushed her face in for a closer look, pushed some of her a-little-too-intense Chanel into Hewitt's sinuses.

"Well, it's a solitaire with a princess cut. Looks like at least a full carat. It's as clear as you'd ever want. Not even a hint of color."

There was a wistfulness, almost a mournfulness at the end of her evaluation. And Hewitt knew with four-Cs-clarity why. You didn't study up on diamond engagement rings like she'd obviously done unless you coveted one. Unless you coveted a life that included, with you and your two-year-old-daughter, a man who had at least tendered the damn offer.

"Wilmette must be treating him pretty well," Jen added.

"In every other aspect of his financial life, he's the cheapest guy on the planet."

Jen's game face makeup was still intact, but her girl-to-girl interest in Hewitt's news had siphoned some of the intensity from her face.

"And he's okay? From the . . ."

Mentor time. Protocol 137. How to speak delicately about the critical wounding of a colleague. Especially when the colleague was your future husband and the bullet had originally sailed past you.

"From the hot one he took in his pasta station?"

Jen's body and head did a hiccup-startle.

"Those wouldn't have been my words. But yeah."

"He's fine," Hewitt told her. "The penis nerve wasn't hit."

Whoever had stepped into her peripheral vision just outside the door had heard every word of that. As decorum would have it, it was her job-shadow's father. And from the look on his face, the appropriateness of her remark and the shiny new thing on her finger were the furthest things from his mind.

4

THEY met behind closed doors in Spangler's office for about five minutes, during which Hewitt was able to make out fragments of their communication from her strategic position in the hallway. But the words all kind of ran together, and it was more like a dog listening to the pitch and volume of the voices of its human family to know whether life was rosy, shitty or somewhere in between.

For Ed and Jen Spangler, it was in between. Because Dad was skewing shitty and daughter was doing her best to make the world—the sick killing world—smell better than it had any right to.

To Hewitt, a father-daughter conflict like this had been an inevitability since the day Jen had announced her intention to transfer from the Psychology Department to Criminal Justice at UIC. To Hewitt, that move had seemed inevitable too. While Captain Spangler had put out an initial vibe of being surprised by the decision, Hewitt knew better. The ingredients were all there for a criminology career stew. You had the father, already a prestigious player in the field. You had a sister figure—an older sister figure—with whom you were competing, consciously or not, for your father's attention. And you had the big wooden spoon that stirred the whole thing. The fact that the father had already undergone two serious heart procedures. So his ability to give attention—to decide who deserved the attention—was something that wouldn't be there forever, was something that could be taken off the table at any time.

And, of course, relative to all that, was the other reason—the most compelling of all. *The Grand Fuck-Up*. Not that any reasonably well-raised human being could look at Jen's beautiful, two-year-old daughter and hang any such label on the circumstances of her birth and Jen's best single-mom attempts to take care of her. But if anything in the Spangler family was up for review—and a make-good—it was that.

A quiet armistice of no more than thirty seconds ensued before the door swung open and Jen Spangler stepped into the second most interesting day of her life—assuming the day she gave birth would hold on to first. Not that it would ever be a justifiable comparison. Not that the fluid-drenched birth of a baby could ever be whispered about in the same hall of confession as the fluid-drenched death that had whipped up the inner office controversy.

"Take her along," Ed Spangler said with icy resignation. "Let her see."

At that, Jen Spangler found Hewitt's eyes, conveyed a small but bawdy pride over her victory. Hewitt didn't acknowledge it. She knew too well the hollowness of such a win. And she wasn't exactly happy about having to drag a college student with her through the first phase of the investigation, virtual family member or not.

TO her credit, Jen Spangler didn't puke. She didn't double up in dry heaves. She didn't so much as gasp. But what she couldn't control for public consumption was the draining of blood from the surface of her skin. Most notably, her face.

It was as if the outrageous volume of spilled blood in the master bedroom of the Naperville Cape Cod—almost all of it contained by the bed—was scaring Jen's own blood into hiding. That and the female body that had been left there, lying on its back, but no longer with the option of staring at the ceiling. Even with dead eyes.

"Still no head."

As reports went, it was as succinct as they came. Hewitt turned to the Naperville PD detective who, upon their arrival, had been the first to inform them that the head of the victim hadn't been located anywhere on the premises to that point. This was his follow-up. And Hewitt knew it wasn't made for the purpose of their edification only. The other motive, the prevailing motive, was to get another close-up sniff of the attractive lady cop.

The way he was staring at her made Hewitt decide to intervene. Or to backtrack to what would have been a preemptive strike.

"I should have introduced you when we came in," Hewitt said, eyes to her student shadow. She shifted her look to the detective, all the sandy-haired, azure-eyed, six feet, one-hundred-seventy pounds and less-than-thirty years of him. "This is Jen Spangler. Captain Ed Spangler's daughter. She's a student in the Criminal Justice Department at UIC."

"I'm job shadowing," Jen volunteered, telling Hewitt, with a dip of her eyelids, that she could handle Detective Testosterone just fine herself.

"You picked a hell of a day for it," the detective advised.

"I'll be all right," Jen advised back.

The detective waited for more. When he saw it wasn't coming, he evanesced into the buzz of the crime scene, like cigarette smoke into a smoke-eating fan.

"They won't find it," Hewitt told Jen. "Not anywhere near here. If someone went to all the work of separating the head from the body, they did it with some bigger purpose in mind."

"Any thoughts?" Jen asked, pulling back with her shoulders as she realized she was crossing the acceptable boundary of Q&A—a gesture Hewitt knew had been conditioned through the years with her father. Hewitt gave her a nod—a *go ahead and take the last dinner roll* nod.

"That's where we earn the money," Hewitt said, with an amalgam of smile-grimace. "Trying to get inside that. Trying to get some sneak peek into why a human mind would even imagine something like that, much less act it out."

Jen Spangler raised her hand to her face, took a strand of her long, straight, coffee-brown hair. For assurance. A move Hewitt read as vestigial, infantile. *Holding Mommy's hair while sucking?*

"The blood," Jen said with a shudder in her breath. "It's hard to believe it could all come from one person."

5

THE headless soul had once been a living, breathing being known as Rita Vandermause. Among the other skills she may have cultivated in her life, decorating was one of them. Interior and, as Hewitt was now aware, exterior.

In a pool of sunshine that might have actually been more voluminous than the blood in the bed, Hewitt and Rita Vandermause's next-door neighbor and almost-close friend, Megan Fitch, sat at a white, wrought iron patio table in the two matching chairs that were two chairs short of a set.

"I've never sat here before," Megan Fitch volunteered, with a numb face and eyes that looked as if they had just been returned from a hypnotist. "She would sit here with girlfriends. One on one. It was always just two of them. But me—she never invited me to sit."

Jen Spangler had pulled up a padded deck chair. Not all the way up to the table. Leaving just a few feet—her observer's distance.

"She would sit here with Joe too. Sometimes for coffee. A drink. Not real often. Lately, not at all."

"How long ago did her husband move out?"

"Almost four months. It was sad. Just not what anyone ever wants to see."

"Did Joe Vandermause ever exhibit any violent behavior—physical, verbal?"

"Toward Rita?"

Hewitt nodded her head in a leading, coaxing way.

"Everyone argues. I mean Joe hated to lose—at, you know, games, sports. I know he kicked in the TV one Sunday when the Bears lost to Green Bay. That was the worst I ever heard about. You can't be thinking Joe did this."

"Right now I have to think anyone could have done this," Hewitt responded. Then, to herself: *Especially someone who really, really hated to lose.*

"HOW long do you think she'll sit there?"

Hewitt's mind had been tracking Art Tatum's right hand as she drove. On the stereo, Tatum was playing a two-handed piano version of "Love for Sale" half a century ago. As much as Hewitt had studied the art of jazz, she could still only track Art Tatum one hand at a time. And right now she wasn't all that happy to take her focus off Mr. Tatum and retrain it on the image of the neighbor they'd left sitting alone on Rita Vandermause's patio.

"Who knows?" she said against a jailbreak of piano notes. "People stare out the window long enough at something they covet, who the hell knows?"

Jesus. Not exactly the sweetest thing she could've said. Ah, hell. She was getting married. She'd have plenty of time to sweeten up, to dress in white and work her way to the top of the cake.

Less than twenty minutes later, the Mazda 6 pulled up in front of a cute—*old lady cute*—bungalow in Bensenville. Technically, it was the house that belonged to Joe Vandermause's mother. The octogenarian was in *managed care* now. Megan Fitch had referred to it as that. After living in an apartment for a couple of months after the separation, Joe Vandermause had moved into the bungalow when his mother and her dementia had moved out.

"I'm afraid I can't take you in," Hewitt told her shadow.

"Understandable," Jen Spangler said. "I'll wait."

"Want me to leave the music on?"

"That's okay. I like piano. But not quite so many notes."

Hewitt took the humor of that with her up the driveway until she hit the stone walk that led to the front door. Then the adrenaline spigot opened. At the sound of the doorbell, she reached inside her summer blazer to nudge her service revolver.

A second ring of the bell. A second no-answer. Two rounds of fist-to-door with no response either. Hewitt tried the old-lady-cute door-knob, felt her adrenals open up some more when it moved, when it turned all the way, when she shouldered the door open.

She swept the house in textbook procedure, regretting a little that Jen couldn't be there for that. The house was clear.

Though it was a cute old lady's house, it had definitely taken on the smell and the decorating mutation of a forty-five-year-old man. A forty-five-year-old man whose mother, through no conscious thought of her own, had abandoned him. A forty-five-year-old man with a marriage that had disintegrated and an almost ex-wife who, at least according to a window-watching neighbor, had recently started seeing someone. A forty-five-year-old man who, in a Greek epic version of his life, would have been known as *Joseph, Destroyer of Televisions*.

If Joe Vandermause had taken out his abandonment anger—all of it: mother, wife—hell, maybe even Walter Payton—then he obviously wasn't coming back to the most obvious place the law would come to look for him. He wasn't going to go *Rear Window* and bury his wife's missing part in some flower bed for the neighbor's dog to dig up.

There was more to do in the house, but she calculated it would be okay for Jen to join her. So she went outside, invited her job-shadow in.

There was an antique writing desk in the second bedroom, which had now become more of a den with a bed. Joe Vandermause had left the first bedroom—his mother's—intact. But he had definitely spent a lot of time in the second room. At the writing desk. Hewitt needed to spend some time there now.

Jen followed her to the room, lingered at the door as Hewitt began to poke around the desk. Moments after Hewitt discovered the travel reservation for a trip to Cancun, she realized that Jen had moved off somewhere into the residence. But the airline reservation, the date, the destination of that place in the sun were Hewitt's immediate focus, not the shadow that was loose in the house.

While Hewitt tried to deconstruct the thought process behind the Mexican getaway, Jen Spangler was making her way to the kitchen. Jen noticed the coffeemaker, a white Krups autodrip that had been used daily but hadn't been cleaned even monthly, if at all. An old lady wouldn't have done that. *Useless information.* They were looking for Mr. Decapitator, not Mr. Coffee.

There were plants on a low shelf in front of the windows that exposed the backyard. Plants that were still alive, but losing their will to live. Jen thought of watering them. But that would be disturbing the crime scene. But this wasn't a crime scene. Was it?

Her thoughts went outside the house. As she approached the back window, her eyes were instantly drawn to the pretty flower garden, a storybook English garden, that rose up just beyond the flagstone path. Her eyes tele-zoomed to the bone-colored surface of the stones, made whiter still by the hard sunlight.

The dark red spots began to occur on the fifth or sixth stone her eyes engaged. And that, of course, engaged all the blood in her heart. She should tell Hewitt. But that thought never made it out of the kitchen.

Hewitt had probably heard her as she exited through the back door, even though she'd done it with minimal noise. Jen told herself this as she descended the back steps, her eyes making contact with the red spots on the flagstone. Hewitt would come outside and find the red marks too. But she had found them first. And she would be the first one to find whatever there was at the end of the stone path that led her now into the exploding colors of the English garden.

He had buried it here. She was certain of that much. But she wanted to find the site, the little patch of disturbed ground. Ahead of her, the path veered into an open space in the middle of the garden. But that was okay. The blood continued to show the way. To draw her forward as she made the little turn. As her eyes startled upon the shoes, the legs of a man.

6

THE digital camera flashes and clicks and captures the image of the groom. There is no need for a second shot. So the photographer moves to his next subject. With the bride already in her position on the pedestal, this requires only a minimum of movement. The digital camera preserves this image for posterity as well. Again, a single shot.

Frozen in time.

It was the idiom often used to describe one of the functions, one of the benefits, of photography. But was it really a benefit to be frozen in time?

The bride and groom were certainly preserved in such a way now. It would be just that. The frozen moment. The frozen intention. The frozen betrothal.

The tea kettle is beginning to bubble. *Silly.* His thought, the composite of a boiling tea kettle and a frozen moment in time.

The physics, the micro-machinations of the universe, cooperating, conspiring to create one tiny bubble. Only to have that bubble exist for a blink of an eye before it burst and was reassigned, reabsorbed by the universe, by God's next inhalation. And all around that one bubble, the same universal drama creating and destroying, creating and destroying. Each one in its tiny, temporary bubble of existence, a frozen moment. So that if a person utterly ignorant of the process were to look at a photograph of any one of the bubbles, the transparent sphere would assume a solidity, a permanence as luxurious as any planet that circled a smiling sun.

A frozen moment, in a boiling kettle.

Silly, silly, silly.

So silly, too, the looks on the faces of the bride and groom. Those looks, frozen solid inside the screaming cauldron. So that someone utterly unfamiliar with physics and human psychology would be compelled to believe they, too, would orbit their smiling sun in such a fixed and wondrous state.

The tea kettle whistles with the collective screams of a billion bubbles all disappearing, in one great inhalation, into the lungs of God.

7

HEWITT had never heard her name screamed at that pitch before. Not that it hadn't been totally warranted. A discovery like that had a way of raising the pitch of everything in a human body.

On her run to the backyard, Hewitt's jangling eyes had spotted the dried blood on the stone path. She knew Jen had taken the same tour moments earlier. Time had done little to evaporate the blood that had flowed onto the white stones from the neck of the male body lying between the bee balm and the irises.

The passing of recent moments, however, had diminished the garden's other spilled liquid.

By the time the first emergency vehicle arrived, the contents of Jen Spangler's stomach had ceased dripping from the nearby rhododendron. It was a good sign that Jen had puked. The way she handled the first crime scene had been a little unnerving to Hewitt. If Jen had processed this discovery with the same nonchalance, it wouldn't have been altogether human. And if there was one thing you absolutely needed to be in this inhumane line of work, it was human.

"Just so you understand," Hewitt said. "It's not like this every day."

Jen looked embarrassed, still somewhat shocky. She forced a little show of teeth that fell short of a brave smile.

"Is it the husband?" she managed.

"The ex-husband."

"I thought their divorce wasn't final."

"It is now."

S ITTING in an English garden, waiting for the sun . . . Hewitt had heard numerous jazz versions of Beatles songs. But to her memory, never that one. As the crime scene unit processed the grounds around her, her mind attempted to translate the melody of "I Am the Walrus" into a jazz arrangement. It would have to be a sax on the lead. Played hard. Overblown. She heard Sonny Rollins doing it, making it work. Taking something that unlikely and making it jazz. So that even the most serious buff would say: *I Am the Walrus. Sonny Rollins. Too cool.*

There had to be a lover. Factored into the Joe and Rita Vandermause marriage dénouement, there had to be a lover. Because this wasn't just a case of blood boiling over. The heat of passion it would have taken to drive someone to commit stereo decapitations was impossible to gauge.

"Is the younger woman your partner?"

Christ. Hewitt turned, saw the only face the words could have come from, saw the map of the world there. The primordial world. The world before oceans. The world before life.

Hewitt remembered hearing that the man behind the voice had left the Du Page PD to take a job in another community. She hadn't remembered it was Bensenville. Now she would never forget it.

Captain John Davidoff smiled at Hewitt, and the primordial, pre-life planet smiled with him.

"No," Hewitt answered, finding a smooth place to land with her voice. "She's Ed Spangler's daughter. Jen Spangler. She's job shadowing. Why *today* you'd have to ask an oracle."

"If I run into one, I'll make sure to pose the question. What else do we know?"

"I assume you heard about the first victim."

Davidoff nodded. "Headless bodies have a way of crying out."

"All indications are that this is the first victim's husband."

"So, suspecting the husband, you came here. But I'm guessing not expecting to find him like that."

"No," Hewitt demurred. "That one I didn't see coming."

"Life is full of surprises," Davidoff said, saying more with the way his eyes passed lazily over Jen Spangler, who remained in recovery mode, away from the garden and out of earshot.

Is the younger woman your partner?

Hewitt knew Davidoff had scoped her engagement ring before he'd stepped forward to address her. But he'd played through. You didn't lose your face in a tragic accident and continue advancing in your field unless you knew how to play through.

The younger woman.

Hewitt understood that her reaction made no sense. Granted, her psyche had once been the executive producer of an erotic dream involving Davidoff. But there was nothing inside her that had ever suggested she would go anywhere beyond simulated, symbolic Eros with him. Then why were tiny beads of jealousy forming on the inside of her skull?

"No ring," Davidoff said.

Hewitt saw the hand he was looking at. The cold one on the ground, on the left side of the body.

"You said *husband*," Davidoff pursued. "Can I assume, at the least, estranged? Unless we have some kind of ring stealer."

His eyes did a fly-by of Hewitt's left hand.

"No," Hewitt said, looking straight into those eyes. "The ring went missing before the head."

8

SHE can't see his face. Not because his face is hidden. There is plenty of light in the room, more than she is comfortable with. She can't see his face because she can't open her eyes.

He is forcing her to keep them closed. Forcing her, not through some imposing of the will, not through some physical restraint. In fact, it is his wild, unrestrained actions that are forcing her to keep her eyelids sealed.

He is on her. He is in her. But he is not *of* her.

This is the last time she will make love. She knows this. There is no voice telling her this. There is just this sense. And not simply because he is the only man she has ever known in this way. Yes, definitely, this is her final time with him. And while there is another man, a man she has already begun to touch, she cannot see beyond the climax of this final act. She cannot see beyond the closing of the curtain on this play.

"I love you," he says to her. But he has always offered those words in the final moments before he releases. So it is always a short-lived love. A shuddering countdown of love. A gasp of love.

The night train of his nervous system has already sent the signal for the long, lonely wail that accompanies the release. And immediately she goes to work on what is left of him, to finish off her own little gift to herself.

If this is the last time, it would be a shame not to have that as a little pink trophy to take with her.

As she feels the river of both of them beginning to flow out of her, she opens her eyes to her husband's face. But his face isn't there to be seen. His torso, still straddling her, collapses all at once, on top of her. All his weight. Everything.

Everything but his face. She cannot see it, cannot superimpose his old face in its absence. She can see the rim of hair around it. She knows it's there. But her mind refuses to let her see it.

Her eyes close again. In this moment, and for eternity now, he will be a body without a face. A body whose face had made its exit from her life even while another part of him was still inside her.

9

ERIC Hubertus, MSW, LPC, LMFT, was late for his first appointment. Given that it was a noon appointment, it was a lot less forgivable than a 9 A.M. Hewitt had no complaint. It wasn't her appointment. But the couple seated across from her in the hallway waiting area on the second floor of Big Shoulders Marriage and Family Therapies were the rightful owners of the appointment and, apparently, a docket-full of personal grievances. His on a white legal pad. Hers on the linen pages of a fabric-covered journal.

Hewitt was intrigued by the name of the counseling business. Obviously someone had gotten creative. Someone who wanted to pay a little homage to the poet Carl Sandberg for his description of Chicago as "city of the big shoulders." Then, too, there was the other side of the double entendre. Something everyone needed from time to time. A big shoulder to cry on.

Either way, this was the kind of place where marriages went to die. Or when things went well, to be resurrected. Which made Hewitt the odd woman out in the second-floor waiting area. Because to that point she was still a marriage issue virgin, with a gem of hope blazing away on her hand to eliminate any doubt.

So the marriage virgin and the couple in crisis waited, the three of them eyeing one another, but communicating nothing, listening to the ambient Native American flute music that pervaded the place like a second conscience. The husband and wife, sipping from their little cups of complimentary spring water, going over their notes.

Hewitt was working in her own notebook. Already she had sketched the two crime scenes, including depictions of the victims. She figured if it came down to a show-and-tell between herself and the unhappily married couple, her notebook would win the prize for most horrifying. At least for the sake of the couple in crisis, she hoped so.

Show-and-tell wasn't going to happen during this noonday, however. Because the professional pitter patter of Eric Hubertus's moccasined feet was already announcing itself on the wooden staircase.

He was a man well into his forties, a man with a compassionate face, intense blue eyes and the bald front dome and lengthy back hair reminiscent of a latter-day Benjamin Franklin. The blue eyes did a quick freeze frame on Hewitt, then apologized to his clients before his words did.

"I'm terribly sorry for running late. And unfortunately I'm going to have to ask your additional forgiveness for taking a few minutes to speak with an unexpected visitor."

He waited dutifully for the couple to accept his terms—which they did—without consulting one another, without words. Then he looked to Hewitt and, with arms at his sides and palms upturned in a way that felt like he was wanding her for negative vibes, accepted her into his office.

Clearly, in the world of Eric Hubertus, life was hard enough. So there wasn't a single hard edge to anything in his work space. It was as if an interior designer had come up with a computer program for the room, the last command of which was: *Billow All.* Hewitt didn't have time to luxuriate in the softness. There were heads missing, heads that had once butted with one another inside these same marshmallow-coated walls.

"The answering service reached me on the way in," Eric Hubertus said from his overstuffed, zebra-striped chair. "They said you were looking for me. I haven't had the news on today. Perhaps I should have."

Hewitt informed him of what he'd missed.

"Rita V. and Joey? God . . ."

Saying that last word, his face began to move. As if, with a brain that was trained to remain calm at all times, his face became the dumping ground for any traumatic overflow.

"I'm sorry to have to tell you this," Hewitt continued. "I'm sorry I have to keep going with questions. But you were their marriage counselor. It's possible they would have confided in you."

The movement of his face steadied. He engaged Hewitt in a vacant stare. The pupils in his eyes were small and fixed, like a doll Hewitt had loved as a child. A doll named Rosie. He exhaled heavily, let the zebra chair swallow him even more than it already had. "So what do you want me to tell you?"

"Well, first, do you know if either of them was seeing anyone else romantically?" Hewitt posed. "And second, was there anyone in either family who would've been opposed—seriously opposed—to the idea of their divorce?"

10

ERIC Hubertus grew very concerned over the suggestion of a third party in the dissolution phase of the Joe and Rita Vandermause marriage. So much so that he chose not to respond to Hewitt's question without first consulting his co-counselor and, as it would turn out, his cohabiter in a marriage-license-defying dance of middle-aged hormones. This was apparent after he returned to the Room Without Edges with his partner, having excused himself and having apologized to the crisis couple in the waiting area, promising them they would still receive their full fifty-minute hour.

Middle-aged hormones didn't have anywhere near the powerful kick of the younger variety. But infatuation was infatuation. And this couple showed every sign of that—Hewitt's first clue being the way they stood together to face her, hip-to-hip, one hand of each finding its way into the pants pocket of the other's ass.

Autumn Fournier had a mass of color-enhanced auburn hair that looked like it could have only attained its intricately braided splendor through the efforts of a village of third world weavers. She carried about twenty pounds more than she needed on her modest frame. The huge hair, however, forgave most of it. She had a look of perpetual curiosity sketched into the lines of her face, as if the answer to all her deepest questions might very well be behind the next door she opened.

"If this is true, this is a horrific tragedy," she said, in a voice much more diminutive than her queenly hair would have suggested. But the way she said it wasn't as curious to Hewitt as what she said.

If this is true . . .

"It's true that two of your clients have been murdered," Hewitt said. "And I'm wondering if you can tell me, for starters, if one or both of them had become involved with someone else during the separation."

One, or both, had. But the affirmation existed only in the single windshield wipe it took for the co-counselors to clear their faces. They didn't look at one another then, but a consultation clearly took place, and Hewitt had to assume it was conducted either via telepathy or some hand-to-ass code.

"We both have clients waiting," Autumn Fournier advised, with her partner bobble-headedly agreeing.

"What's happened is horrific, but it's happened," Eric Hubertus said—they'd both used *horrific* now. "But these people, these clients outside are in crisis right now. And they're counting on us to be here, come hell or . . . *this*."

Hewitt bought the argument that they had needful clients. But she also perceived that the counselors had their own need for a session, a little heart-to-heart among themselves. Hewitt was fine with that. Because if there was something they needed to conceal, the more time they took, and the harder they tried, the more obvious it would become.

Human beings were lousy spiders. The webs they spun had one inevitable function—to entrap the spinner.

"When would be a good time to catch up with you?"

Via back pockets, the co-counselors apparently checked each other's calendars.

"Six o'clock," Eric Hubertus answered. "We'll be home. You're welcome to come by."

Autumn Fournier was doing the nodding this time. Not so much a bobble-head as one of those nodding dogs in the back window of a car. Eric Hubertus was already scribbling an address on the back of one of his business cards.

"Unless you insist on making this an official visit to your place of . . ."

The pause allowed Hewitt to insert her own absurdity. *"Inquisition."*

Something in his disapproving eyes and supereducated forehead suggested it to Hewitt. But no word—absurd or otherwise—followed.

"No," Hewitt said. "Your place will be fine. Thank you."

She had taken the card, was processing the address.

"It's just a few blocks from here," Autumn Fournier said. "We have a loft in The Regency."

How sweet, Hewitt thought. On nice weather days they could walk to work together. Hand-in-hand. Or if the hormones moved them, hand-to-ass.

11

FUCKING Hegel.

Hewitt remembered it distinctly. The philosophy course at UIC, sophomore year. The section on a Mr. Georg Wilhelm Friedrich Hegel.

The Hegelian Dialectic. The philosophical theory that had gotten inside her head then and had seemed to inhabit her existence ever since. And never more so than the last few days. It was the idea that the human experience could be broken into three distinct aspects, all of which were connected, interwoven, and as much as people tried, impossible to escape.

Thesis. Antithesis. Synthesis.

It was laid out by Hegel as a three-stroke process, a self-perpetuating three-stroke process. And the beauty of it was that it pretty much explained *everything*. At least as it applied to human history, human evolution, human nature and every skirmish, conflict, battle and full-scale war the species went through—collectively or personally.

Thesis. This was the initial action, act of will, act of fate, act of God. It was something someone or some group did. Action. Event. Cause.

Antithesis. An event, movement, force that manifested in the face of the thesis. To reflect it. Challenge it. Push it. Fight it. Fuck with it.

Synthesis. The results of all that reflecting, challenging, pushing, fighting and fucking with. The end result of which would be some measure of evolution, of learning, of cooperation, of *growth* that would generate another action, movement, cause. Another freaking *thesis*. So the whole wild ride could start all over again.

She'd seen it, had gotten to know it intimately in the deaths of her parents. Of course, she'd been too young to understand the philosophical architecture when her mother died. But she did understand it was the meanest trick the world could have played on her. The way it finally came about, after all that waiting, in the same week she had her first-ever real boyfriend. And her dad . . . Well, given the shape of his arteries as revealed in the autopsy, the heart attack could have come at any time. But the fact that it happened in the same month she was named a Special Agent with the ISP. Well, there were only two words for that too.

Fucking Hegel.

And now she had this. She had become engaged, to be married. Elizabeth Taylor Hewitt had finally found a man willing to roll those crazy dice. And the next fucking Hegelian day, a couple in marriage counseling had turned up with their heads missing. Which meant she was now knee-deep—hell, crotch-deep—in the *synthesis* act of the play. And the damn thing was, there was nothing she could do to make those Hegelian forces stand down. At least nothing she'd learned since her sophomore year in college.

Fucking Hegel.

Her phone was ringing. Hegel calling from hyperspace with some friendly advice? No, Brady calling from his own car, with a verbal pick-me-up bouquet.

"So how's your day going? No, let me guess. Some underwear shopping at Macy's. Some book browsing at Barbara's. Back home for a light lunch. Then a little nap with the Oscar Peterson Trio."

"Where do I trade in the day I got for that one?"

She listened to his *sometimes the world sucks* sigh in her earphone.

"I think you have to go deep into prayer or meditation—your choice—and when you visualize a glowing complaint box, drop yours in. But be prepared for a wait."

"I've been to that complaint box. I'm still waiting."

"I hope you didn't go there over the ring," she heard him say, as the tip of her thumb nudged the underside of the object in question.

There was such a tone of the little boy who needed a pat on the head to Brady's voice that Hewitt had no choice but to pat away.

"Come on, I love it. It's beautiful. Don't be an asshole."

Her closer made it clear the patting was over. His investment checkup ended there too.

"So what the hell have you got?" Brady asked.

"What have you heard?"

"Two decapitated victims. Separate locations. A married couple."

"A married couple in the dissolution phase of their marriage," Hewitt said.

A long pause from Brady. Something uncomfortable about it.

"Well, they'll stay married forever now," he reflected.

A dark thought came loose in Hewitt's head. She chose not to say anything. But apparently it was dark enough that Brady felt it, even over the phone.

"What?" he pushed.

They were betrothed. And his intuition, his mind reading, would only get better over time. So she figured she might as well start sharing the inside stuff now. "I'm just wondering if the families will bury them together."

"An interment of convenience." Brady's take.

She shuddered a little at that. The gallows humor. Though it was a staple of the profession, it was weird being backstage with the hangman under these circumstances. They had just gotten engaged and here they were talking about an estranged couple who'd been murdered and whether or not their final resting place would be joint or separate. And the damn thing was that Brady didn't seem the least bit fazed by that. If there was some dark-hearted irony, some bleak omen visited upon them, there was no way it was going to rain on his sparkling little parade.

Hewitt flashed a memory of her high school driver's education class. The day they were shown the movie everyone always talked about. The one with several acted-out vignettes of drivers who didn't make smart decisions and, as a result, became the victims of terrible crashes. The kicker was that they would show the grisly aftermath of actual crashes. And there was always someone in the classes who puked at that point—Kelly Krantz in hers—at the sight of the bodies.

Vivid as the memory of those images was, the thing that was really seared in her mind was the reaction of some of the boys in her class. Thirty minutes after seeing the movie, they were in the lunch room, making short work of their food and making fun of the two black guys in one of the movie vignettes. Specifically, the passenger in the front seat who kept telling his driver buddy that it was the middle of the night and they should stop for a cup of coffee.

"Man, you really oughtta pull over for a cup of coffee."

"You falling asleep, man. Come on, we gotta pull over for a cup of coffee."

"A cup of coffee, man."

"A cup of coffee."

"A cup of . . ."

The tires screamed. Hewitt felt her sternum and collarbones grabbed by the shoulder harness. A plastic ball had bounced out in front of the Mazda on the suburban arterial.

No. Shit. It wasn't a ball. It was a Goddamn balloon.

"Hewitt, what the hell happened?"

Hewitt, again.

"I just killed a balloon," she told Brady.

When he didn't ask for further explanation—settling for a description of where she was going and a projection of her availability for the evening—she took it as a good sign. It may not have made him ideal eternal partner material. But at least it removed him from that lunch-room table of Twinkie-popping dorks.

12

JEN Spangler looked in the mirror and saw her father. Not behind her, looking over her shoulder, his eyes checking out the kind and quantity of makeup she was proposing to wear to school. That was strictly seventh grade. By eighth, she had closed the door on such in-house surveillance. No, the Ed Spangler who was looking at her now wasn't behind her, or around her. He was in her. In her face. In the pushed-back set of her shoulders. She could definitely see it in her eyes. Not just the shape, the color, but in the way they looked back at her.

More so today, more so right now, than she would have liked to see. Especially now that the girl in the mirror was twenty-two years old, with a two-year-old daughter taking a nap in the bedroom down the hall.

Jen knew Hewitt had seen the vestiges of her father's face in hers—several times—during the morning shadow session. She'd noted it in those little pauses Hewitt made, those little cocks of her head, those quick *you're weirding me out* glances.

She was pissed at Hewitt, despite her best intentions to override the reaction. Sure she understood it was perfectly reasonable for Hewitt to have sent her home. But she was still pissed.

She took her washcloth from the rack and wetted it. All these years and she still had her washcloth in the same place on the family rack. She had to admit she'd worn too much makeup to the job shadow. Was she trying to look older? More worldly? More *available*? She knew the kinds of men who worked in the business. There were two types really. Those, like her dad, who had their values, their belief systems, and somehow, some way, held the line. And there were the others—clearly the majority—who had their values, their belief systems, but weren't quite so committed.

The thing a person had to do, the thing Hewitt was so good at, was playing in both of those sandboxes. And getting invited to play again.

She took the washcloth to her eyes, stripped off some of the façade. In the mirror, she saw a hologram of her dad looking on approvingly.

She was pissed at Hewitt because she was signed up for a full day of shadowing. It wasn't her fault the day went apeshit insane. She understood why Hewitt couldn't take her to the interview with the marriage counselor. But she would've been happy to sit outside the interview—knowing full well she would've found her way to the closed door for some accidental listening.

Hell, anybody could walk through a garden and stumble over a dead body. But walking out of the garden to figure out why, how and who, that was the hyperdimensional puzzle that addicted people to this game.

She dried her face, took the towel with her as she crossed the house to the door to the basement.

Her dad had died twice on the operating table. If he had died a third time, she would've probably already done the thing she was about to do. She remembered his instructions specifically, remembered the narcotized way he'd delivered them from his hospital bed in the moments before they came to wheel him out for surgery. The words sounded again in her mind as she made her way down the basement steps.

"There's a firearm I've been keeping. Behind the big box marked WORLD BOOK. *It's in a metal box with a combination lock."*

She was under the steps now, her hands reaching behind the big box that housed the old encyclopedia set. Her warm, slightly perspiring hands found the cold of the metal.

"The lock, the combination. It's the numbers of your birthday."

Jen Spangler was clicking those numbers into the box lock now. After the surgery—after refusing to die, twice—he had never mentioned the gun, his staring-death-in-the-face bequeathal of it. And Jen figured he likely didn't remember it. Dying multiple times on the operating table probably hadn't enhanced his short-term recall.

When the last digit of her birthday clicked into place, Jen felt the mechanism relax. She released the lock slowly, taking another deliberate moment to unseal the top of the box. The scent of the gun pushed up into her nostrils. It translated, instantly, into a taste she would never forget.

13

HEWITT had always been a little intimidated by the Catholic Church. When she'd learned that the Vandermauses were Catholic, she'd been hit with a wave of apprehension over having to follow that lead. Raised Lutheran, she had been staked with a certain wariness, pretty much from birth.

The Lutheran Church, with its relaxed rules, its ministers who wore sweaters in the church offices, seemed more accessible, easier to participate in. The Catholic Church, in the years she was growing up, with its opulence, its ritual, just seemed bigger, grander, more *by invitation only*.

The Lutheran Church was field hockey. The Catholic Church was polo.

There were no horses galloping on the grounds of St. Sebastian's Catholic Church in Arlington Heights when Hewitt pulled into the parking lot. For a couple more weeks the adjacent playground would be quiet. But there was noise, visual noise, on the playground on this day as a priest—she assumed *her priest*—rose up from the tree stump where he'd been sitting. Hewitt was just crossing the first of a series of four-square boxes on the asphalt when the priest looked up, beckoning her forward with an apprehensive nod.

Approaching him, Hewitt encountered a chalk-drawn hopscotch game. When she stepped in the first box, she felt a buzz in her foot, a quickening of her nervous system.

"Father Wilson?"

The priest extended his hand, took Hewitt's.

"Everyone calls me Father Brian," he said. "I see no reason why you shouldn't too."

He watched Hewitt's eyes click.

"Yes," he said, no smile. "A little later I'll introduce you to Sister Barbara Ann."

It was obviously a line he'd used in countless introductions. But never, Hewitt surmised, in a situation that approached anything like this.

"I'm Special Agent Hewitt," she offered. "Most people just shorten that to Hewitt."

When your fiancé was included, it was pretty much the whole world.

"Congratulations."

Hewitt didn't follow him. When he nodded in the direction of her left hand, she understood.

"Thank you," she said, smiling slightly but wanting to get the attention off herself as quickly as possible.

"By now I'm rather adept at spotting a fresh one," the priest told her. "And that's a fresh one."

Hewitt declined to tell him exactly how fresh the ring was. And the whole *freshness* thing made her more self-conscious of it than ever—like there was an extra-large, grade-A egg in the setting instead of the diamond.

"I'm still getting used to the concept," she said.

Father Brian Wilson seemed poised to deliver another comment on the ring. But he shifted all at once to the terrible thing they had to talk about, the thing not even the playground setting could pretend away.

"You're sorry we have to meet under such circumstances," he volunteered.

Hewitt projected a grim smile, nodded.

"That's usually my line," he continued. "The preamble to condolences."

Hewitt got that, straight up. The role she had assumed far too often herself with the families of victims. A negotiator for death. An apologist for evil.

"The devil," Father Brian Wilson said, "works in mysterious ways too."

With that, he started walking, dipped his shoulders, invited Hewitt to follow. "If you don't mind. I'd prefer to do this outside. My office has been feeling a little claustrophobic lately."

"Anywhere's fine," Hewitt said. "I'll try not to take too much of your time."

He shrugged as he walked toward the playground equipment. "When I'm finished talking to you, I have nothing scheduled in the next few hours but contemplation. And right now I'd rather talk than think."

Facially, he didn't resemble the original leader of the Beach Boys. But for a man in his early fifties, he had retained most of his hair. It was light brown, and cropped around the dome of his head—not unlike the most recent versions of his famous namesake. And as he turned to her now in front of the swing set, there was something slightly off about the focus of his eyes. Not nearly as pronounced as the more famous Brian Wilson. But definitely a little bit adrift like that.

Sail On Sailor.

The priest had approached one of the swings, extending his hand to one of the chains as if to inspect it. But instead, he used his grip to help him turn and sit down on the swing. Though he wasn't a heavy man, there was a heaviness to the way he sat that seemed sure to test the strength of the chains after all.

"Feel free to pull up a seat," he said.

On the sandy beach of Hewitt's mind, the melodic line of "Sail On Sailor" had dug itself in. She sat down in the swing next to him.

"I'd like to go right to the heart of it. Joe and Rita Vandermause were in the final phases of a divorce. As you told me on the phone, you'd been providing counsel to them over the last several months."

"Yes," the priest said, pushing back with his legs, settling the weight into his haunches, enough to make the chains creak. "One of our duties is to provide counseling for members with marriage issues. Sometimes we can help. Other times there's no help to be had. Sometimes, with some couples, you just come to an understanding . . ."

He relaxed his legs, lifted his feet just enough to let the swing move forward, back, and again, before he straightened his legs to stop. "For me, perhaps sooner than with some others."

Hewitt let her body turn the swing slightly toward him. Enough to let him know he still had the stage.

"Some priests might've hung in there longer with them. But the writing on the wall is the writing on the wall. Especially having seen it firsthand, having been there."

This time Hewitt's swing felt as if it turned without her help.

"You've been married?"

He smiled benignly. "I don't know why that surprises so many people. It's not as if I'm the only priest on earth who lived one life before finding another."

"I guess you just don't think of priests being married."

"I guess you don't think of priests as being widowers either."

"Oh, I'm sorry," Hewitt offered. "I assumed you were talking about a divorce."

The priest smiled patiently, as he would with a child who'd given an impassioned but incorrect answer in a religion class.

"I'm afraid the Church wouldn't approve of such a personal history. A divorced Catholic man is not permitted to enter the priesthood. My wife and I were well on the way to that eventuality when she got sick. To some men, maybe that wouldn't have mattered. I chose to stay with her—literally by her side, until the end."

By now the movement of their conversation had created a kinetic effect in the movement of their swings. Father Wilson was staring at the ground. Hewitt joined him in the vigil, let him decide when it was time to move on. It ended up being seven swings, by Hewitt's count.

"Okay, so what can I tell you?" he said, to himself as much as to Hewitt.

"Well, what I'm really looking for at this point is the existence of a third party in the Vandermause's situation. Given the nature of what we found. The two separate crime scenes. The rage one person would have had—at both of them. In your conversations, your observations, was there anyone?"

Father Brian Wilson's swing stopped its movement. "Someone who would decapitate them and take their heads as souvenirs?"

"I just want to know who else might've been a player in the drama. The odds of this being a random killer—someone who didn't know the victims—are remote. As it is, I'm in a big apple orchard right now, Father, and I have to shake every tree."

The priest capitulated with a little forward roll of his shoulders.

"I've been in that orchard," he said solemnly. "If the person I have to tell you about wasn't one of our parishioners, I wouldn't be so reticent. And if he wasn't one of our deacons, it would make it a hell of a lot easier too."

14

IN the old days, they would have taken a shower together after sex. They had put in the big ceramic-tiled shower when they remodeled their home, in part, for the ritual rinsings.

Sometimes, their feet struggling to grip the big ceramic squares, they'd indulge in a command performance in the hot spray. Either way, encore or not, he would finish off the water games by pouring his own golden libation in the general direction of the drain. Somewhere along the line, some urologist had put into his mind the importance of flushing the tubes as soon after intercourse as possible.

She had always detested it. But not enough to detest it out loud.

Well, all that was over now. He could shower the next woman in his life with that lovely experience. What had happened that morning was a good-bye fuck. She knew it. She had known it all along. He, despite the *I love you*, had known it too. Afterward, when she confronted him, asked him if he had come over with the intention of ending up in bed, his answer had been a believable *no*.

The proof was in the process. The only foreplay had been psychological. Intensely psychological. He had made the first move. A biggy. His willingness to settle it all, to settle out of court. It had surprised her. Enough that she'd revealed it. Enough that twin rays of appreciation had escaped from her eyes. Rays that hit him, hit his switch. And from there, well, fuck happened.

It was over. And the bath she was taking, in the tub that was within spitting distance of the master shower, was an immersion in the finality of it all.

There was so much of it, the ending, that she didn't know where to begin. Or she didn't know, couldn't tell, exactly when the ending would finally be over. So she had stayed there, sitting in it, for more than two hours now, adding new hot water as needed, draining old lukewarm to make room. She'd gone through half of a new aromatherapy candle—sandalwood, for the occasion—and there was no guarantee she wouldn't take the second half right down to the dish.

And all that—the time and the water exchanges and the candle melt—had become an issue now. But especially the time. Because if she didn't get out of the tub in the next thirty seconds, when would she? It was a question that begged an even bigger question.

Why wasn't she getting out?

She remembered a little piece of paper her mother had once left on the supper table for her father—her midlife-depressed father, she now realized. It was the 1970s, the middle of the decade. And the handwritten saying was one of those leftover peace and hope and *Love, American Style* sayings from the era.

Tomorrow is the first day of the rest of your life.

They were both gone now. Tomorrow would be the first day of the rest of their afterlife. If she didn't get out of the bathtub in the next thirty seconds, when would she?

It was over, the marriage. For all intents. But it wouldn't be over, officially, until she left this watery holding tank.

If she was trying to hold on to something, it was pointless. In water, there was nothing to hold on to.

If she was afraid of letting go, it was displaced fear. The letting go had already happened. Tomorrow was the first day of something. But she couldn't see it, couldn't sense anything about it.

15

HEWITT couldn't remember ever having heard a jazz rendition of "Sail On Sailor." So she knocked the melody around in her head until it landed in the mouth of a tenor saxophone. Not the tenor sax belonging to Sonny Rollins. For this specific melody she had another reed player in mind.

Mr. Julian "Cannonball" Adderly.

There had always been something lonely, longing about his playing. Out there on the sea, with nothing but your soul for company. Cannonball Adderly was definitely the captain for that ship.

Hewitt stood at the far end of the swimming pool, the deep one. On the coach's whistle, the members of the men's swim team emerged from the side of the pool, each as if he had been lifted by a dolphin trained for such purpose. It seemed that smooth. That synchronized. That sensual.

Then again, Hewitt had always had a thing for swimmers. She'd dated a couple of them in high school. They had both been a little too athletically arrogant for their own good. But those bodies.

There were a dozen of them coming at her now. But twenty-plus years were twenty-plus years.

When the young men peeled away into the locker room, it was a good thing. Nineteen- and twenty-year-olds weren't the true object of her desire on this late afternoon. It was their forty-seven- or forty-eight-year-old volunteer, off-season coach, a former collegiate swimmer himself who looked like he could still give the younger men a run for their money.

He was approaching her now, his whistle still in his mouth, as if he might call her for an infraction of protocol at any second.

"I'm Dr. Boccachio," he said. "Gerry. I already know who you are. But as for the *why*, there you're going to have to help me."

He didn't extend his hand. But the recently placed breath mint made it into her personal space, cutting through the chlorinated air.

"I met with Father Wilson a little earlier," Hewitt said. "Have the two of you talked?"

The mention of the priest's name drained some of the confidence from his face.

"Is there somewhere you and I could talk privately?" Hewitt asked.

There was. The little coach's office in the corner of the complex. It was there Dr. Gerry Boccachio made Hewitt sit and wait in a plastic swivel chair that looked like it had been salvaged from an old bass boat. As it was, the chair wasn't the only thing making her uncomfortable.

It was clear that the inner office door led directly to the locker room. It couldn't possibly have been more clear. Because the voices of the men's swimming team were streaming under and through the closed door. The showers were on and Hewitt knew the whole freaking bunch of them was standing under those industrial-issue faucets, like extended cousins of Michelangelo's *David*, without the long hair.

Hewitt had a thing for swimmers, and this preposterous manifestation of it seemed almost biblical to her. To the point that she expected no one less the tempter than the devil-snake himself to come slithering into the office, wink and say: "How 'bout them apples?"

But the entity that entered the office fifteen seconds later couldn't have been more human. Although the look on his face was infinitely more hellish than what she'd seen previously. And she knew she had been made to wait with the showering young men so their coach could make a phone call to his Beach Boy priest.

"I, uh. I . . ."

He circled his desk with the same imprecision as his words, struggling just to remember how to move his body into a sitting position.

"I understand," Hewitt said. "You'd rather hear it from him. But please let me say how sorry I am."

Her words bounced right off him, fell to the tile floor.

"I don't know why you're apologizing to me. I'm hardly the next of kin."

"No, but rumor has it you're the next of sin."

She thought it, didn't say it. Although she had a feeling Father Brian Wilson would have appreciated the pointedness of the comeback.

"They were in the final stages of a failing marriage," she said. "If you had already started some involvement, it would be perfectly understandable."

The pain in his eyes was so quickly and quietly displaced by anger that she found herself questioning whether the pain had been there, or whether she'd just superimposed it.

"Thank you for helping me to understand the human dynamic of that," he told her. "When you met with Father Brian, did he mention what kind of doctor I am?"

He hadn't, but now Hewitt could guess.

"I've been practicing psychiatry for seventeen years. Not that that should discredit your ability to pass judgment on me. But please understand, you're not the one whose judgment I'm beholden to."

It didn't register with her until he had completed the statement, how his eyes had locked on hers, with a look of unadulterated accusation.

Stone her, stone her—Hewitt's inner voice shouted.

"Trust me, nowhere on my business card does it say anything about rendering judgment. I get paid to analyze information. And as best I can, to understand people."

"Not unlike what I do in my vocation," he said. "I'm assuming that's what the comment and the follow-up smile meant to convey."

His right thumb and index finger were fiddling with a paper clip that was sticking up from the magnetized top of a plastic holder.

"I wouldn't presume to make that comparison," Hewitt said. "Any more than I would presume to know what you're feeling. Given the news. Regardless of your *situation*."

Dr. Gerry Boccachio pulled the paper clip free of the magnet, lifted the linked strand of clips that followed, making a sound that was suddenly swallowed by the opening of the locker room door.

"Coach, I need you to sign—"

A sheet of paper fluttered past Hewitt, close enough that she could feel the breeze against her face.

It relieved Hewitt to see that the intruding swimmer had at least wrapped himself in a towel. It relieved her further that the young man read the situation instantly, retreated without turning around, closing the door behind him.

What wasn't a relief—what was biblically distressing—was what Hewitt had seen through the door in the handful of seconds it had been open. Two of the three buck naked swimmers caught in her viewfinder had scrambled for cover. But the third had just stood there, holding his ground, making no apologies to Hewitt, or the world. And there'd been more. In the look on his face. In the voice in his eyes.

The message, utterly clear. *Come and get it*. Which wouldn't have been so bad if Hewitt had never seen that look before. But she had. She'd seen it in the face and eyes of every man she'd ever been attracted to.

When she turned back to Dr. Gerry Boccachio, she saw that his face had fallen completely apart. There were tears in his eyes. Tears as big as paper clips.

16

IT was the little things, like watching the way her father delicately flaked the meat from a salmon steak with his fork, that Jen Spangler noticed now. The way he put the folded edge of the napkin to the corners of his mouth after every third or fourth bite.

Across the table, his granddaughter wasn't being quite so neat with her fish sticks. They were on the verge of another fork battle—two-year-old Victoria Spangler preferring to use her fingers while her grandfather was about to assume his role as fork enforcer.

What did it really matter at this point? Ed Spangler was quick to respond to his daughter's question.

"If we don't start with utensils *now*, when do we?"

The *we* talk always made her cringe. It was natural for two parents to say *we*. Not so natural for solo parent and solo grandparent. And she cringed not because her father was making that leap, but because she had put him in a position where, to his mind, he had no choice but to jump in.

The universe, however, had pretty much opened the door and cleared the space for that. Her mom had been gone only a few years. But in that time, in her walk through the motherless desert, she'd managed to get pregnant, have a baby and drop out of college, only to re-enroll in a new department, on a new career track.

"Someday Victoria will be invited to her high school prom," Jen said, in the lecturing voice she'd co-opted from her father. "She'll go to a nice swanky dinner. And I guarantee you, when her salad comes, she won't eat it with her hands. So somehow, between now and then, the miracle of the fork will happen."

Her dad was grinning slightly. Part amusement. Part negotiation tactic. It was a look he'd mastered while eating his way up the criminal justice food chain.

"As her mother, though, wouldn't you rather have her learn the nuances of the fork from *you*—as opposed to learning about it on the street?"

Now it was her turn to grin. But she didn't, couldn't let him see it. Her negotiation tactic was to be chronically unimpressed, terminally bored. So that when she did allow someone to get a rise from her, she could steer their future behavior by using it as a reward.

"And, of course, on the mean streets of Skokie, we know fork disinformation is a major problem."

On the disastrous surface of the high chair tray, Victoria Spangler had shocked the world by lancing a piece of fish stick with all three tines of her safety fork. When she didn't raise it to her face fast enough, Ed Spangler reached his hand out to her elbow and gave her forearm some directional encouragement.

"I found the second body."

"*No. Yucky,*" Victoria Spangler entered in the opening her mother's statement had created. With her non–fork hand, she pushed her grandfather's hand away.

Jen could feel her father's face radiating surprise. She didn't look up to confirm it.

"I thought Hewitt—"

"Is that what the report said?"

"I didn't read the report. I just figured—"

"You just figured she's the one with two degrees and fifteen years experience."

Jen looked up now, saw her father was radiating something besides surprise—an almost embarrassed interest in her as a human being.

"I was looking out the kitchen window. I saw blood on the flag-stones that led to the garden."

The two-year-old had started banging her controversial utensil on the high chair tray in a rhythmic way that suggested that, despite her latest rejection, she was ready to play the fork game again.

"So you told Hewitt what you saw."

There was a hitch before Jen's response, a hitch that became a full-blown hesitation as the fork pounding continued.

"No. I went outside to check it out."

"By yourself?"

"It was pretty much just me, yeah."

Jen Spangler saw her father straighten up, heard his vocal cords prepare to call the room to attention. As if the table was peopled by a division of detectives and not the only two members of his immediate family.

"Rule number one. You never separate from your partner without telling them where you're going. I mean, for God's sake, the killer could've been lying in wait."

The timbre of his voice had caused the fork pounding to cease.

"I mean I'm pretty sure this little girl would like to continue to have a mother who has a head on her shoulders."

"Dad, there were no signs—"

"There are never signs!"

The timbre of his voice silenced all dining-related activity this time.

"Christ, Jennifer, do you really want the last conscious thought of your life to be *Oh, shit?*"

"I'm sorry," Jen said hollowly. "But once I saw the blood, I was thinking victim more than perp. And I thought someone might still be alive back there."

"That's a perfectly reasonable thought to have had," Ed Spangler allowed, his voice backing away from the briefing room podium. "That's a normal instinctive reaction. But that's level one instinct. If you're going to do this—and I still hope you think long and hard about it—you'll need to learn to override that base-level response. You need to develop a whole second tier of responses. More informed than instinctual. And that comes with training. And experience. The result of which is that you would *never again in your life* walk into a potential hot zone with a killer, unarmed and, well, clueless."

Jen was squeezing the big-girl fork she held in her hand. If the look of her eyes had stayed on the utensil, she would have bubbled the silver plating.

"Don't worry," she said, shifting her eyes to her father. "That will never happen again."

17

THE world without edges did not follow from Eric Hubertus's therapy den to the loft condo he shared with Autumn Fournier. Instead, it couldn't have been a less accurate predictor of the home decorating scheme of the loving pair of marriage counselors.

The best description Hewitt could come up with was *neo-Scandinavian, with nowhere to hide.*

The space was cavernous. And unless there were some secret rooms on the other sides of hidden panels, it was just the one big-ass open space, including the sleeping area. The designers had the good taste to put the his 'n' hers bathrooms behind closed doors. But apparently that hadn't been a consideration for the bedroom. And having total visual access to the place where the couple slept—and no doubt, conducted more elaborate forms of hand-ass activity—was a discomfort and a distraction for Hewitt. Especially after her eyes had wandered to the arrangement of oils and lotions on the nightstand.

The emollients weren't the only collection in the condo that troubled Hewitt. Much more unsettling was the collection of licensed therapists in the living room quadrant of the great space, the lot of them settled into the configuration of Nordic body supports disguised as furniture.

Besides her hosts, there were two other couples present. Hewitt grouped them as couples in the sense that they, like Hubertus and Fournier, worked as two-person therapy teams. That, Hewitt learned, was the basis, the gestalt, of the marriage counseling practice at Big Shoulders Marriage and Family Therapies. Following an initial consultation, the husband in crisis would pair up with the male counselor of the team. The wife would work with the female counselor. After a few sessions of working individually, the couples would reunite for joint therapy sessions.

It was all nice and neat and comfortable and oh so helpful. Which was exactly the feeling the assembled business partners were projecting in their collective appearance. Which was exactly why Hewitt's brain had gone to the red flag.

And again, Hewitt was the odd woman out. Not just because she wasn't a licensed family therapist. But because she was the last to arrive, and the post-modern Viking couch and two matching love seats that formed the sitting and socializing three-quarters rectangle around the big teak and glass coffee table were already claimed. Hewitt settled for a chair on loan from the dining table.

Six to one was never a good ratio. Unless you were a street evangelist on your first day on the job. But Hewitt was no evangelist. And these six were no adoring flock.

"I have to say I'm surprised to see such a turnout," she shared with them. There was food on the table—guac and chips. There were beverages. Something in the spritzer family.

"We're all absolutely sick about what's happened," Eric Hubertus offered, in a tone that would've been just as appropriate for offering her one of the mystery drinks. "We felt we needed to get together to talk about it, as a group. To come to grips as best we can. And to make ourselves, as the six principals in the partnership, available to you at the same time."

At that point, Hewitt had no cause to believe they had done this for reasons of conspiratorial advantage. If they had calculated it that way, it would ultimately become very transparent. The classic tactic of conspirators was to unify and synchronize their stories, to prevent an investigator from separating the members for individual questioning.

"Would you care for a Zinfandel spritzer?" Hubertus asked.

"Not while I'm still on the state's clock," Hewitt responded.

The four therapists whose names she still didn't know all nodded as one to her statement. As if they understood precisely. As if they possessed some kind of a priori knowledge of her thinking, her motivations. It was the same way of acting, of behaving that had always creeped her out with certain types of mental health professionals.

The introductions came then, as they went around the room at Autumn Fournier's prompting.

"I'm Dennis Fassbender," the largest man in the room said from the Scanda love seat to Hewitt's left. She had a pretty good feeling that when all the male voices had a chance to sound, his would be the lowest. By at least a fifth. Maybe a freaking octave. As he continued talking, Hewitt secretly dubbed him *Dennis Foghorn*. "I want to say how sorry I am that we've been brought together under these terrible circumstances."

Dennis Fassbender fell into the category of ruggedly handsome. But not just rugged in a common sense. His was the Baja Peninsula of rugged handsomeness. He looked like he'd either done some serious boxing, some serious sunbathing, or some serious boxing in the sun.

The commensurately small woman beside him on the love seat also fit into the south of the border motif, a strikingly attractive Latino perhaps twenty years his junior. As it turned out, she was *Mrs. Junior*.

"I'm Lourdes Fassbender," she said in a voice considerably more mature than her young face would have suggested. As she continued, the voice revealed only the slightest vestige of an accent.

"My heart breaks for this. For them. For the families. My heart breaks."

A hand that seemed so big she could have laid her entire head in its palm came up behind her and settled on her upper back and shoulders.

On the opposite side of the table, in the matching love seat, another arm moved in a gesture of reassurance. This time, a classic male hand to female knee.

"I know Lourdes speaks for Maya and me as well," the man with the handsomest face and most expensive haircut said. It took Hewitt a moment to find his eyes through the lenses of his designer frames.

"I'm Steve Norris."

His hand was still on the knee of the forty-ish woman next to him, the woman whose straight blond hair had been died such an extreme blond it was almost albino.

"And I'm Maya Macy," she offered. "Obviously this shakes us to our core. We were just talking, before you arrived, how there's nothing in a person's professional experience that could possibly fortify you for something like this."

Hewitt felt a rattle of capitulation move through the assembled therapists. A rattle that ultimately circled all the way to her.

"I've seen things you wouldn't even want God to see," she told them. "And this one's definitely on the list."

18

IT was the twenty-four-hour anniversary of their engagement. And strange as that seemed to Hewitt, Brady wanted to celebrate. At least that was the vibe Hewitt had gotten from him over the phone. When he arrived at her condo an hour later, he didn't need words to reiterate it. The pheromones he shot at her, with water cannon force, pretty much did the trick.

And so, officially off the State of Illinois clock, with her official fiancé all over her, Hewitt went to the park and laid out a blanket for the fireworks.

It was a loud, intense, but surprisingly brief show, scar tissue tickling and all.

She had never heard a jazz version of David Bowie's "Suffragette City." But there was a line from the song that came to mind for those times when a gentleman caller popped the cork on the Asti Spumante a little too early.

"Oh, man, wow," Brady's whisper exploded into her ear after he fell dead on top of her. But he could have quoted the Bowie line just as easily.

Wham, bam, thank you ma'am.

Given the context, with a double homicide that had sunken both sets of teeth into her, Hewitt had no serious regret at the uncharacteristic brevity of the event. Weird thing was that Brady didn't seem to have a hell of a lot of regret himself. On the occasions when he'd fin-

ished fast in the past, there had been at least some show of regret.
Once, even a hilarious *oops*. But this one was passing without comment. Just another day on the mattress. But hell, this wasn't just another day. It was their twenty-four-hour anniversary. He'd said so
himself.

Brady didn't disengage from her as much as he rolled off. Or maybe
he'd separated with his usual care. Maybe her inner thoughts had made
their way to the surface. Maybe she'd helped him off. Maybe she'd
pushed him.

"In boxing they give a guy a minute between rounds," he said, sug-
gesting he had, in fact, detected her use of force. "Maybe we can give
it another go."

"I'm good," Hewitt said. "My head's not here anyway. I think I left
it with the marriage counselors. They're probably still sitting there,
passing it around in a circle. Like a magic eight ball."

"Hopefully they won't get any guacamole on it."

He had opened the door for her to pick up on the little sharing session she'd initiated within minutes of his arrival at the condo. But now,
within seconds of their first anniversary sex, she wasn't so sure she
wanted to resume it.

"You know we don't have to talk about this," she said. "I mean I
told you what I know. So we could lie here under the sheet and speculate on a profile of my killer. Or we could talk about the two cold cases
you've got. I mean how are we going to handle this? *How the fuck are
we going to do this?*"

Hewitt had always had a problem with drama queens. So she definitely had a problem with the way her voice sounded in the asking of
those last two questions. She could see Brady wasn't exactly loving it
either.

"One day after the proposal you find out you're marrying a psycho
bitch," Hewitt said, bringing her voice back into the reasonable zone.

"Trust me. I factored that in long before I walked into Zales."

"It just seems to me if we're going to have a life together, we should probably start with a life."

She felt his hand reach across the bed and take hold of the baseball. There were no baseballs in the bed, of course. But the strength of the grip and the way it encompassed her pussy made it feel like he was ready to take the hill.

"Stop talking," he said. "Better yet, stop thinking. Don't worry, the psycho bitch will still be there when you get back."

THEY had mixed their sports metaphors. His, boxing. Hers, the national pastime. But the end result had been a little something in the victory column for both of them. This time he took his time—enough that she could get off with him. Not the longest coital union in human history. But better than the first rendition of David Bowie. This one, to Hewitt's calculus, was more of a *Wham, bam bam bam bam bam, thank you ma'am.*

It wasn't at a conscious level that she had pelted him with pheromones when she'd first made his acquaintance at the Poe-themed crime scene in Wilmette, the first time he'd poured his Luke Skywalker voice in her ear. But she must've. Or he was just that hot to trot. Hot enough to have manifested in her hospital room after she'd survived her own Raven attack, as if she'd wished him, conjured him there. And a year later, after he'd survived a year as her boyfriend, a little thing like a near-death experience on her behalf hadn't scared him off. And to pop for a diamond—four Cs and all—after getting popped in the gut, well, hell, any combination of *wham* and *bam* was a gift from God, the universe, the bridal registry at Target, Tiffany's. Who knew? Who cared?

Hanging out in the living room now, in the post-sex semitorpor, Hewitt turned her focus to assigning a lead player for her jazz rendition of "Suffragette City." This was a tough one. No "birth of the cool," no "hard bop" player popped to mind. It had to be someone more *electronified*. Once she made that leap—into the modal-electric later sixties, she settled on a player from the Miles Davis camp, a "Bitches Brew" alum.

The sound of the Fender Rhodes piano in Hewitt's head had temporarily drowned out the audio portion of the movie Brady had joined in progress on cable—*The Godfather, Part II*. The quintessential guy movie. On the screen, Fredo was telling his nephew—Michael's son—his secret for catching fish. The *Hail Mary Soliloquy*.

Brady, sitting on the floor in front of the coffee table, was all over that scene. Almost as much as he was all over the pizza he'd retrieved from the fridge no more than five minutes after the second game of the sex double-header had concluded.

While Hewitt imagined Herbie Hancock playing David Bowie, while Brady watched Fredo Corleone go fishing, she continued her ramped-up activity in the notebook.

Her first new page was the most interesting artistically. But the most appalling, given the reality it was based on. It featured sketches of the victims—Joe and Rita Vandermause—in before and after versions. *Before* showed the couple standing together, holding hands. *After* was the same couple, no longer holding hands, no longer with their full complement of physical parts.

Taking the heads. Why would the killer take the heads? In the psycho killer world, it was a common practice to keep a souvenir, a trophy. But the keepsake was usually a little smaller, a little more *portable*. Two heads were a lot of work. To go to all that trouble, the heads had to have a purpose, *a life* beyond ornamentation, beyond a basement rec room display next to the autographed baseballs.

Baseball again. She could feel Brady executing the split-finger fastball, even though he was currently across the room, reciting a sympathetic series of *Hail Mary*'s under his breath.

A gunshot echoed over the lake.

He was going to use the heads as part of a bigger plan, a project, a staging of some perversely impossible dream.

"Killing your own brother," Brady muttered, in lieu of *Amen*.

Yeah, this was nice. A softly lit living room. The two of them just hanging out. She with her artistic pursuits, he with his film studies.

This was nice. This could work.

19

NAOMI Nelson was awake for no more than a couple of breaths when she heard the sound again. The same sound that had worked its way into her dream in the form of a gold wedding band falling and hitting the smooth surface of a lake and disappearing into the water. Followed by another ring. And another. Then, a windswept spatter of them. And finally, the skies opening, the torrent of gold rings.

He had come back. Of all the bad ideas, he had come back. And not only that. He had turned it on. He had turned on the damn shower.

Christ, whatever happened to bowing out gracefully? Did he really expect his water invitation would get her out of bed and into the bathroom with him? What the hell was he thinking? And what the hell had she been thinking when she'd agreed to that last meeting? Not just the meeting, but the way she had let it happen as the good-bye hug turned into a farewell fuck.

"You have to leave!"

Yelling at one o'clock in the morning, without any warm-up, gave her voice a matronly harshness that came close to her mother's yelling voice.

She waited inside the echo of that old fear for a response. But none came from him. And somewhere in the next half-minute, the old fear of her mother crossed over to a more immediate trepidation over what the hell he was proposing to do in her bathroom, her house, her life.

They had a deal. They had sealed it in body fluid. But now here he was, with some outrageous let's-take-a-shower addendum.

"Ted, you can't be here. You can't do this."

There was the chance he hadn't heard her initial yell over the sounds of the running water. If that was the case, he definitely hadn't heard this. Mindful of steering clear of any vestige of her mother—even if in audio memory only—she had definitely been less forceful with the second call.

She sat up in the bed, pushed the sheet and blanket off. But the bedding seemed to fly from the mattress, as if pulled by a ghost. *Mother, God dammit!*

She was already yelling at him by the time her bare feet hit the hallway floor. But not in a way he could hear. The inner yelling was something she had been doing since childhood. The inner *yelling back*.

She would open up soon enough, use her outer voice. A few more steps down the hall . . .

She approached the closed bathroom door, found it locked.

"God dammit, Ted—open the door! What the hell are you doing in there?"

The shower was on. The door was locked. His lips were sealed. Well, he could bet his hairy ass that her lips were sealed now too. Upstairs and down. And no amount of shower foreplay was going to change that. The asshole had a better chance of penetrating the Venus de Milo.

"What the fuck are you doing in there?"

In the bathroom, the shower continued to run. Cleanly. Unimpeded. Meaning there was no *body* interrupting the flow. So he'd turned on the shower but he hadn't gone in. Which meant this was really fucked up. *He* was really fucked up.

"Dammit, Ted. Quit fucking around."

And just like that there was a new person in the hallway. Not the royally pissed off almost ex-wife. This was someone softer, more human. Someone who was hoping the almost ex-husband was *only* fucking around.

The lone being in the universe who could hush her into fear so quickly was her father. It was his ghost awake now inside the house too. And she was reacting to him the way she always reacted, when he'd come home from the nights out, his drunken presence, the sound, the smell, the *force* of it filling the house instantly.

She had learned the quick cool—from angering to humoring—from her mother. Because it was when her father came home from such nights and turned to the dark side of himself that his wife knew when to put aside her rage and smile in a sweet-sick way and ask him if he wanted a warm bath. Just to get him to the warm water, where he would fall asleep and remove himself from the potential to become violent. Only problem was she didn't always get him to the bathtub.

"Ted, come on. It's late and I'm tired. I just want to know what's going on."

There was a groan from the bathroom. But not the groan of a human voice. It was the voice of the shower itself, the disturbing sound it made when the water pressure dipped below a certain level and the pipe that delivered the water was suddenly short of air.

It was a groan that came when another water source was turned on in the house. A toilet. A faucet.

Please, Daddy, don't hit.

She could feel her face, her hands pressing into the cool wood of the bathroom door. She turned her head, put her ear to the door. She would've heard the toilet. What she was listening for now was the faucet. Her ear and her brain and her heart worked to find the sound of that, to separate it out from the sound of the shower and its groaning.

There was an obvious pitch difference between the running water of the shower and the faucet. But the faucet's higher pitch was either evading her detection, or it wasn't there at all.

Without moving the rest of her body from the stability, the protection of the door, she allowed her right hand to slide up the right side of the doorframe, continuing to the top of the frame, where her fingers found the tiny doorknob key.

"Ted, I'm going to unlock the door," she called, her mouth so close to the door that the wood conducted the vibration of her voice back into her forehead. As she inserted the lock-popper, she flashed two pictures of him. Neither one good. The first was that he was just standing there inside the door, waiting for her to take this action. Maybe he had removed his clothes. Maybe he was jacking off. Disgusting as that would be, it was better than the other picture.

The lock popped. Her hand was on the doorknob. She waited before turning it for any sense of a hand holding its counterpart on the other side of the door. And even when she began the turning, she did so slowly, still waiting to feel some resistance to her forced entry.

The doorknob rotated, undeterred. She pushed the door open.

The vanity lights were on, dimmed, but giving plenty of light for her to register that the room was empty. But there was still one place he might be. Behind the drawn curtain of the shower which, with its solid blue hue, revealed no preview of its contents.

The ceramic tile was cool to the bottoms of her feet as she crossed the room, but also damp from condensation.

People slit their wrists in the bathtub. People did that. But that was people. This was Ted.

The shower curtain rings screeched against the rod. The fabric of the blue curtain rattled like the wings of a hundred peace doves. But the nothing she discovered was immediately filled by the presence of the person who had joined her.

The face of the man standing in the doorway was covered by a mask. A mask of a face that had been *erased*. The arms of the faceless man flexed, lifted, projected to her the real face of her husband, still attached to the head, the heaviness of which she would have never guessed until she raised her hands to catch it.

20

HEWITT had been walking the same path for years. Her route, her early morning course, due west of the condo complex on a mile-and-a-half of faded asphalt, patched countless times but never redone. It was convenient, accessible, with an easy-to-grasp beginning, middle and end. The beginning and end were the same square of sidewalk at the base of her back porch. The middle was the woods and the yellow warning sign that proclaimed it an official DEAD END, to drivers and pedestrians alike.

Three miles round trip. Thirty-five minutes of aerobic exercise before the start of the day, give or take, depending on blood pressure, mind-set, case load. In a less crazy world, it would have been the ideal path for walking meditation. And maybe she actually did use it as that on some occasions. If deliberating on the mind and motives of killers could slide into the meditation column. She had to assume the Dalai Lama wouldn't exactly endorse that as the best way to practice meditation. Although she figured if he did dismiss it, he'd do it in the kindest way possible.

On this morning, she left Brady asleep in the big bed. Her walk, to that point, had included an opening topic, followed by a trip, literally, down memory lane. So after starting with a mental rundown of the Vandermause homicides, Hewitt found herself wandering in the memory fields of the two cases that had spent the most time walking alongside her on the morning path in recent history. Beginning, of course, with the specter of a great dark bird whose in-flight shadow would never quite leave the Illinois landscape.

She remembered the first manifestation of *The Raven*, the diminutive version in the form of a crow on one of the lawns, in the final stages of succumbing to the West Nile virus. To think that bird would foreshadow the Poe-based killing spree that followed made her shiver even in the early morning warmth of a firm, ripe August sun.

Then there was the other case that had attached itself to her shadow. The more recent. The musical killings. Murder set to music. The piano compositions of a French-Polish genius motivating the mind of a long-abandoned boy. A boy who'd grown into a man with powerful hands and a penchant for nylon stockings.

And now, of course, there was the latest edition of murder-to-walk-by. Just a few minutes before venturing out, she'd received a call from Bernard Padgett, the forensic toolmark specialist at the State Crime Lab. His conclusion had been as clean and precise as the type of blade he ascribed to the killings. *A sharp, flat sword. Extremely sharp.* The kind of thing you were a hell of a lot more likely to see in a Samurai warrior film than in the suburbs of Chicago.

Hewitt's semimeditating eyes made first contact with the DEAD END sign that preceded the woods by about a hundred yards. For a moment, her brain replaced the words on the sign with the symbol of the murder sword as she imagined it. And beyond that it was pretty easy to conjure the pictures of all three players in the empty lot that bordered the woods.

Chopin at the piano. Poe composing at a writing bureau next to him. And rounding out the triumvirate, some nameless, faceless master of the sword, performing to the music of the piano, the sweeps of the quill pen.

And it got even crazier, when another of the bad brains that had infiltrated her psyche rose up. Really, the first one. The one she tried hardest to avoid in her dreams, her waking states, The one who not only thought but *knew* he was no less an entity than God himself. The one who had taken his ten-step program of retribution to the streets and homes of Chicago. The one who had gone face-to-face, soul-to-soul in mortal and immortal combat with the only other man in the world she would have married.

She closed her eyes, did her best to delete the images. When her eyes opened again, it was to her own shadow on the road surface. In late August, the length of her shadow was considerably longer than her actual self. Maybe it was that taller aspect of herself that triggered what came next in that black-on-gray reflection. She saw her father, his gait suggested in the movement of her shadow. And it wasn't her current shape that reflected back to her. It was the boob-less, hip-less version of herself that had accompanied her father on all the neighborhood walks, the State Park hikes, the universal path of Dad and daughter. Sometimes Mom was with them. Her shadow had been the first to fade. His had kept walking for many more years. The daughter of those shadows was the only one that remained.

Her current shadow, a few feet out in front, reached the end of the asphalt before the rest of her did. She had reached the woods. It was definitely time to turn around.

21

BEING a homicide detective on a weekend was like being a doctor on a weekend—with an avocational measure of Dada artist thrown in. When you had an active case, you were always on call. And even if you didn't get a call that required specific outbound action, you were always a captive of your own inner studio, immersed in abstract process, creating, raging, hallucinating. Doing everything in your power to meld minds with the demented muse who had come to cohabit your life.

For Hewitt, it was just another Saturday morning in paradise. Now that her first official anniversary had come and gone, it was back to business as usual. Back from her walk, she was in the kitchen, at the table with her morning cup of Swiss Miss, her notebook open as she added to the profiles she'd started for the key players in the theater of the absurd she was now in charge of managing.

She had done her little caricatures of each, along with her comic book–style handwritten comments.

Father Brian Wilson. The surfing priest. Her drawing of him reflected that inanity. He was also a widower—something not yet reflected in the drawing. So Hewitt sketched two circles in the sky above the waves where the priest was surfing, turned one into a wedding band, the other into a Roman collar.

Dr. Gerry Boccachio. Shrink. Church deacon. Swimming master. For his sketch, Hewitt put him in a church pew, in a coat and tie, his note pad on his lap, his whistle around his neck. His right hand was holding a pen. His left hand fell to the side and rested on the seat of the pew. Beside his left hand was another hand—this one feminine—connected to a wrist and forearm that weren't connected to anything else. It was the hand of Rita Vandermause.

While considering the sketch, Hewitt had the thought of adding an open door behind and over the shoulder of Dr. Boccachio. An open door to the youthfully arrogant swimmer she had caught in her headlights and who, apparently happy to be there, had caught her in his. But nudes had never been her forte. And a swimmer's body always shaved a good twenty points off her IQ.

Brady was up, making his way to the bathroom. After watching brother kill brother in *Godfather II*, Brady had grown irretrievably melancholy before bed. He'd moped through some ESPN Classic boxing—Sugar Ray Robinson and Jake LaMotta, she recalled—before excusing himself and going to bed without her. So there'd been no David Bowie encore of any degree of wham-bam intensity. Which left the door open to some kind of morning reprise. He was too far away in another part of the house for a pheromone spray. But maybe a little telepathic suggestion would help.

Ground control to Major Tom . . .

She was looking at her marriage counselor page now. She had chosen to keep all six personalities on the same sheet of paper because they had worked so hard, done their damnedest, to appear to be on the same page for her enlightenment at the loft apartment conclave.

For purposes of historical accuracy, Hewitt used a bird's-eye perspective in arranging the six therapists in their original love seat configuration.

She took two sips of hot chocolate, heard the sound of Brady turning on the shower. Hewitt's eyes were drifting over the notation she'd added to the therapist schematic. There had been no shortage of therapy-speak at the meeting. These people were in the business of being relentlessly helpful, even if, on this occasion, they wouldn't be able to bill Hewitt's group plan for their efforts.

Eric Hubertus and Autumn Fournier were the only members of Big Shoulders Therapies who had worked with the victims. In so doing, they had followed the practice's therapeutic template for couples in crisis. After an initial meeting of all four parties, Joe and Rita Vandermause had gone their separate ways—the husband to work with Hubertus, the wife with Fournier. They would have a gender-matched session or two as both a cooling off and a getting-to-know-you exercise. This would be followed by a meeting of all four, in which the male therapist would facilitate for the male client, the female for the female. This was the case, primarily, in the opening phase of the joint session. The gender advocacy lines would blur as the session progressed. Hewitt figured that at the end of all that blurring, some kind of fuzzy group hug would have been the ideal outcome.

Following the heterogeneous session, the male-male and female-female teams would break off again into separate sessions. To regroup, reconnoiter and plan for the next joint session. This therapeutic arrangement could go on for weeks, months, years. Until such time that the couple reconciled, gave up or were killed by a sword-wielding freak.

In the therapeutic process, Rita and Joe Vandermause had eventually hit the wall, an assessment corroborated by their ten-hanging priest. According to their former therapists, the Vandermauses had spent nine months in the program before deciding, mutually, to move to dissolution. That decision had been reached a little less than a month earlier. There had been no subsequent sessions for either one with Big Shoulders Marriage and Family Therapies.

On the subject of Dr. Gerry Boccachio, Hubertus and Fournier had been the picture of cooperation, a picture Hewitt sensed was a little too perfect. Yes, they knew of Dr. Boccachio. But only in the context of his place in the wider therapeutic community. They did not volunteer any knowledge of the psychiatrist's spiritual and other possible dalliances with Rita Vandermause.

By the time Hewitt set her notebook down, Brady was out of the shower and on his way to the kitchen. Hewitt's head had been so into her notes that she hadn't been audiotracking his movements like she typically did. So she couldn't say whether or not Brady had stopped in the bedroom. But she thought maybe he hadn't.

Which would have been odd. Odder still was the evidence Brady presented seconds later at the kitchen door. Naked as the day he was born, with one exception. Unless he had been the first baby on record born in a pair of white sports socks.

She looked at him, tried to stop him with her look. But he and his crotch chimera waltzed right by.

"I like to air dry sometimes," he said, more to the coffeemaker than her as he began the process of brewing a four-cup pot.

"Well, I guess that explains it," Hewitt replied.

"Sometimes if I'm hurrying and I put my underwear and my T-shirt on too soon after a hot shower, it sticks. So . . ."

Since he was filling the carafe with water and hadn't turned around to address her, it was a little like his ass had done the talking. No, it was a lot like his ass had done the talking. As he lifted the carafe to pour the water, he flexed the muscles of his shoulders upward, like a boxer setting to throw a punch. And that sealed the deal on the thought that had been poking at Hewitt's brain.

It was a boxer's body. In a world where bodies were categorized by type of sport, Brady's fit best in a boxing ring. As opposed to, well, a swimming pool.

So the verdict was in. The judges had reached a unanimous decision. The man with whom she would share her life—and, possibly, her genetic code—had the body of a fighter.

But this was a good thing. For a marriage and a career. There was very little life of the smooth and gliding nature in a detective's world. But there was a hell of a lot of dirty infighting. Taking your shot at the opponent when the opening came. Protecting yourself at all times.

That was the vocational side. On the love life side, having a boxer was a good thing too. Boxers stayed in there, battling, hugging, bleeding. She'd dated swimmers in high school. Swimmers always swam away.

"Ever do any boxing?"

The question surprised Brady. When he turned around, Mr. Happy seemed a little startled too.

"A couple bar fights," he told her. "I wrestled in high school."

An ex-wrestler. Not exactly the boxer she'd romanticized. But close enough.

"Want to put me in a full nelson sometime?" Hewitt asked.

"Depends," he said.

"On what?"

"What you're planning to put me in."

22

BLOOD matching the husband had been found at the scene where Rita Vandermause had been murdered. Which would have been great information, homicide-charging information, if the husband were still alive, if his estranged wife had fought back in a final attempt to save her own life, drawing blood, making him bleed. But now, with the husband dead in the same manner as the wife, it only made the bloody mess that much worse.

Life, as much as the pretty flowers in the garden hoped to suggest otherwise, could be a brutal, fetid quagmire. For proof, all Jen Spangler had to do was look and breathe. She tried to do as little of both as possible when she changed her daughter's diapers. Other than a quick scientific check to make sure nothing anomalous was going on.

Weird poop.

She'd heard other moms use that lovely term to describe their children's atypical movements. But like most of the shorthand slang in the baby-raising realm, it got the job done. Nothing weird on this occasion. At least not in the realm of poopdom. But in the world of blood and bone and missing heads, weirdness continued to rule.

She sealed the Velcro on both sides of the diaper, listened as her father listened to whatever Hewitt was imparting to him on the phone in the next room in his first business call of Saturday morning.

"You're right," she heard him say. "It doesn't mean he was killed there too."

There was another pause, long enough for Jen to put the diaper into a plastic garbage bag for disposing.

"That's possible," he resumed. "I mean we don't know until one of them turns up."

They were talking about the heads. Obviously the heads were the key. Find the heads, find their keeper. If he kept them. And even if he didn't, he'd kept them long enough to leave something behind. Something that could be traced.

Her dad had signed off, and Victoria wanted up. At two years old, this wasn't accomplished by a cry or a kick. It was signaled by standing straight up on the changing table and looking at her like: *What the fuck? Come on, Mom. Shit happens. Life goes on.*

"I all done, Mommy. I all done."

There was that way too. And it sounded a lot better without the profanity embellishment. She picked Victoria up, let her down to the floor.

Shit happened. And you couldn't pretend it didn't. The only way you ever got to smell the flowers was to clean up every damn stinking mess that came your way. Eventually, there'd be a break.

She followed Victoria into her father's bedroom.

"Yucky die-pee bye-bye," the little girl announced.

"Good, honey, good," her grandfather responded, his mind miles away—in all likelihood, in the passenger seat next to Hewitt.

"Dad, I want to participate in the case," the bigger of the two girls in the room announced. "I think I can help. I think I can help Hewitt."

23

BYRON Biffle had been expecting a check from one of his key advertising accounts for three days. So when the Saturday morning mail arrived at the *Mundelein Dispatch*, he fished it out of the front door mailbox and riffled through the stack.

Since he was chief financial officer, editor and layout artist of the weekly community paper, everything in the box was ultimately earmarked for him—including, on this morning, the large tan envelope with the single word WEDDINGS printed in 24-point Courier on a strip of label paper that had been affixed neatly beneath the address label. That label, too, was printed in Courier, 12-point. There was no return address.

Odd. And not just because the labels seemed odd. The whole thing felt strange. Stranger still was his strong sense that the oddness theme would continue with the envelope's contents.

It was, as his father used to say, *a dancing hair feeling*. But there were other items of business that were rattling Byron Biffle's skin on this morning. Like whether or not Carpelli Motors had graced his enterprise with their ninety-days-past-due settlement on an accrual of almost five thousand dollars for ad space.

The tan envelope would have to wait. Because the white one, the business-size, with the Carpelli Classic Autos logo and return address was the one . . . Ah, yes. Halle-freaking-lujah. He could pay the printer and pay his freelancers without dipping into his line of credit.

Byron Biffle walked the final steps back to his office, set the rest of the mail on his desk, sat down to open the Carpelli Classic Autos envelope. He hated this. Hated cutting it so close. Hated the creative balancing of accounts. Robbing business account Peter to pay business account Paul.

The envelope was open now. The payment was in his hand. As his eyes read the details of the salmon-colored check, his face went from natural to amber.

Twenty-eight hundred. Twenty-eight God damn hundred. John Carpelli had told him himself. The ninety days past due would be paid in God damn full.

He picked up his cell phone, found John Carpelli's number. On a Saturday morning, Carpelli would be in. When the receptionist picked up, it felt like she'd been waiting for him. It wouldn't have surprised him if she brushed him off with a *Mr. Carpelli is with a customer.* But she didn't. She put the call through.

By then, Byron Biffle's fingers had separated the gummed flap from the body of the tan envelope. He slipped his fingers inside.

"Byron, listen. I need another week and then I'll bring the whole account up to speed."

The CFO and editor versions of Byron Biffle measured their response to John Carpelli carefully. But before the words fully formed, the layout artist pulled the five-by-seven wedding photograph from the envelope. He wasn't used to getting printed photos anymore. Most newlyweds had gone to the JPEG.

"Holy fucking shit."

"Christ, Byron. You don't have to swear at me."

Byron Biffle failed to register the car dealer's words. Nor were his eyes able to accept what they saw staring back from the matte finish of the wedding photo.

24

IRONY was served up like a double Manhattan for Hewitt—despite the fact she never drank hard liquor. If she was ever going to start, this would've been the day. The first, the most glaring irony, was the fact that the biggest story the *Mundelein Dispatch* had ever uncovered was its own. The second head-shaker was the other major story involving Illinois law enforcement. The breaking news that Jennifer Spangler wanted to partner up with the same woman over whom she'd displayed every form of petty jealousy, if not contempt, in a contest for her father's affection.

But the Jen Spangler situation would have to simmer, fascinating as it was. Because all of Hewitt's attention was focused on the hideous piece of mail the U.S. Postal Service had delivered to a Mr. Byron Biffle earlier in the day.

"There was nothing else inside the envelope?" Hewitt questioned. "No note, anything like that?"

Byron Biffle remained slumped in his desk chair, his expensive Herman Miller spine-saver. He was in his early fifties, the perfect age when degenerative discs trumped the need to be fiscally conservative with personal office furniture.

"It's the first thing I looked for," he mumbled in the direction of his desk blotter. "I'm a news guy. What—was I just going to miss something like that?"

"Most people—news people or not—would've been understandably shaken after a discovery of that nature."

Byron Biffle's face rose up from its desk-ward tilt. The eyes took a couple of seconds to join it.

"I can't tell you I've seen worse things," he said. "But I've seen enough. My father was a crime reporter for the *Tribune*. When I was a kid, I'd hear the stories. On one occasion, I found some unpublished crime scene photos in his file cabinet at home. Unpublished for a damn good reason. Once I knew where he kept the pictures that didn't make the paper . . . Well, kids are curious."

"May I ask your father's name?"

"His real name was Carl Biffle. But his pen name was *Carlton Ritz*."

Hewitt knew the name instantly. It was a name she had encountered originally as an adolescent, when she first started taking an interest in the daily newspaper as a tenet of civilized life.

"Well, of course I know who your father was," Hewitt said, with what she considered an appropriately reverential tone. She also knew the appropriate tense for referring to him was *past*. Carlton Ritz had died a little more than two-and-a-half years earlier, under circumstances that would have made his crime-reporting heart flutter—if it hadn't been snuffed out in the process.

It was obvious his son didn't want to talk about it or him. Because he knew the item that had landed in his lap was today's screaming headline. It wasn't every day that the decapitated heads of a once happily married couple showed up photo-shopped onto the tuxedoed and gowned bodies of a classic wedding couple.

"Can you imagine the day they took their vows that anyone in attendance could have possibly envisioned . . ."

"That the happy couple would end up like this?" Hewitt assisted. "No. Not unless the devil was sitting in the rear pew. And even then, he would've had to be in some kind of manic high to dream this up."

Dismal as the day had become, Byron Biffle paused for a moment to admire Hewitt's remark, to admire *her*. He sighed like a man who had seen it all but was resigned there was still more to be seen.

"So the questions are: *why me,* and *why here?*"

"Any light you can shed on either question would improve the world dramatically," Hewitt said.

"Trust me. I've thought it through. The only person who desires to understand this more than you is me. And to this point, I can only come up with two angles. First, that I'm one of a handful of community newspapers that still does the weekly wedding column—with photos. And the second is that my father—his life, his death—would make me a more visible target than the editors of those other papers."

"How long have you had your offices here?" Hewitt inquired.

"More than ten years now."

"Are there offices upstairs as well?"

"No, that I left as a living space. On occasions, when things are running late, I'll stay here for the night. I was thinking of renting it out at some point to a small business. But I wasn't sure I wanted to have the commotion overhead."

Hewitt was inserting her next clip of questions for him when the gun went off. Not in the form of Fredo Corleone being shot in the head. But in the audio report via Hewitt's phone from Captain Spangler, conveying the news that two more headless victims had been found. Another married couple. Another married couple in the end stages of that holy institution.

She closed down with Byron Biffle, asked for and received the photographs as evidence, as well as his verbal pledge to keep word about them as mum as a newspaper owner could.

25

WITH a homicide, the first one on the scene was also the last one. Not necessarily physically. But always psychologically. Being the sole discoverer imprinted the experience in a way that made it impossible to ever truly let it go. It was the seconds, minutes, sometimes longer, when it was just you and the discovery, alone together, that lit a kind of eternal flame in your mind for the victim. Others could come and witness. You, however, you were the keeper of the flame.

It had happened to Hewitt numerous times, and each one was housed in a special place in her psyche. Jen Spangler, owing to her garden discovery, was now a member of that club. As was the extremely tan, athletic-looking woman in the aquamarine track suit, Kirsten Hill, whom Hewitt was debriefing on the front porch of the latest victim's split-level ranch in Roselle.

Kirsten Hill had had an appointment scheduled with Naomi Nelson that morning. When she arrived to pick up her friend, no one had come to the door. Finding the door unlocked, she went into the house, called out a couple of times. She sensed the worst even before she entered the bathroom. It was there she discovered her friend's body, in the unthinkable condition it was.

"You said you had an appointment with Naomi Nelson. What had you planned to do?"

To that point, Hewitt had avoided sitting down next to the woman in the open half of the double Adirondack chair on the porch. But based on Kirsten Hill's facial response to the question, Hewitt claimed the seat now. "I'm sorry if that was the wrong question."

For a moment Hewitt fought off the impulse to console the woman physically. But her left hand took flight and landed, in a kind of slow motion, on the right hand of the slumping soul beside her. Hewitt's new diamond exploded in the sunlight at the same moment Kirsten Hill detonated her held emotions.

As the heaving cries sounded, Hewitt found her hand functioning more like a restraint on an electric chair armrest—at full juice—than a quiet hand of reassurance. In that moment, it had to be both.

If Jen Spangler was so hell-bent on this career track, she should've been there to job-shadow this wonderful side of it. Not just to see it from a few feet away, but to feel it reverberating up your arm bones, through your shoulder, your neck and straight up through the top of your head.

Hewitt held on. And when the tumult had subsided, her own head, despite the exit wound, was at least still connected to the rest of her.

"We were going to get our hair done," Kirsten Hill's voice managed. *"Our hair."*

Hewitt felt a revulsion plummet through the core of her body that seemed like it would never find bottom. A revulsion caused by the knowledge that Naomi Nelson's hair was, in all likelihood, still scheduled for a styling at the hands of the image-maker who had taken her life.

"Whoever did this to Naomi did it to Ted too," she heard Kirsten Hill say. "Like that other couple. The couple that was all over the news. That's what happens. Only now it's Ted and Naomi Nelson of Roselle."

Hewitt gave a slight nod. "Theodore Nelson's body was found at the apartment complex where he'd moved after the separation."

"The Eastbrook Apartments. That's where the men go when it all falls apart. And least the ones in my small circle."

Hewitt had the sense there was one man in particular, in the innermost part of that small circle, who had sought refuge in the Estranged Husband Apartments. She didn't have to poke at it to have it confirmed.

"My Andy too."

Hewitt could see the extrapolation playing out in Kirsten Hill's eyes.

"It could've been Andy and me," she said.

Within minutes of her statement, however, the ISP's Pete Megna called Hewitt from Unit 6 of the Eastbrook Apartments with information that strongly suggested Andy and Kirsten Hill would have never made the list.

P ETE Megna had been hunching his shoulders all his life. It was so ingrained that Hewitt figured he had probably developed the habit *in utero*. When he appeared at the front door of Unit 6 to greet her, the latest dramatic turn of that lifetime-plus of hunching knocked her back a half-step on the welcome mat. Because if Frankenstein ever had a brother, this latest incarnation of Pete Megna would've been him. A couple of weeks earlier, when Hewitt first learned Megna's car had been hit from behind and he'd suffered a whiplash injury, she assigned it to whatever strange neck karma was being played out in his life and vertebrae. Now that he'd been fitted with the cervical collar, all he needed was a pair of big black boots and a little sciatica problem on one side—enough for a limp—and it was time for the villagers to light their torches.

Megna handed her the professional invoice in question.

"Thickens the borscht a little, doesn't it?" he said.

"And, one hopes, eventually tightens the noose," Hewitt said back.

That one, unintentionally, hit Megna where he lived. Necks. What the hell was it with necks?

One thing she had now was a connection between the necks and *shoulders*. As in Big Shoulders Marriage and Family Therapies, the logo of which was there for all the world to see at the top of the request for payment—*second notice*—Pete Megna had found on the desk of the almost-divorced husband.

Inside the almost-bachelor pad, the crime scene unit was processing the wretched details. Theodore Nelson's body had been found in the bathroom, in the tub, clothed in gray sweatpants and a white T-shirt that now looked like a bad tie-dyed job in the red section of the RIT color palette.

"It's like the Queen of Hearts left Wonderland and came to Illinois," Hewitt said as she observed the body.

In lieu of cocking his head, Megna blinked his eyes quizzically.

"Off with their heads," Hewitt explicated, with just enough of an English accent to creep out Megna and scare the hell out of her own inner Alice.

26

IT is time for the photo. The subjects are waiting. So he leaves the little tabletop studio he has arranged and ventures to the kitchen, to the
refrigerator.

He feels the imaginary chill of a December day as he opens the
door. Reaching inside, he takes the first item into his hands and pro-
ceeds to carry it to the kitchen counter. He sets it down, the index
and middle fingers of his right hand lingering on the perspiration
that is already forming on its surface. This he tastes. This reconsti-
tuted water. Not holy water. But not unholy either. Simply the water
of life.

All that remains now is the removal of the cork. Of this he makes
short work. Removing the foil. Loosening the cap holder. Lifting the
bottle and, with a couple of powerful twists, liberating the bung.

There is no other sound like it. The physics of the popping. The
sound of the cork hitting the ceiling, the floor.

As tempting as it would be to allow himself a sneak sip, he knows
it is only appropriate to wait for the others. So he takes the bottle and
delivers it to the studio. He returns then to call for the first subject, returns to the refrigerator.

Ladies, as always, first. Once the bride is positioned for her sitting,
he returns to the kitchen one more time and appropriates the participation of the groom.

Into the three champagne flutes on the table he pours the bubbly tribute. Again, the lady first. The husband second. Their photographer and, for this occasion, toastmaster, third.

Gently, respectfully, he places the first champagne flute so its rim is just inches from the face of the bride. He does the same, right beside her, for the groom.

He pauses now to take the mental picture of the two of them thus posed. Then he half-circles the table to retrieve his own champagne flute. This he raises before him, before them, before the eyes of all the unseen who now bear witness.

In his mind, he offers the toast.

The first sip, then, is his. And it is delicious, precious, unforgettable. And now it is time for the couple to partake. Positioning himself to accommodate the bride, he takes her glass and lifts it to her lips, closes his eyes while she sips. Then it is the groom's turn. Again, a raising of the glass to the lips, a second closing of eyes.

An effervescent moment later, the light flashes, the camera clicks, the couple smiles for the ages.

27

SHE would always be suspicious of flower deliveries. Having an admirer leave eleven white roses on your doorstep—as a prelude to killing you— would put a long-term chill toward the surprise bouquet in anyone. And her recent thoughts of *The Raven* hadn't helped. This delivery, however, wasn't exactly being done surreptitiously. The big yellow delivery van with the white letters DAISY'S FLORAL SERVICE couldn't have been any noisier.

Nor could the timing have been more impeccable. Because Hewitt had been back at the condo for no more than ten minutes when the flower power bus rolled into her life. It was the second day of her engagement, and the first day of her weekend. Obviously she wouldn't be taking a lot of time to celebrate either. But this fragrant little breath of life would be a welcome interruption in her workday. And her fiancé— Jesus, was she actually calling him that now?—had done good, *damn good*, to throw a little sunshine her way.

She set the flowers on the kitchen table, being mindful not to set them in the spot where she'd placed the white roses all those months ago. Purely superstitious. But if you were cross-referencing your own near-death experience, a little superstition had its advanced logic.

The flowers were in a vase, wrapped in noisy delivery cellophane. Feeling edgy as it was, all that rattling plastic wasn't going to soothe her. So she went slowly in liberating the flowers—tulips, from the smell. Which was pretty damn impressive if her fiancé—what the hell, he was earning the title—actually recalled her favorite freaking flower.

Careful as she was with the unwrapping, the cellophane still made enough of a commotion that she didn't hear the intruder on her porch step until the screen door was already being pulled open.

The cellophane cacophony ceased. She heard hands, fingers against the front door as she caught the first glimpse of the faces of the big laughing tulips. She picked up her jacket from the kitchen chair, withdrew her service revolver, the tip of the weapon brushing one of the tulips as she did.

Working her way to the front door, trying not to let the wood floor creak, trying not to announce her appearance.

Outside, the hands stopped making noise. Hewitt crouched down as she reached her side of the door. Her skeletal system began a slow straightening. When her eyes reached the first of the two small, inset windows, she found the owner of the futzing hands was not in her sightline. But all that changed in her next breath of tulip air, as the face rose up to mirror hers. Although as reflections went, it was a decade-and-a-half younger. And a whole lot perkier. She opened the door, startled the visitor—which she figured the visitor deserved, for starters.

"What the hell are you doing?"

Jen Spangler didn't like being caught, didn't like being startled, didn't like being scolded by the older sister she never had and never really wanted.

"Leaving you something," she said, pissed off at herself, or at least her luck.

By then Hewitt had seen the business-sized envelope taped to the outside of the door.

"I didn't see your car in the lot. I figured you weren't home."

"I parked on the street," Hewitt informed her. "It's a faster in-out."

Jen's eyes were on the envelope that had now found its way to Hewitt's hands. The envelope with the communiqué she had intended for Hewitt, but not under these circumstances.

"And now I've screwed everything up," Hewitt said, in a tone that was mostly conciliatory, but still a little put off. "You went to all the trouble to write something and now you're stuck with telling it to my face."

"What if I didn't write something? What if the envelope contains compromising pictures of you and the Prince of Wilmette?"

Hewitt had always enjoyed her status, generally speaking, of being the smartest one in a roomful of cops. Even dearer to her heart was her reputation of being the smartest smart-ass. But this comeback from Jen Spangler was impressive, damn impressive.

"That's a nice thought," Hewitt allowed. "But I'm afraid it's an impossibility. Mr. Richter and I have never been in a compromising position. We're saving that for a special occasion."

Jen gave her a disarming, self-effacing smile. "Can I come in? I promise not to take too much of your time."

"Sure," Hewitt said, sounding accommodating, but feeling exposed. This was Jen Spangler's maiden voyage into her personal space. She knew the junior detective's mind would be in full reconnaissance mode.

To begin the tour, Hewitt led her into the kitchen.

"Can I get you something to drink? I have sour orange juice and flat Coke. But the Swiss Miss was flown in fresh today."

"I'm okay," Jen said. "Wow, nice flower delivery. Looks like I interrupted you during the unveiling."

"Yeah, I guess the Prince of Wilmette was feeling romantic," Hewitt said. "Or guilty."

Jen had moved to the kitchen table for a closer look.

"I love tulips."

"You can take some with you," Hewitt offered.

"Shit."

A startled *shit*. Not angry. Not nasty. And it clearly involved the little gift card that had been knocked loose from the presentation during Hewitt's unwrapping.

"These are from my dad."

Hewitt's eyes sailed through the kitchen, saw Jen's mixed-up face, saw the big tulips laughing again. But now, laughing at Jen.

"It says: *Congratulations. Ed.*"

Two good things about that for Hewitt. First, that her boss had finally acknowledged that he knew. She couldn't imagine he hadn't noticed the ring the first day, during the whole job-shadow imbroglio. And in typical Ed Spangler fashion, he'd waited until he knew she needed a lift. The wedding photos had been the bucket tipper. So that was good. And the second good thing—really good—was the fact that he hadn't signed off on the laser-printed card with the words: *Love, Dad*.

Though from the look on Jen Spangler's face, he might as well have.

28

SHE wonders about him. Even as she describes her week to him, she wonders about his willingness to tolerate her suggestiveness. There was no question she had pushed things into the overt column now. There was no more chalking it up to accidental spills of feeling.

She wonders, too, about his willingness to schedule an appointment on a Saturday afternoon. A single appointment on what was otherwise a day off. Yes, after the Friday cancellation—on her terms—she had been the one to bring up the possibility of a weekend appointment, unlikely as that prospect seemed to her.

It wasn't unlikely now. He was sitting right there, listening like he always listened. But he was looking at her differently. He was assessing her in a way that would have unnerved her ten years earlier.

But life was life now. With death ten years closer, life wasn't something you could wait to participate in when you felt a little more up to it.

"And how is your daughter's therapy going?" he asked, setting his notebook down, the signal they were nearing the end of the session.

"It's a struggle," she said. "I could tell you it's getting better. I could say she's making progress. But I'd be trying to fool both of us."

"I'm sorry to hear that. Dr. Pappas is an excellent therapist."

"To tell a family secret, I think I'm the problem."

She watched him smile his disarming smile, felt herself exhale more than just her previous breath.

"Well, that makes for an easy solution," he said. "All we have to do is eliminate you and everything's fine."

It was such a Gerry-ism, she had to smile.

"Of course, denying the world one of God's truly lovely creations would be a tragedy."

"I'm afraid this lovely creation isn't all that lovely in my daughter's eyes. But see, that's the thing. It's not just Brooke. It's how I look at her. How I see her. Because when I look at Brooke, I see *him*. I see Ian. Because she's so much like him. His personality. Even his mannerisms. She's so much like him. And so not like me."

On the wall were the four clocks that had piqued her interest the first time she'd walked into his otherwise conventional office. Four identical schoolroom-style clocks on the far wall. Beneath each was the name of a major world city, starting with Chicago, set to the local time. This was followed in order, from left to right, by Paris, Athens and Calcutta, all set to their own local times.

There was a fifth clock. The one that had always interested her the most. A clock set to no time at all. Because the hands of this clock had been removed. And beneath it was the location of the place where time-keeping wasn't needed. *Heaven*.

She saw Dr. Gerry Boccachio's eyes reading the blank face of this last clock as he composed his next thoughts for her.

"I guess we all want to be loved for who we really are. But as importantly—ultimately, more so—we don't want to be hated for something we're not."

His eyes left the handless clock and settled on her face. And for all she could tell, he was looking not at her eyes but at the space between her eyebrows—that part of her forehead. And it struck her that if her face had been the face of a sixth clock, the hands, as read by his compassionate eyes, would have been pointing straight up at twelve.

Which translated into one of two possibilities for her. Midnight. Or high noon.

"I'm scared to death of what I'm turning into," she said in a bottomless whisper.

"Don't be," he said. "In this world, there are no ugly butterflies."

29

SHE agreed to Jen's terms. In the loosest sense, the least binding way she could concoct. The only other option would have been flat-out rejection. And given how rejection had covered Hewitt's condo like bad inherited wallpaper during Jen's visit, it was never really an option.

"I don't want to sound pathetic or anything, but I'd love to get some action like that."

That had been the quote. That had been the vocalization of the 800-pound gorilla Jen had let loose in the condo. Which meant what? My father never gave me flowers. Or I wish someone, anyone, preferably a nice guy under thirty with a career who didn't have a problem with marrying a young woman with a kid, would send me some freaking flowers. Tulips preferred.

"Maybe if I would've married him—Victoria's father—maybe there would have been a few more occasions."

But that hadn't helped Hewitt either. All it had done was release another 800-pound ape into the wilds of Hewitt's home.

Flowers from the husband who loved her? Or from the dad—because she had followed the relational protocol he approved?

"But I couldn't marry him. I couldn't marry a guy who was so *hands-on*."

Jen hadn't spelled out the full meaning of that. There'd been no reason to. The hurt in her eyes spoke for the hurt wherever those hands had gotten rough.

Which meant Gorilla 3 was uncaged in the living room. And this one was prone to violence. Among its own kind. Though she already knew the answer, Hewitt asked Jen if her father had ever been told about the hands-on activity.

"It wasn't anything where you throw the book at someone," Jen demurred. "It was basically some over-the-top stuff when he drank. When he didn't get what he wanted soon enough. It wasn't hitting. It was *squeezing*. Hands. Neck."

"He choked you?"

"I'm sure there are some people who would've passed it off as rough sex. And you know, maybe that's like an idiosyncrasy you learn to live with. But there were times"—she tried to toss a little laugh at it—"when I was worried about, you know, the whole breathing thing."

Through the doorway to the living room, Hewitt saw the pop icon Sting manifest, standing chest-up strong in a yoga pose, wearing nothing but a loincloth. Or was it a Speedo?

Every breath you take . . .

"There was something so inside, so primal about it, I got the feeling counseling wouldn't really be much help," she heard Jen say.

"How much contact do you still have with him?"

"Minimal. He has no real interest in caring for Victoria. And I have no interest in encouraging it. So it's me and Gramps—keeping the smiley beach ball in the air."

It all sucked. Hewitt understood that now, understood just as clearly why the appearance of the flowers had pushed the suck of it all the way into confessional articulation right there in the Saturday afternoon kitchen.

Jen's mascara had begun to run. After she excused herself to the bathroom, Hewitt ignored Sting's astral projection—it had been an off-white Speedo after all—and took the opening to read the note Jen had printed out for her. It was a nicely written single page, wherein she respectfully requested the opportunity to offer her services to Hewitt as an assistant, an intern, a hot chocolate runner, whatever, insofar as it related to the case of the missing heads.

When Jen returned to the kitchen after the touch-up, her appearance improved even more with Hewitt's *yes*. That yes, of course, was contingent on a second *yes* from the applicant's parent or guardian.

O N the Edens Expressway, with Jim Hall playing "Angel Eyes," Hewitt explained to her supervisor the nature of his daughter's first assignment.

"I'd have her do some backgrounding on Carlton Ritz," she said, the round tones of Jim Hall's guitar forming harmonic bubbles around each word.

"Carlton Ritz is dead," Ed Spangler responded. "I wasn't aware you had time for cold cases too."

"Byron Biffle, the owner of the *Mundelein Dispatch,* is Carlton Ritz's son."

Jim Hall filled the ensuing emptiness with a lush arpeggio.

"Are you fishing for a connection between the murders of the estranged couples and the murder of Carlton Ritz?"

"No. If I was a betting woman, I'd put my money on any connection as incidental. As in Carlton Ritz is the victim of an unsolved homicide. His son runs a newspaper, one of the last, that still runs wedding photos. As imaginative as fate can be, I can't see a killer taking out Carlton Ritz and then, two-and-a half years later, coming after his son to play head games."

"Pun intended?"

"I'm not that clever."

Another pause from her boss. Enough for Jim Hall to paint the ending of "Angel Eyes."

"So what is this—an academic exercise for Jen?"

"Essentially."

"So you're sticking her in right field."

"Yeah, but even from there, she gets a chance to dig into an interesting case and stretch her mind a little."

On the car stereo, Jim Hall was sketching the opening to " 'Round Midnight." By now Hewitt was more than convinced Mr. Hall was the perfect guy to play the jazz version of "Every Breath You Take." Hell, she'd let Sting play bass. As long as he reprised the Speedo for the session.

"So what the hell do I do if she solves the Ritz case?"

Hewitt counted the breaths it took for her to answer. *Two and a half.*

"I guess you'd have to hire her."

30

THE smell of unbridled sex hung in the air. Maybe it was more *unabashed* sex. For the unbridled part, she'd have to see a video replay. Hell, maybe she and Brady could learn something from watching. If not a new position or two, definitely something from the secret life of emollients. On a Saturday afternoon the unmarried marriage counselors had been getting in touch with their own inner feelings. Until Hewitt's drop-in.

If Hewitt hadn't followed an elderly resident into the building, the counseling team wouldn't have been forced to hit the PAUSE button and respond to the insistent pounding on their condo door. They wouldn't have had to scramble for their bathrobes. They might've even had a chance to straighten up the lotion station before their company came calling.

In the center of the open living space, Hewitt waited now for Eric Hubertus or Autumn Fournier to respond verbally to the news that another couple on their client roster had turned up dead in the same godforsaken fashion as the first.

Hubertus and Fournier were well-educated, *super*educated people. They were trained to solve problems, determine probabilities, synthesize potentialities. Hewitt could feel the fuel of that intelligence displacing the shock of the information almost immediately. She could practically smell the fumes of the burn as the two minds supercomputed. Thankfully, although only temporarily, the exhaust of that activity masked the original scent of the Saturday afternoon lovefest.

"I'm sorry to have to share this news with you," Hewitt offered. "But the rest of the world will be finding out soon enough. I figured you'd appreciate some advance notice."

"One minute you're fornicating like there's no tomorrow. The next minute there is no tomorrow."

Neither Hubertus nor Fournier said that. But Hewitt's inner voice had no problem sending it up. Inappropriate as the words would have been to the situation, they were totally appropriate to the looks on their faces.

"Jesus Christ."

There, that was an appropriate response—from Hubertus.

"I can't believe . . ."

Hewitt waited for Fournier to complete the thought. When she didn't, Hewitt threw out some unspoken options.

. . . this is happening to people we know and care about.

. . . this is happening to us.

. . . this is happening to me.

. . . you interrupted my Category Five orgasm for this.

Unable to find the words, Autumn Fournier let out a sigh that released the already low-hanging fruit inside her bathrobe.

"We're absolutely . . ." Eric Hubertus looked at his partner as if he was seeking approval to use a word she already knew. Fournier consented with a little flicker of her cheeks, her invisible cat whiskers. ". . . devastated."

"For the couple who lost their lives," she added. "And for their families. But also for our family. For Dennis and Lourdes."

The skin at the base of Hewitt's back did a little crawling then. Not just at the notion of having to bloody and otherwise sully yet another couple's Saturday afternoon. But at the thought of getting another private tour of a second therapy couples' personal space.

31

SHE had never been drilled on a desk before. She had thought about it. Many times. Did it qualify as a page one fantasy? No. But she'd been in enough offices—where there'd been enough of a sexual tension between the desk chair and the visitor's chair—that her mind had opted for that little mental break. It almost always proved a lot more interesting than the business at hand.

Maybe *drilled* wasn't the most flattering way to refer to it. There had been enough of an exchange of human touches—tenderness on her part, something closer to chivalry on his—that it wouldn't have been a lie to say that love had been made on the desktop.

Sex act semantics aside, what had happened was not an undesired result. Thinking back, she couldn't really pinpoint one moment in her therapy sessions that had been the turning point. There was no architecture to such things. No blueprint. It was more like a watercolor painting. Little swatches of blue here and there that eventually became the sky.

The sky was fully blue today and she had about as good a view of it through the moon roof of the Pacifica as you were ever going to get. And so she laid her head back on the headrest and tried to relax for the first time since she'd left Gerry's office.

Gerry. She was definitely on a first-name basis with him now. He, at her request, had been calling her *Laura* since their first appointment. There had never been any *Mrs. Pennington.* Because by then *Mrs. Pennington* was the last thing on earth she wanted to be called.

She was Laura now. She would be Laura forever. And for just as long, she would be a member of the desktop drill team. She was okay with that. She was *good* with that. For Christ's sake, it was the first non-self-service orgasm she'd had in over a year.

For Christ's sake. There was that aspect of it too. With a psychiatric practice that didn't pretend to keep his Catholic faith cloistered—not that he shoved it down your throat. But it was a presence. Invisible, but always there. Kind of like God. And with her being a fallen Catholic . . .

She'd fallen a little farther now. And he'd been right there with her. Like two skydivers. Instructor and novice. One on top of the other as they fell. Well, they'd landed on the neat, well-kept desk. And they'd walked away uninjured. Whether they were undamaged, only God knew.

And yes, absolutely, there were the questions of where things went from here. Was the desktop the beginning, the middle or the end? Looking up into the buzzing watercolors of the sky, however, she didn't want to taint the perfection of it with such trifles.

"What are you doing?"

As always, in the fourteen-year-old voice, it wasn't a question but an accusation.

She turned to see her daughter, fresh from the tennis lesson. Gym bag over her shoulder. Bug up her ass.

"People were all looking at you. Like you're drunk or something."

"I just got my brains fucked out. What would you like for dinner?"

Oh, the personal mercy of that. If only she could have permitted herself to say it out loud.

"It's a beautiful day. I just thought I'd take a moment to appreciate it."

Her daughter had climbed into the car with her, the gym bag flying between them toward the backseat.

"It's a beautiful day if you don't care how other people might be feeling. Other people who might not think everything's so beautiful."

Laura Pennington started the car, put up the side windows, closed the moon roof as the AC kicked in.

"They say it's all in the eye of the beholder," she told her daughter. "It's there if you choose to see it. It's not if you don't."

"SHUT UP!"

It was a scream with vowels and consonants.

Some man was going to have to listen to that someday. Which was turnabout, fair play. Her daughter had learned it from a man. Who had learned it from his mother. Eventually, if her daughter had a son, she would teach it to him.

Where the hell would it all end? What could be said, done, to break the chain?

"I just got my brains fucked out," she said quietly. "What would you like for dinner?"

32

I T was a Tiki Room, a world-class Tiki Room, the living space shared by Dennis and Lourdes Fassbender. Walking through the front door of the latest condo unit in her life, Hewitt felt more as if she were walking onto a movie set.

Bamboo up the wazoo—Hewitt's snap take on the set design.

Lourdes Fassbender ushered Hewitt inside, apologizing as she had done during Hewitt's phone call for the fact that her husband was at a weekend retreat and would not be available.

With a name like Lourdes, it was odds-on that Mrs. Fassbender had been raised in a Latino Catholic home. As they sat down on the lime-green and coffee-black padded chairs in the living room, Hewitt could see the twin candles of a deeper belief holding steady in Lourdes Fassbender's eyes, despite the news that her business, her vocation, her life was being targeted by the sickest soul on earth.

"Ted and Naomi Nelson were your clients," Hewitt said. "From my understanding of your process, you would have spent more time directly with Mrs. Nelson."

There was a drop-off in the candlepower of Lourdes Fassbender's eyes. Whatever thought had come to her mind was going to preempt Hewitt's line of questioning.

"I'm sorry. If you'll excuse me for a moment. There's something I need to get. It might be useful to you."

Hewitt watched her go. She was so little that Hewitt could almost envision her giant husband picking her up like a child. And there was another undeniably juvenile aspect of her. Though she was well into her thirties, there was something about her face, her eyes, that seemed as if that part of her would never be any older than sixteen.

Lourdes Fassbender returned to the room, holding a photograph in her hands. She sat down, laid the photo on the glass-topped bamboo coffee table. It had been a while since Hewitt had been forced to suppress a gasp.

"One of the things we do with couples is ask them to bring in a favorite wedding picture."

Hewitt watched as the little hands—dainty, really—picked up the photo and stood it up against the centerpiece of the table—a Tiki god statue of cut stone. The Tiki god of *what* Hewitt had no idea. Maybe the god of coffee tables.

"Once we initiate therapy and set a course, we'll use the photo as a kind of touchstone. A way of getting back to a clearer space for the couple. And we'll ask each to describe themselves as they remember being the day the photo was taken. What their feelings were. What their hopes were. And often, most revealingly, what their concerns were."

Of all the things that might have been whispering a warning in the minds of Theodore and Naomi Nelson as they stood smiling on the steps of the church that day, the thought of someday having their heads photo-shopped on a ghoul's computer wouldn't have been remotely possible. But that was the one thought ringing the bells in Hewitt's head as Lourdes Fassbender continued.

"I felt as long as we were going to be talking about Naomi and Ted, it would be helpful to see an image of them. So they're not just the latest victims. So we can put a face with a name."

If Lourdes Fassbender was a demonic imp sent just to fuck with her, it was a hell of a performance. But Hewitt's gut told her there was no chance of that. Not unless Byron Biffle had broken his promise to keep quiet and had shared the information with privileged members of Big

Shoulders. Her cerebrum joined her gut and declared that an impossibility as well.

"May I ask where this practice of using the wedding photos in therapy came from?"

The candles in Lourdes Fassbender's eyed flared. Not with fear, but with what Hewitt assessed as pride.

"It's something Dennis created—several years ago. Before we started working together. I was the one who encouraged him to make it a regular part of the practice. But it was his idea. It was Dennis's brainchild."

33

THE problem with entering *Carlton Ritz* into a Google search was that most of the responses came back in the form of a pricey hotel chain. So Jen Spangler added the word *murder* to the phrase, and that lined up the search engine ducks in a neat but bloody row.

Her father had informed her that the Carlton Ritz case file, the actual case file, complete with ketchup, mayo and coffee stains, would be made available to her on Monday. But that was distant future. It was Saturday evening in the present. Her daughter had conked out early. And her dad was floating in an isolation tank—the Spangler bathtub version of one. So unless somebody called her for a date in the next hour, her Saturday night was set.

She had an Uno's pepperoni pizza with her name on it in the freezer. Obviously not as fresh as a dining trip to the real deal would have served up. But it was a deep-dish, with plenty of cheese goo, seasoned tomato sauce and enough pepperoni to remind your taste buds they were alive for a reason.

As a citizen of Greater Chicago and a daughter of a state police official, Jen was aware of some of the elements of the Ritz case. Other details quietly made their way to the pages of her notebook as she conducted her web search.

Carlton Ritz, award-winning crime reporter for the *Tribune*, had been the victim of a homicide. There was no disputing that, even though his body had been found on and around the inbound railroad tracks about a mile north of Union Station, fueling early theories that he'd been the victim of a horrible accident late one night while pursuing a story. The story: the unsolved murder of Loreena White, a twenty-year-old woman whose body had been found dumped—in one piece—along those same railroad tracks five months earlier.

As was his custom, Carlton Ritz had gone beyond the typical reportorial avenues and had put himself inside the story, refusing to let the story fade when police attempts at solving the murder began to fizzle. Early reports of Ritz's death suggested he had been poking around for evidence when he either suffered a heart attack or fell into the path of an incoming train. So the first question had been whether or not he was still alive when the inbound Amtrak from Milwaukee—*The Hiawatha*—turned him into pieces.

The Medical Examiner's conclusion was that Carl "Carlton Ritz" Biffle was already dead when *The Hiawatha* hit him. And not dead from natural causes. The reporter's head had been bashed in by repeated blows from a blunt object. Not even the train had been able to hide that.

She heard the inward burp and swirling sucking sound as her dad pulled the plug on the bathwater. Her first interview—her closest and most convenient—was sitting fifty feet away in a bathtub, doing his usual post-bath ritual. Sitting there in all his middle-aged glory, waiting for all the water to exit the tub before he did. Jen understood. Those three or four minutes were precious alone time. Thinking time. Contemplating the fate of humanity time. Contemplating your own little life time. And what better way to do it than in the wet naked form you were born in?

Who needed a fancy rebirthing experience in some expensive spa when you had the classic porcelain of suburban Skokie?

Without question, Ed Spangler knew details of the Carlton Ritz investigation, cold, aborted, failed as it was. But if she went to him, she would have to keep going to him. And that wasn't her way. He was a good dad. But he wasn't a coddling dad. He was a *this is your fork, I suggest you start using it* dad.

If she went to him, she would be obligated to follow his lead. But this was no family wedding reception. For this, she would dance alone. She could never get those damn polka steps anyway.

There was something not quite right about Carlton Ritz. Beginning with the way he looked. She was looking at an online photo of him from the *Tribune* archives. Mostly, she was focusing on his eyes, their *lack* of focus. No, that wasn't quite it either. It wasn't that the eyes weren't focused. They weren't focused on the same thing. One eye was trained on the camera. The other eye seemed to be looking at something behind it. Something at the far side of the room, maybe the far side of the world.

There were two eyes focused on her now. She could feel them against the back of her neck, her shoulders. That prickly feeling that someone knew more about you than you did about them. And there was another thing that signaled the presence of the watcher. Irish Spring.

"You're really good at sneaking up on people," she said before turning to see him standing there in his old blue bathrobe.

"Not quite as adept as some people out there," was his cryptic answer.

Translated: *I still don't like you doing this. But if you insist, watch your ass. Watch your ass closer than you've ever watched it before.*

"I was wondering if you could do me one more favor," Jen ventured.

"If it's reasonable, I'll do my best."

"The case file of the woman who was murdered near Union Station—Loreena White—the one Carlton Ritz was investigating. I'd love to get a look at that file too."

34

I N the memory, it is always a late summer day. The smell of August air. The smell of summer, past peak. The sense of it, that the most intense living of the flowers, the trees, has already been lived. The frenzied growth of June and July has run its course.

There is something sad about this to the young man. To the older man who watches him from the future, there is something tragic about it. The waning of summer. The fading of something never to be known in the same way again.

The young man—the boy, really—is standing in the garage, poised before the twin metal garbage cans. It has not been a decision easily reached. For boys of twelve, few decisions are.

It is a decision several days in the making. The decision to retrieve the book. In the days since it was thrown away, life, damaged as it is, has gone on. And so, the trash of life has gone on, continuing, as it does, in the endless stream of things consumed, things used, things dumped, destroyed, left to rot.

He smells this. The smells of life already lived, already gone bad.

Mercifully, the garbagemen will come tomorrow. For the sake of the smell. For the sake of him, maybe not so merciful. If he is to retrieve the book, he must do it now. While he has the opportunity. While his parents are gone. It would be easier, of course, if they never came back. If they were gone forever. But he is not a child anymore. He is not a little boy. Wishing them dead is a waste of time.

If he does retrieve the book—and they find out—he may wish *he* were dead. In fact, he can't think of anything he could do that would be more outrageous to his parents than to retrieve the book.

What would they think? What would they do? Better not to find out. Better to leave the book in the metal can on the right, beneath the several paper grocery bags of expired life.

In the memory, it is always that August day. And in that moment of the memory, the older man always sees the young man take the first step toward the garbage. The first irreversible step. He sees the hands reaching out to the cover of the can, the fingers touching, feeling the surface of the metal, like the fingers of a blind person reading a stranger's face.

The hands move to grasp the handle, lift the lid.

There is a slight hesitation. As if the young man is considering putting the cover back and avoiding the massacre to follow. But the older man knows he is just pausing to decide where to put the cover so he can proceed. On top of the other garbage can. Of course, as twins, the perfect fit. And so he sets it there, listens to the words his mind sends him to describe the smell that has been released into the sad August air.

The paper bags have been weakened, wettened by the decomposition. So he must handle them carefully as he sets them, one by one, on the concrete floor. Six bags total. And then it is just the book at the bottom of the can. The book that was never to be seen again. In its spoiled white cloth cover. With gold letters spelling out the names of the man and woman and the date when they became one.

35

DENNIS Fassbender took one of the longest pisses Hewitt had ever witnessed. Not that she was in the habit of watching men urinate in the wild. But she'd been around enough men—father, boyfriends, colleagues, the occasional fiancé—that she'd seen some, heard plenty. And what she saw now as part of her surveillance informed her that this man had an aquarium for a bladder.

It was always best to present yourself to a person of interest when they had their guard down. Zipper down was even better. But she waited him out, in the sallow light of the partial moon. She figured he deserved the courtesy.

"Mr. Fassbender?"

He turned like a startled bear. From her position in the trees on the other side of the hiking path, Hewitt felt, suddenly, like food.

"Apparently you don't know the meaning of the word *retreat*," Dennis Fassbender announced in a voice that, given the context, couldn't have been more ursine.

As Hewitt stepped toward him, she expected him to follow up with a big, bassy *"Only you can prevent forest fires."*

"I'm sorry," she said. "But I have some terrible news."

She watched as he read her, read the situation. Putting it together. How her car was parked in the adjacent lot. How she'd been observing him in his role as leader of the men's weekend retreat until he broke off to take a leak.

"Lourdes called me," he said. They had drawn to within ten feet of one another. Close enough, for now, for both.

Dennis Fassbender expressed his deep shock and sorrow in therapeutic style. The shock and sorrow were in his voice, but not his moonlit face. Maybe in the sun it would have been more obvious that he was appropriately distraught.

"Is there somewhere we could sit down and talk for a few minutes?" Hewitt posed. "This just doesn't feel like the most conducive place for a heart to heart."

"I'm on a men's retreat," he said dissuadingly.

"If you're trying to tell me it's *no girls allowed*, you needed to post a sign before you opened for business."

T HERE was a campfire smoldering about a hundred feet from the main fire circle of the men's gathering. Dennis Fassbender stoked the fire, threw a couple of pieces of hardwood on it, blew into it a couple of times with lungs Hewitt assumed were only slightly bigger than his bladder. In effect, the counselor had allowed her into the men's club without actually letting her in. Although to Hewitt, the distance from the men didn't matter. From the way the dozen or so estranged husbands were staring at her, she might as well have been tied up nude on a spit over the main hearth.

As her fireside chat with Dennis Fassbender ensued, she couldn't help thinking how possible it actually felt that she might end up there. With this gang of disenfranchised husbands, their fires, their drumming, their secret rituals in the dark. And then to have a vestal virgin drop from the heavens. Well, that aspect she didn't have to worry about. The record indicated she was no virgin, vestal or otherwise.

She covered the predictable territory with Fassbender. Background on the two victims. An overview of their joint therapy. Nothing there that fanned the investigational flames.

"Well, the one thing we really need to start looking at is the possibility that someone has it in for you, one of your colleagues, your business. Or all of the above."

Dennis Fassbender got that, told Hewitt with his eyes that he'd already been there in his own thinking.

"But that could be anyone," he said. "Collectively we've had hundreds, thousands of clients. Professional and personal relationships. We've all written articles, made public appearances, media appearances."

He paused then, his eyes settling into the flames of the campfire. "And then, of course, there's Maya's book."

Maya's book. *Maya's book*. If Maya Macy had a book, why hadn't it shown up in Hewitt's top line background check? Any www search would have coughed that up.

"It was almost fifteen years ago," Dennis Fassbender volunteered. "She published under a pen name."

That made the world make a little more sense. Even in the context of campfires and estranged husbands of the forest.

"May I ask the pen name?"

"Amanda Lilliput."

Hewitt filed the name. But even as she was filing it, she bumped into a file that already seemed to exist.

"I wouldn't have brought it up if I wasn't willing to share," Dennis Fassbender continued. "You would have found it eventually anyway. It's not like it's been sealed away from the world. Although if Maya had the power . . ."

Three minutes of campfire crackling later, Hewitt understood why Maya Macy would have envied such power. Any book titled *Learning to Love Your Inner Slut* was going to attract some serious lightning to the rod. Funny thing—outrageous thing—was that Hewitt not only remembered hearing of the book, she remembered holding it in her hands. Paging through it at a B. Dalton. Damn near buying it. *Damn near* to the point of eyeballing the cashier to see if she felt comfortable revealing that much of herself to a bookseller.

Ah, the wondrous unpredictability of life. She would've never imagined a men's marriage crisis retreat would be the thing to make her revisit her decision on *Learning to Love Your Inner Slut.*

"So you're aware—familiar—with it?"

Now she was going to buy the freaking book after all. And Dennis Fassbender was going to ring her up.

"I've seen it," Hewitt said. No need to pretend she hadn't. Dennis Fassbender was apparently pretty adept at spotting pretenders.

"Have you read it?

"Paged through."

"Never bought one?"

"No."

"Never was willing to let it into your home?"

He didn't look at her when he said it, pretending to be more interested in the snaps and swirls of the campfire flames than in her reaction. But clearly he was going for a reaction. And she wasn't sure why. Which made her feel like toasting a stick-full of marshmallows and shoving them in his face.

Hewitt tried to put in the curbs on her emotions right there. She knew it was true that cooler heads prevailed. But fantasizing about rubbing hot marshmallows against an opponent's face had its momentary merits too. Not that Dennis Fassbender had just like that become her opponent. But his comment about not taking the book home had taken the conversation not only into her house but into her private space.

"And how did it feel taking the book into *your* home?" Hewitt asked him, with a point blankness to it that made his face less bemused and more perturbed, pained, more marshmallow-coated.

"I didn't have to take it home," he responded. "Because I had the dubious fortune of living with it."

Dennis and Maya sitting in a tree. F-U-C-K-I-N-G.

A smile came to his face at the same time it would've if he had actually heard Hewitt's thought. But Hewitt recognized the expression as preconfessional.

"We were just a few months into the relationship when it was published. It was pretty cool at first. Seeing the person you're involved with taking flight like that, you know, and you being the confidante. But then the outside world started to report in. As it always does. And a lot of times that's not terribly pretty. I don't have to tell *you* that, do I?"

He lifted his eyes from the fire, cooled them against Hewitt's face. Hewitt chose not to answer, responded instead by reaching into her bag and withdrawing a framed photograph. Dennis Fassbender wanted to know all about it immediately. That was abundantly clear to Hewitt from his reaction. The needful, almost lustful look in his eyes, the way his hands became active against his bent knees.

"Just one last thing for you," Hewitt said as she handed him a picture from her parents' wedding.

He took it, turned it, let out a half-sigh, half-laugh.

"I'd like you to tell me what you see in these two people," Hewitt said.

His larger-than-normal brain did the analysis in a matter of seconds.

"I see two very happy human beings who will someday raise a very inquisitive and ballsy daughter."

36

SHE is dancing with her father, and at first she doesn't understand where. Even less does she understand why.

She had danced with her dad only a handful of times. Yet she had a sense for how he danced. And this was it. How he moved. This was how his body felt. He was never a great dancer. He knew his steps well enough. But as far as movement above the hips, there was something reluctant, almost apologetic about the way he engaged a partner. Or at least the way he engaged his dancing daughter.

This is the last time they will dance together. The awareness of this hits her all at once. And the dread of that notion turns her skin cold, throws her nervous system into chaos.

She feels like she will fall. She feels like her father will let her fall. As if he has no choice but to let this happen, to let the thought realize its potential, to let the dread fulfill itself.

If she falls, there will be no floor to stop her. Her balance is gone now. Her legs are searching for some sense of structure. Her entire body, her entire being, rattles in a furious hot-for-cold exchange.

The world, the dream, *everything* goes white as she begins to fall. But just as the ocean of whiteness starts to claim her, she feels his strong hands grasp the bones of her thighs.

How can his hands be grabbing her bones? She feels it unmistakably. His hands, not grabbing her by the skin and muscle, but by the bones, the femurs themselves.

It is from this base of strength, these rods of power that her father snaps her—the rest of her—pelvis, spine and head into their original positions. And she is there with him, in his arms, face to face.

There is a price to be paid for her rescue, her salvation. And she sees this now, sees it in the face that looks back at her, in the face she now realizes she is seeing for the first time in the dream.

She understands. Only one of his eyes can see her. She knows intuitively. Physically, she can tell by the way the eye, the left one, moves with her, reaches out to her, communicates with her. *I will hold on as long as I can.* She hears the thought, her thought, in his voice, but as if it has been spoken by the eye. The left one. And she understands she must confront now the other eye. So she does. And what Jen Spangler sees is what she already knows.

His right eye is sightless, blank, vacant. His right eye is already dead.

37

HEWITT had never been much of an incense burner. Given the smells she encountered on the postmortem side of life, the other side of day-to-day existence usually smelled okay enough without the need for enhancement.

But this incense was a different story. It didn't have the psychedelic sweetness of typical exotics-shop incense. No, this was special incense. Delicately rendered. Reverential. This was God's incense.

Hewitt remembered encountering the scent, the feeling for the first time at a Catholic wedding as a child. Sitting between her parents, she had observed with rapt attention as the Catholic faithful entered the church, dipping their fingers in the little font of holy water and touching their foreheads. She remembered some of the older church members genuflecting. And then there was the kneeling in prayer. But all that was for them, for the Catholics only. For people like Captain Ed Spangler. And his daughter, a former choir girl with a voice so pretty, her father teared up a little whenever he mentioned it. And, of course, Mr. Brady Stephen Richter, former altar boy. One of the fortunate ones.

The incense that burned during the walk-in, the processional, however, was something Hewitt had always considered public domain. Sitting in her aisle seat in the third-last pew of the church on this Sunday morning, she had the thought that it would be nice to have a home supply of that incense. It was that good. That *pure*. By now the processional incense had already faded. The reading of the second gospel had just been completed. Father Brian Wilson had risen from his ornate, wood-carved chair and crossed the altar to deliver his homily.

"As most, if not all of you, already know, St. Sebastian's has suffered a great loss."

He had spoken these words with his head lowered to the polished marble floor. He lifted his head now. Then, with a deep inhalation, his shoulders. A stillness inundated the church, a stillness even a fussing infant and a couple of chatty toddlers were at least temporarily compelled to observe.

"Joseph and Rita Vandermause. By now I'm sure you know. How could you not know? And as I thought about them, Joe and Rita, as I prepared this homily, the first thing I had to decide was the words I would use to describe their deaths."

Father Brian Wilson was one of those public speakers who could cast his eyes out over a large room and make each individual think he was zeroing in on them. In the early parts of the mass, he had caught Hewitt in that hold several times. But she was so far back in the church she had attributed it to just that—effective mass eye contact.

This time, however, his eyes didn't leave her in their wake after the usual five or so seconds. This time the feeling of being caught in the priest's headlights held. And the pause that followed was so dramatic, and the look so penetrating, the little Lutheran girl in Hewitt thought she was going to be asked to stand and sing a solo.

"How do we describe deaths like this?" he asked Hewitt instead. "Often we hear a death referred to as a *passing away*. So, yes, we could say that Joe and Rita Vandermause passed away. But would anyone really believe that? Would anyone accept that as an accurate description of what happened to them?"

His eyes left Hewitt and drifted to the front of the congregation. The infant began to fuss again. But other than the breathing of hundreds of hushed souls, there was no other sound in the church.

Hewitt was one of those hushed souls. Hushed and a little stunned. Hushed by the priest's piercing presence. Stunned by the brutal honesty of his reflection. And Hewitt found it all the more compelling because she had a very strong feeling Father Brian Wilson had never surfed in such brutal waters before.

"So I contemplated that. An honest, accurate way to talk about it today. Because there's no *not talking about it* in this church, this community. And between you and me and God, there's no talking about anything else until we've talked about this."

He had frozen Hewitt in his headlights again—at the *you and me and God.*

"Joe and Rita Vandermause didn't pass away. Joe and Rita Vandermause didn't slip away. Joe and Rita Vandermause didn't leave this world."

He took in a long breath. Not just for himself. But for everyone else in the church.

"Joe and Rita Vandermause *lost their lives.*"

The way he said it—the way Hewitt decoded it—clearly communicated that this was not a case of having wandered off the path and gotten lost. This was a case, the worst kind possible, of being ruthlessly attacked and dragged away and thrown into the abyss. And for that, there was historic precedent in Christendom. There were enough martyrs and victims to fill a sea. And given the identity of their leader, that sea was named Galilee.

"He was crucified, dead, and buried."

Father Brian Wilson allowed the words to hover on the Sunday morning air. Until, after several seconds, his next words came, at an unexpectedly high volume, and with a rupture in the pitch of his voice.

"He descended into hell!"

It was here that he left such a gaping silence Hewitt imagined the organist must have been twitching to fill it with an interlude.

"He descended into hell!"

Louder and, definitely, with more feeling.

"We say these words. We say them together each time we gather. But who among us—the man standing at the altar included—has ever actually considered the full weight of those words, the full depth of those words?"

As his eyes found the polished floor of the altar, he allowed them to rest there.

"And some of us—the man at the altar included—may have asked ourselves: Why would God allow such a thing to happen?" Here he looked up, to address the next question to everyone in God's house. "How could God allow his own son to spend even one hour in hell? How could God allow two members of this church to spend even one minute in the hands of a killer?"

A collective murmur was undulating through the church. Not a murmur of words, but a murmur of shifting bodies. Uncomfortable bodies, sensing additional discomfort to come.

"Now some of us might think there is no answer to these questions, to questions of this nature. The man at the altar would have once believed that to be the case. But today I am willing to offer you my understanding of an answer. And I do so, I offer this, for the sake of Jesus Christ. For the sake of John the Baptist. For the sake of un-fathomable numbers of Christian souls. For the sake of Joseph and Rita Vandermause."

At some point during that pronouncement, the priest's eyes had left their tending of the congregation. His gaze had lifted above the heads of the flock and was focusing not just over them, but beyond them. And Hewitt had a strong sense of what he was looking at.

That he was staring at the face of God explained the look on his own face, but only partly so. To Hewitt's mind, it was also the fact that he wasn't seeking permission from God to make his next statement. He was giving God a heads-up.

"But there has to be an answer," he said, first to the Supreme Being, then, with a nod of his head, to the members and guests of his church. "Do the souls of all those prior—and Joe and Rita now—do those souls not deserve an answer?"

There was a sweep of breeze through the opened windows of the church that Hewitt felt against her moist palms. As if God had sighed, Ed Spangler–style, and said: *"Fine. Let them see."*

"And the answer is this. God did not *allow* these things to happen. Because God was *powerless* to stop them."

There was a collective gasp from the parishioners at that. And why not? This was awesome stuff. And Hewitt's own head was buzzing with the amazing possibilities this surfing holy man was presenting.

"And God was powerless because, even though he has the power, to intervene would have meant breaking a universal covenant that, it is clear, he has agreed to observe. And that is the *covenant of opposites*. Of one force engendering its inverse twin. So that there could be no light without darkness. No good without evil. No God, at least as we understand God to be, without his opposite."

Hewitt felt another sigh against her damp palms, this one her own.

"Hegel," she said in her mind—with enough conviction that her lips moved to form the words. *"Fucking Hegel."*

38

AND fucking David Byrne. The Talking Heads version of him anyway. Because it was his song, "Life in Wartime," that had turned Hewitt's pituitary gland into a twirling disco ball, and the inside of her head into a throbbing dance club. Not that "Life in Wartime" was disco. It wasn't. But it was definitely dance. And the lyrics that accompanied that bump and grind of the mind were the thing Hewitt couldn't shake.

This ain't no party, this ain't no disco, this ain't no fooling around.

Hewitt could reasonably assume those lyrics had never been used by a Catholic priest to establish a context for the battle between good and evil. At least not until this Sunday. Not until a nice Lutheran girl in the back of the church had made the inexorable connection.

Of course, that would have all been fine if it was just the song that had gotten into her head. To play once or twice or several hundred times in the juke box of her thoughts. But now, as was her MO du jour, she had to commission a jazz artist to interpret it.

And it wasn't like she didn't have other things to figure out. Like, for starters, how to keep her composure and look like she belonged in the Catholic communion line, especially the one she had gone out of her way to switch into. It was comforting, at least, that she knew the protocol for pretenders. Father Brian Wilson had enunciated that clearly enough in his pre-Eucharist instructions.

"For any visitors who are not Catholic and who wish to come for-

ward, please cross your arms like this as you reach the front and you will receive a special blessing."

She was only five spots away from the front of the line now. And the one older man who had been keeping a suspicious eye on her since she made the line switch had now received his wine and host, had crossed himself and proceeded on his way.

Four spots to go, and still her Eucharist minister had not recognized her. Then again, it wasn't his job to look down the line and see who was coming. It was his job to look into the eyes of the one before him, to commune in that moment with the God they shared and with the body of his son.

Three to go. She could hear his voice clearly now.

"The body of Christ."

Two . . .

"The body of Christ."

As he raised the host for the last soul in line ahead of Hewitt, his eyes hit her, but only with a glancing blow. He wasn't about to let some interloper deprive an eminently deserving church member of their moment with Father, Son, Holy Ghost and multitasking Deacon.

"The body of Christ."

Hewitt stepped forward, assumed the position, folding her arms in an X that crossed her chest.

She looked for everything here. In the watery fonts of his eyes. The same way she would be looking at his eyes the next time she approached him. Which, according to her plans, would be before either of them had a chance to exit the big, sad, Hegelian church.

39

IN accepting heaven, was there a part of you that had to die on earth before the rest of you did? Jen Spangler reflected on that thought, concluded she was the only person on the planet contemplating that exact question while spreading Welch's grape jelly on a piece of Roman Meal toast.

She was alone in the house, alone with her thoughts. And being it was the house she grew up in, it made her thinking all the more alone. Especially with her mother already gone and her father with one eye already fixed and dilated.

She took a bite of toast, took memory-comfort in the taste of the Welch's, unchanged since her childhood, since the days when her father would take *her* to the park and her mother would be alone in the house with her own thoughts.

Solace swept over her at the kitchen table. A lucid realization that you were never really alone. As long as you had grape jelly in the house. Or God. But God was a lot more work. A lot more to reconcile. Especially if you died one eye at a time. She knew the man in her dream who had seemed to be her father wasn't really him. That was why, for the first three-fourths of the dream, she hadn't been able to see his face.

She got up from the table, went to the counter, to the coffeemaker, found it in the state she always found it. Except for those rare occasions when she was actually up before her dad.

Eight-and-a-half cups of less-than-fresh-brewed coffee. The ten cups he always started with—to brew less would have been an admission that his wife and the mother of his daughter and the grandmother of his granddaughter was never coming back for one more cup. That starting ten minus his own single one with breakfast, minus the half-cup he took for the ride into work.

So she brought the carafe down to seven-and-a-half cups, returned to the table, went back to work on the jelly toast, went back to work on the Carlton Ritz case. She knew him now. Because it had been him in the dream. Her mind had disguised him as her father at the end. But the man with one eye already dead was the already dead Carlton Ritz/Carl Biffle. And what Jen regretted was that she'd totally screwed up the dream from there.

It was a dream that definitely fell into the nightmare category. And in nightmares, the disturbing shit always cried out for the spotlight. Of the two eyes on the face of the Ritz/Biffle entity, the light had come to the disturbing one, the opaque one, the already-dead one. And being already dead, there had been nothing there for her to see.

And that was exactly where she'd blown it. Because the knowledge that only one eye was dead meant what? That the other freaking eye was alive. *No shit, Sherlock*. The other eye was alive, with a story to tell. The story of what it had seen in those last crazy hours of life. And more importantly, what it had seen in the days or weeks before those final crazy hours. What it had seen that had put Carlton Ritz on a one-way, one-eyed journey to oblivion.

40

"WHY didn't you tell me you had treated Rita Vandermause as a patient?"

Dr. Gerry Boccachio had taken a donut along for the walking interview he himself had suggested—ostensibly to get some air and some circulation after an hour-and-a-half in church. But also, Hewitt was certain, to get away from the church and the roving eyes of the departing membership.

Hewitt had declined to take a donut for herself. As she watched her fellow walker take his sweet time in finishing his, she was revisiting that decision. Maybe not a donut. But a banana nut muffin had called her name at least twice.

"Patient-doctor privilege," he said, with his mouth not quite empty. "Respect for the deceased."

Respect for the dead Hewitt bought. But it was a little early in the game to be playing the patient-doctor privilege card.

"We're a small parish," he continued. "And Chicago, despite being the third largest city in the country, is still a small town."

His brown wingtips were marking steady time against the sidewalk, slightly syncopated, his left foot lagging a little behind the beat. And, of course, the damn rhythm of it was close enough to Hewitt's brain-track selection that "Life in Wartime" was suddenly breaking out all over the sun-coated suburban neighborhood.

"Go to Disney World and a thousand child mannequins will tell you *it's a small world after all*," Hewitt offered. "But it's only going to get smaller if you withhold information—information Rita Vandermause might have imparted during your sessions—that could help us stop a killer from killing again."

His left foot picked up the pace.

"I would hardly refer to that as withholding information," he said, in a voice that had quickened its pace too. "I would put that in the category of information that was never requested."

It was clear to Hewitt that he was one of those self-ordained men who always had to be the smartest one in the room. Or in this case, the smartest one on the sidewalk.

"But as a Christian man, a Catholic, if you had something that would help, why wouldn't you offer it?"

The left wingtip decelerated first, then the right, until both stopped moving entirely.

"If there *was* such information, there's only one way it could help you stop the killer," he said. "And that's if the killer is me."

The birds of waning summer had been singing all along. But their song took center stage in the quiet that ensued in that shared square of concrete. And something about the wild, voluminous intensity of it solved one of Hewitt's Sunday morning problems.

Coltrane. She came within a flutter of her larynx from saying it out loud.

"Obviously that's what you're doing here today," he accused, like some giant scolding starling. "I'm sure you didn't come all the way out here on a Sunday morning for the free fellowship and Father Wilson's homily."

"It was a hell of a homily, wasn't it?"

Hewitt's comment, her unwillingness to engage his calculated aggression, knocked him back a little. Into the heel of his left shoe first, then his right.

"I mean you have to admit it isn't every day you see a priest get up God's nose like that."

That pushed a few more pounds of him into the heels of the wingtips.

"He's angry," the psychiatrist said, reclaiming his deacon's voice. "Innocent people have been brutally murdered. That makes some people very upset."

His weight was moving to the front of the shoes, and the shoes were moving toward Hewitt. Just a half-step each, but enough to send a message. Hewitt let him have the space. A single square of concrete in Arlington Heights wasn't worth fighting over. Not at this point.

"You want to know if I was in love with Rita Vandermause enough to kill her."

If they had been engaged in a short-distance, Western-style gun draw, she wasn't sure she could hit him first. He was quick, cagey. And if he wasn't always the smartest guy in the room, he was enough of a performer to convince the room he was.

"I don't draw conclusions until they're reasonably defensible," Hewitt told him. "But the society I work for expects me to draw inferences pretty much every fifteen seconds."

"So what inference are you drawing—or should I say creating—right now?"

"Right now I'm positing that if we don't resume our walking, the people looking out the window of the white split-level ranch are going to think we're either beginning an affair or ending one."

As Dr. Gerry Boccachio silently capitulated and resumed his walking, just a step in front of her, it gave Hewitt a moment to confirm her selection of John Coltrane for the David Byrne composition. There was no other choice. Just as in the mid-1960s there was no one else who could have taken a song from *The Sound of Music* and turned it into a jazz masterwork. Now "My Favorite Things" and "Life in Wartime" couldn't have been a wider ocean apart. Julie Andrews as a nun versus David Byrne as a punk. Yet here Hewitt was, bringing those entities to the same bedroom. At some level, envisioning their love child. But first she had to envision their love.

"You know, there's a type of man who would be attracted to you," the strolling shrink offered, in a tone that framed the statement in potentiality only. It was clinical, dismissive that way. As if in Hewitt's almost four decades of existence it had never happened, but there was always a chance.

"I hope he's a handsome prince with an even handsomer horse."

Dr. Gerry Boccachio turned, looked at her for a moment, came dangerously close to acknowledging her as a near-equal.

"You see. That's just it. The biting wit. The razor-sharp teeth. There's a type of man who's attracted to the danger of the iconoclast. A risk-taker."

"A man who doesn't mind getting a few tooth marks on his male ego," Hewitt extrapolated. "As long as it gets the job done."

"You're a quick study," he told her, with a muted grin of admiration. "You take no prisoners. Unless someone is brave enough to touch that heart of yours. And then you give them the keys to the prison."

"That's very poetic," Hewitt said. "I guess I'm wondering if your answer to my next question will be just as lyrical. Did you ever treat a Theodore or Naomi Nelson?"

He knew the names. That much she could see instantly. What she didn't know was whether he knew them from personal experience or from any of a hundred breaking news reports on the city's airwaves. He professed to the latter.

"No," he said. "You're welcome to come and look at my patient logs. I know who they are. I'm sorry for what happened to them. Whether that's a poetic answer or not, I don't know."

"Doesn't matter," Hewitt told him. "That's not what I was looking for."

41

IN Chicago, all roads lead, eventually, to Union Station. So when she left a note for her father, saying she was going to UIC to do some library research and could he watch Victoria for another couple of hours, it wasn't exactly a fib. Union Station was on the way, more or less. Maybe not exactly as the crow flew. But she wasn't exactly flying there with a flock of crows. She was rolling with a pack of Sunday morning expressway drivers. And she, or rather her vehicle, was getting the usual glances of interest. And once the looks went from the exterior of the vehicle to the front passenger seat, the interest, of course, grew.

It wasn't every day you saw a twenty-two-year-old woman driving an unmarked but very official-looking police vehicle. Then again, it wasn't every day your dad could get you a killer deal on a retired police fleet sedan. So the gray Crown Victoria with its side-mirror-spotlight had become her official ride, and her unofficial badge-on-wheels. And her official theme music was whatever was playing on the smooth jazz station the radio was tuned to. She liked smooth jazz. She knew Hewitt would probably consider it pussy music. But she enjoyed it. It made her relax. Unlike the supposedly *real jazz* Hewitt listened to. Some of that stuff got a little too frenetic for its own good. Kind of like its famous listener.

Driving into the area north of Union Station, Jen was happy she had such a square-jawed, don't-fuck-with-this-one car. But once she got out of the vehicle, she was just another criminology student on a field trip. Especially since she'd opted not to include her father's heirloom re-volver in the occasion. Well-connected criminology students packing heat on a field trip were prime candidates for the evening news.

The well-connected thing she couldn't do anything about. It wasn't as bad as being forced to wear an orange windbreaker in the field so everyone would know who she was and give her a little extra consider-ation. Her father's shadow was a big one. But she had two feet of her own, and the closet-full of shoes to give her whatever level of mobility she needed. On this occasion, the Diesel running shoes.

From archived newspaper reports, she knew, within a hundred yards or so, where the reporter's body had been found. And given that it had been hit by a train, it wasn't like you could've put a typical chalk outline around it. You would've needed a marker with a seriously larger perimeter. More like the kind of thing they used to contain oil spills.

There was a high, chain-link fence bordering both sides of the tracks. As with any chain-link fence, Jen knew there would be a human-made opening somewhere. A force of nature come to bear. A force of nature with a wire cutter. What would compel you to want to get down to some train tracks enough to cut your way through, who the hell knew? Maybe nothing. Maybe just a general dislike of chain-link fences, and what they represented to some wandering soul's sense of freedom.

Sure as shit, she found an opening. Within seconds, she was expe-riencing the chain-link liberation herself. And just as quickly, she was experiencing the creepy feeling of wading into the tall grass sanctuary of a thousand grasshoppers. And it wasn't just the hopping kind of grasshoppers. Also present were the kind that creeped her out the most. The kind of grasshopper that could jump and really take to the air and cover some serious distance. The grass-*flyers*.

She was coming down the embankment toward the first set of train tracks when the first grass-flyer buzzed her face. Not as if it had gone out of its way like some scout sent to intimidate her. It was just following its nature. To leap out of the grass and fly around to see what was going on.

At the bottom of the embankment, her intrusion sent up a legion of common hoppers. The majority of them were just returning to the tall grass when another grass-flyer took a direct flight pattern at her face, causing her to duck forward and close her eyes. She heard the sound of a hard smack at the same moment she felt an explosion of nausea. And her last thought was that she was going to black out before she could throw up.

42

HEWITT'S left hand was flying. And there was something totally liberating about it. This wasn't the first time her hand had flown. She'd been there many times before. Just not in a while. Her first time, of course, had been in the family car. The Buick wagon. Riding where she always rode, in the backseat behind her dad as he drove. The idea of rolling down your side window and letting your hand out for some air surfing was the kind of escape you came up with when you were ten years old. Or thirty-eight. With a brand new ring on your finger. With a diamond cut just right for you. Because you were a princess dammit. Even if your mom and dad weren't around to tell you.

Hewitt might not have had her parents in the car. But she did have her latest family. Her *case* family. The motley group of players that had come careening and crashing into her life since Captain Spangler reported the first missing head.

As case families went, this one was in its own league. Beginning with an odd family of family therapists. And in classic family mode, they'd been on their best behavior for public consumption. Like a big extended family coming together for a big extended family photo. She was up to her eyeballs in family drama with this case family. Problem was she didn't have a lead character.

The sextet of therapists had given her their best smiling family photo. But no one had called out across the coffee table or whispered in her ear: *I know we're all fascinating people, but I'm the one you want to go to dinner with for an exchange of secrets.*

Each player, however, had given her some behavioral moments that had given her pause. Especially with Dennis Fassbender's history of creative uses for wedding photos. But enough to suggest he or any of the rest of them could have been a prime mover in what had been done? Enough to take group immolation to that exponential extreme?

No and no.

And yet there was something there that she couldn't absolve them of. Something in their collective attitude, their group culture—their smilingly benevolent exterior with its kinky underside—that Hewitt couldn't reconcile.

Well, her little Sunday afternoon research quest was designed to shine some light into those murky waters. But her destination was still five minutes away. Which gave her a little time to contemplate the two other branches of her investigational family tree.

The next family unit would have been the most socially controversial at first blush. Because it was a family headed by two dads. One a deep-thinking, God-loving, holy-water-dispensing herder of lost souls. The other, a deep-thinking, head-shrinking, Eucharist-dispensing shaper of young men whose bodies had already been shaped to Hewitt's personal standards by thousands of hours of work in chlorinated pools.

Of all the players she'd encountered, the psychiatrist–deacon–pool boy had given her the most to think about. To say the man was a walking and/or swimming contradiction was obvious. He was a faith-based psychiatrist. A scientist of the human mind in a world of mysticism, ritual, faith. A medical doctor certified by the American Psychiatric Association who, in the shrieks and sobs of a difficult case, would ultimately have to ask himself, *What would Dr. Jesus do?*

On the search of the Ted and Naomi Nelson home, they'd found no evidence of any relationship with the psychiatrist. She would send

Megna on Monday morning to take the doctor up on his offer to view patient logs. But given that he *had* known one of the first victims, Rita Vandermause, professionally and personally, and had remained unwilling to discuss his experience after the post-mass hike, Hewitt now had to ask, *"What would detective Jesus do?"* To her mind, there was no question that the messianic detective would have put a twenty-four-hour tail on Dr. Gerry Boccachio. So if the good doctor didn't already have an invisible friend, he had one now. Hewitt had been happy to see to that. Where it would lead was anyone's guess, God included.

Which led her to her last family. The smallest and, as it stood, the most broken. *The Biffles.* A father-son family unit whose only possible family reunion would be someday, somewhere in the afterlife. At which point they could invite the mother of the family, Stephanie Biffle, to the reunion too. She'd been waiting a long time. According to Hewitt's information, seven years since her death from a brain aneurysm.

An afterlife family reunion. That was all Hewitt needed. That neuro-reactive concept. The questions were popping like an end-stage microwave bag of Movie Time. Would there be picnic tables at an afterlife family reunion? Would there be an outdoor pavilion in case it rained? Would grills be provided? Did you have to bring your own meat? If cream soda was the only soft drink left in the big ice tub, would there be a vending machine within walking distance?

Oh, shit. And then there was the almost-family member so close to her she'd damn near forgotten about her. The almost-sister she'd done her best to keep busy but to keep on the sideline for her own good. She'd have to check in as a courtesy. Next time her cell phone hand wasn't busy flying out the window.

She had parked the car, was out and on foot, taking her musings into the bookstore. Right until the moment she made partial eye contact through her big Chanels with the first of the two booksellers at the counter. A woman well into middle age, with a diamond wedding band—God, was she really looking at that stuff so closely now?—who gave off the matronly vibe of an empty-nester who was working at a bookstore to help put a little something back into the nest egg.

"How may I help you?"

"I believe you're holding a book for me."

Apparently the woman hadn't been earning extra cash long. Because she turned quickly to the young man beside her for guidance.

"It's for *Hewitt*," the customer said.

The young man took his time in taking a good, hard look at Hewitt. Which gave Hewitt a chance to read him too. Everything about the guy screamed trendy, with the exception of his Civil War sideburns. Although Hewitt couldn't rule out their trendiness either, having been a while since she'd done any serious paging through *Vogue*.

Mr. Post Modern Antebellum hesitated just enough to let her know he'd been anticipating her arrival. Not *her* arrival specifically, but whoever would be coming to pick up the last copy they had in stock of *that* book. The big Chanels over Hewitt eyes had kept him from recognizing her—or maybe he didn't catch much news, being so busy coordinating his wardrobe and growing those sideburns.

And the true pisser of the delay was that it wasn't just him. Because in a couple of tick-tocks of bookstore time, the young man managed to share a little look with the middle-aged woman, unlikely conspirators though they may have been. She was old enough to be his mother. And now that Hewitt caught a look at the woman's face from a new angle, she saw she had some pretty good sideburns going too.

Obviously there'd been some sort of conversation between them about the book. Speculation about who the buyer would be. The kind of person who would walk into their store and walk out with a copy of *Learning to Love Your Inner Slut*.

The young guy rang her up, and it was pretty much just business then, with all the proper *thank-yous* and the obligatory *Are you a member of our special Whatever It Was program?* And, of course, Hewitt was right there with the perfunctory *I don't need a bag*.

It was then, as her hands picked up the book, that she dialed up the controversy of her bookstore appearance.

Sir Sideburns noticed the engagement ring first. But it was his bookstore mom who fixated on it until her eyes radiated their disapproval outward into the rest of her face. And Hewitt was left to exit the bookstore not as a future bride, but as a blushing slut-to-be.

43

SHE is tickling her face. Victoria is tickling her face. But her head hurts too much to open her eyes, to do anything. The sun is up. The day is already bright. Way too bright.

She feels her eyelids trying to open. But each attempt makes her head hurt worse.

Victoria is tickling her eyebrow now. Enough to cause a twitch that unseals the eyelid. To the total sun. Both eyes opening to the total truth. That the soft, exploring fingers of her daughter have become the hard, hunting legs of insects.

She bends her knees, rolls to her side, feels herself throwing up. But nothing comes. She looks to the place in the grass where the contents of her stomach should have been, sees only the grasshoppers that have dropped from her face. As if she has thrown up *them*.

She feels her pockets. Finds her keys. Her wallet.

Then what has been taken?

Ice coats her skin, even in the heat of the summer sun. She feels under her skirt, her privates. Not with her fingers, but with her mind. A quick mental inventory. She feels dry. Doesn't feel violated. Thank God.

Feeling with her hands now. Her skirt, her panties. Everything there.

She takes out her wallet. Twenty-six dollars in cash. Her one credit card. All there.

With these things determined, the bomb of her head goes off, at the back of her skull. Here she knows she has been violated. She feels for the wound, is surprised to find no blood. There is a swelling of the bone. But not a knot. As if she has been struck not by a gun butt or a club, but by something flat. A board. A heavy book.

She is sitting up now. Having assessed the shape of her head, she now assesses the perimeter of her crime scene, realizes, as she does, that this should have been her first priority. To make sure whoever assaulted her is no longer a threat.

It takes her a moment to reclaim the gyroscopes of her inner ears enough to stand up. But life has hit her in the head before. And so she finds her balance, finds her strength.

What the fuck happened?

The answer comes in the voice of an approaching train. Or is it still the rumble of her head? Or are the grasshoppers, the flyers, all beating their wings, revving their engines for some kind of all-at-once attack?

Jen Spangler is alone on the wrong side of the chain-link fence. The train rolls closer. Relentless, unstoppable now, the energy, the force of it. And her head hurts like hell. And the vibration of this incoming train is only going to make it hurt more.

But there is good news. Christ, is there good news. She has been assaulted, but she has not been violated. She has been hurt, but she has not been badly injured.

No one has to know. No one. But especially him. Her father doesn't have to know. This is not something she can ever forget. But it is at least partially, maybe even mostly, erasable.

Like the train that's coming. A big, crazy, earth-dominating minute or two. But then passing into the past, into assault-of-the-senses history. And this, what has happened, passing similarly into assault-of-the-body history. She will have the rest of her life to reconstruct it.

The inbound train's time is now. She sees the long silver exoskeleton of the Amtrak. Like a string of monstrous metallic grasshoppers, end to end. Coming. Coming. Until it is on her, of her, the engine breaking the seal.

She is okay. *She is okay.* A deep breath is what she needs now, to deflate the concussion of the train. She breathes, her chest expanding against the tight hold of her T-shirt. And it is at the apex of that, or maybe just slightly on the other side, slightly into the exhalation, that she realizes she is not okay.

She knows this because she knows her body, knows her skin, knows her breasts. There is no further analysis needed. No confirmation with hands and fingers. Because the feeling of it against her skin is as loud and metallic and screaming as the wheels of the giant grasshopper train against the tracks.

There are eyes on her now. The faces of the passengers as they roll by. The steady beat of them as the train slows in its approach to Union Station.

And they look at her, this lone woman on the wrong side of the chain-link fence. As if they, too, know that someone has gone to the trouble of removing her bra and returning it to her body, inside out.

44

THE world is a good place. He truly believes this. He can't conceive—
he has tried—that the ultimate, the natural state of the world is bad.
This is why he has returned to the wedding albums again. The two versions. To revisit his actions. To revisit the timeline. To consider his actions as a boy versus his actions as a man. And so he takes his time with
the albums. Because he wants to give the world every opportunity to
recognize its true potential, to realize its true form.

Bad people are not bad from the beginning. They are all born *good*.
It is what happens then. What is *allowed* to happen that turns the mirror ugly.

It is not the mirror's fault. It has taken a while, but he understands
this now. *The mirror is not to blame.* The mirror can only reflect what
the world presents. The mirror cannot take bad and make it good. Just
as he knows the world does not have the power to take what is good
and make it bad.

Of course, he doesn't have the first album. After he made the mistake of retrieving it from the garbage, his father had eventually found
it. And the beating he'd taken had been no surprise. The only surpris-
ing thing was the moment when the beating stopped.

And now all this time later, to have found another album. To be sitting here with it now, open to the pictures, pristine once more. Innocent once more. The married couple in the photos was a good couple
then. They had yet to appear in the mirror.

It's a little funny. The thought that he could do with the heads in the new album what he'd done with the first. But this is impossible. There is no reason. There is no one left to see them. His parents, himself as he'd been—they are all gone. The only ones who make any sense to him are the people who are here now, the people who no longer have a need for a wedding album of their own.

A thought climbs the white staircase in his brain. He stands up from the desk, takes the wedding album, keeping it open to the second front-facing page.

He crosses the room to the wall mirror. Slowly, he raises the album, the first page, to face the mirror. Seeing it now, it confirms his thought. It is not the mirror's fault. The mirror sees only what the world puts before it.

45

IT was a little after noon and Hewitt was in her car, in the parking lot of the coffee shop where she'd indulged in a store-bought, way-too-hot cocoa. She was sipping and grimacing her way through the opening chapter of her slut manual, wherein the author laid out her premise that human sex was a form, arguably the highest and purest, of human art. It was the notion that any action, embellishment, articulation, touch beyond the bare necessities of animal-style coitus was, by its very nature, an act of creative expression. And as such, on the female side of the gallery, the ones who were driven to the most passionate expression of their art form were to be praised, revered, loved.

Byron Biffle's phone call put an end to the opening argument. And that was a good thing for the starving artist in Hewitt who had subsisted on bedroom mac and cheese in the years B.B. *Before Brady*. But the interruption was a bad thing, the worst form of bad, with the kind of art she and Byron Biffle would now be adding to their photographic exhibit.

If there was a crazed fan in the bedroom shadows of *Learning to Love Your Inner Slut*, he had just dialed up the crazy level. Forgoing the U.S. Mail for a personal delivery was a clear expression of a desire for more intimacy. And Hewitt, given her recent reading, felt like the perfect woman for the job.

She found Byron Biffle sitting on the front porch of the two-story Victorian, like a kid waiting for a friend to stop by. Knowing from the time he was a kid that you didn't mess with potential evidence, he had left the envelope where he'd found it, leaning against the wrought iron porch railing.

"Needless to say, I wasn't expecting that," he said as Hewitt used a gloved hand to pick it up.

With the envelope in her hands and her mind already connecting with the contents, she heard his words but didn't register them.

"When was the last time you were here?" she asked.

"Friday. End of day."

"And no one was here yesterday?"

"No. With the exception of the person who left this. But no one who works with me."

"Can we step inside, please?" Hewitt asked.

Byron Biffle took a lingering look at the street that felt odd to her. As he opened the front door, his next comment felt equally out of joint.

"You're getting to be a habit with me. You and these deliveries."

Inside, he led her to the production room. As she followed, Hewitt noted the precision with which the second envelope had been labeled—in virtually identical style as the first. This was a neatnik they were dealing with. And Hewitt knew her own neatness, gloves and all, was in all likelihood a misappropriated virtue. Forensics had come up empty on any leave-behinds from the first mailing, other than what Byron Biffle had inadvertently deposited in handling the envelope and its contents. Past that, it was clear the photographer had been working in pristine, controlled conditions.

At a table in the production room, Hewitt used an Exacto to cut the top edge of the envelope as Byron Biffle observed, commented. "If it's not another horrible wedding photo, we'll be disappointed, won't we?"

A flashbulb went off in Hewitt's memory. The man with the camera was Jimmy Stewart. In *Rear Window*. But it was Grace Kelly's line about what awful people they were to be disappointed at the thought that the neighbor-man across the way might *not* be a murderer.

"If it turns out to be a picture of Grace Kelly and Jimmy Stewart, I'll be so happy I'll do a cartwheel for you on the front lawn."

He didn't like that he didn't get it. But she could see from his eyes that he wasn't going to give up on it.

Her fingers were inside the envelope now, finding the single enclosure. The photo. The one she knew wouldn't take her anywhere close to a cartwheel. But the power of the suggestion, the childlike freedom of it, managed to float a kite across the back of her mind. A kite with the faces of Kelly and Stewart stretched over the frame. The faces she pulled into the light, however, were much more grossly distorted.

Moments later, Hewitt and her parting gift were exiting the front door of the *Mundelein Dispatch*. There'd been no need to gasp and groan, no need to grope for words with Byron Biffle this time. On the front porch, she turned, offered him surveillance of the property in the event, unlikely though it was, that the deliveryman decided to call again.

"That's your call," he said. "But I would have to question the chances that whoever's doing this would make the same kind of delivery again. Wouldn't you?"

"I'd say there's about a one hundred percent probability he won't," Hewitt responded. "Of course, I'm hoping there won't be an occasion for another delivery."

"Your hoping sounds something less than hopeful."

"Four decapitated victims will do that to a person," Hewitt said. "You'll have to forgive my moment of weakness."

46

IT is after midnight and he is enjoying a late drive, his appointments having been kept. His mission, for the time being, fulfilled. He is driving the maroon Cadillac, an old man's car. And he has found amusement in allowing himself to casually follow a nameless and, until now, faceless woman in a BMW, a woman about whom he is free to speculate.

A married woman. But not looking joyously so. Having pulled up beside her earlier, he had seen the ring. Paused behind her at the stoplight now, he is able to see just enough of her face in her rearview mirror. Just enough that he is able to interpret her expression.

No one has ever really loved me.

Including, honey, and most glaringly, you. Because, really, where is it written in permanent ink that the capacity to love *unconditionally* is on a short list of humanity's greatest attributes? Human history wasn't exactly a heartfelt, starry-eyed lovefest. In fact, if it hadn't been for a short list of avatars through history, there would have been no road map to a realm called *Love* whatsoever. Historically, the only thing human beings were better at than breeding biologically was breeding intolerance and contempt for all the other types that bred around them. Without the love-blind avatars and the romantically delusional poets, a human world was not exactly the most compassionate place to get dropped from the sky. So the idea of love in some true form being an entitlement, well, you could pick out a star in the black night and make a wish to it for exactly that, but you might be waiting a long time for your star to get back to you.

At the next stoplight, another look from the woman, again open to interpretation.

I hate who I am.

But that would presuppose that you've ever actually met *you*. In a species in which hate comes so easily toward those who are not like ourselves, the same hate, or at least a ricochet version of it, would inevitably be turned against one's confused, misunderstood, *different than we would like it to be* self.

Whether she senses him watching her now or it is just time to check the mirror, her eyes find his face through the windshield. Instantly, he dons the invisible mask for her, his expressionless reflex to being caught in the mirror. She does not wait for the light to turn green before she powers away, saving one last glance for him as she makes her escape.

47

MONDAY morning was breathing against her face. Hewitt lifted out of sleep, thinking Brady was next to her, his skin covered with leftover pizza sauce and her DNA, the same way hers was glazed with his. Sunday nights were his Friday night. And even though she was officially back on the clock on Monday morning, a vicarious Friday night was usually too much to pass up.

She had exited sleep before the clock-radio had a chance to kick in its wake-up jazz. But it was time to face the music anyway—the day, the job, the world, in the sorry state of separation it was.

Pit stops at the microwave and toaster gave her time to reminisce over the Sunday night that could have been Friday but turned out to be nothing but a night of solitary sketching and soul searching. Skewing heavily to the soul-searching side.

On the phone Sunday evening, Brady had heard that in her voice. And maybe fearing his soul might be one of those probed, he had acquiesced into his own solitary night of pizza and wine. Although he probably went to Pepsi, not being the type to open a bottle of wine unless there was something in it for him beyond the buzz.

Once Hewitt had gotten her soul into a comfortable chair across the room from herself, she had begun her search with the premise the author laid out in the second chapter of *Learning to Love Your Inner Slut*. The unsavory notion—at least for a recently engaged woman—that men were genetically programmed to be anything but faithful, lap-dog partners. Because, and the author claimed there was scientific evidence for this, men were hardwired to—as the author had put it so eloquently—*peruse the herd* for any and all possible mating options.

And women, according to this same author, were no temples of monogamy either. They were preprogrammed by nature to seek the best package of genetic goods for their needs, the most pressing of which was stud service for producing the best possible offspring. Which was all well and good in a group of primates where Big Daddy could be identified by the fact he could either beat or scare the shit out of all the other males. But in the socially diverse, free-wheeling human world, finding Mr. Genetically Right required some serious shopping. Something most modern women appeared preprogrammed to do as well.

Okay, that was all fine for the smooth-ape side of life. But what about the heart-mind connection? But what about Elizabeth Barrett Freaking Browning? What about those self-stabbers and poison drinkers, Romeo and Juliet? What about Nat King Cole?

L is for the way you look at me . . .

And what about Gabriel García Márquez? What about *Love in the Time of Cholera?*

A call was coming in on the business line. Hewitt answered, listened as Captain Spangler connected the misbegotten dots. She caught the last name of the victims. *Pennington.* How regal, that name would've appeared on the invitations, the matchbooks, the thank-you notes and, now, the death certificates.

With the victims having been found in separate locations in the village of Glen Ellyn, Hewitt wrote down the first two destinations for her new day, knowing there would be a third. And that would be wherever the hell she had to go to pin down a former literary slut and her current business and bedding partner.

"Do me a favor," Spangler said as a prelude to signing off. "When things settle a little, give Jen a call. Her hair is wound about as tight as I've ever seen it. All this Carlton Ritz business. I think it's getting inside her—a little too deep."

"She just wants to show you something. That's what this whole thing is about."

"So far she's shown me nothing," Spangler sighed. "And she's told me even less."

Hewitt agreed to the request, signed off, knowing she'd get to Jen. But that was down the list. At the top was the call she was placing to Detectives Kaya Schiffman and Glen Kurkewicz, her night-to-day shift of the twenty-four-hour watch she'd put on Dr. Gerry Boccachio. Detective Schiffman took the call, was anticipating it. The news of the latest murders was the lead story on *Good Morning ISP*.

Hewitt listened to Schiffman's details from the log of Dr. Boccachio's recent hours.

"He cooked a steak on his patio about six last night. Went inside. About an hour later, he went for about a twenty-minute walk. After that, he took a swim in his pool. More of a workout really. Then he went inside for the night. We haven't seen him or his red Speedo since."

"And you're sure he hasn't checked out of the house," Hewitt said, knowing it fell into the dumb question pile, but knowing she had to ask anyway.

"We've had eyes on the residence the whole time," Schiffman responded.

"And you're dead solid he stayed put all night?"

"Unless he's a very meticulous sleepwalker, dead solid."

48

J EN was lying on the floor with a Sponge Bob beach towel over her head when the case files arrived via courier. She wouldn't know that for sure until she got up and crossed the room to the front door to confirm the presence of the deliveryperson. But she knew unannounced doorbells at a little after nine on a Monday morning meant one of two things—a special delivery or a special message from Jehovah.

As the odds favored, it was the case files, the archaeology of them contained in an oversized Jet-Pak. She opened it on the living room floor, sitting on the Sponge Bob towel now as her daughter pulled on the opposite end of the envelope, every bit as anxious, as possessive of the package as her mother. Once the files were extracted, Jen let her daughter have the packaging, freeing herself for a couple of unimpeded minutes with the archived remains of Carlton Ritz and Loreena White, the two of them inextricably coupled like this for as long as these paper bones would exist.

She treated the first file she pulled like she would treat a report card. Not looking for the results subject-by-subject. But drawing a bead on the GPA.

Case files didn't have grades. But they had bottom lines. If you knew what you were looking for. If you knew where to look. If you knew how someone had looked at you in the same bottom line manner.

It hadn't occurred to her right away. It had taken her brain a while to synthesize the whole fucked-up idea. If the back of her unbloodied head hadn't been throbbing so much, she might've thought of it sooner.

It would be somewhere in the pre-autopsy observations, in the condition of the victim at the time of discovery. If someone had noticed. If there was anything worth noticing.

She looked up, saw Victoria using her mouth to check the Jet-Pak for any possible sugar content, intent on doing as full an analysis as her mom was conducting with the Loreena White file.

"No, Vicky. No mouth, honey."

She pulled the Jet-Pak clear of her daughter's mouth with her left hand as, with her right, she thumbed her way to the report in question. Scanning it, for the grade point equivalent that would tell her if she'd aced the self-exam or not.

It was a single-page photocopy of the original handwritten report. She absorbed it, catalogued it, laid down in the tall grass with it. Relived the grasshoppers. The hit. The sunny-sick wake-up. But she couldn't re-create the one aspect of it that had been crawling on her skin like a hundred hopper hatchlings ever since.

If it had happened, they hadn't seen it, or taken note of it. And that was all the *if* she needed to introduce into her suddenly crashing and burning theory. But after another thirty seconds of paging through the file, and another gentle pull on the Jet-Pak her daughter was now chewing, she found that her gut was still refusing to loosen the knot it had tied around the concept at least a dozen hours earlier.

She wasn't sure if it was the knot loosening or the bottom of her stomach dropping when she found the envelope marked *CS photos*.

She sighed—not just a *do I really want to see this* sigh, but a *do I really want to see things like this for the rest of my life?*

Her face. Oh, Christ. *Her face.*

No, she couldn't think thoughts like that. Couldn't get attached. If she was looking for a pretty profession, she should've enrolled in beautician's school. Oh, that was great. It wasn't bad enough she was all over herself, now her internal dad had to chime in too.

But that face. No one ever deserved to have their picture taken like that.

Loreena White had been lying on her back in the weeds for more than twenty-four hours when she was discovered by a local vagrant—later cleared of any connection to the homicide—who had been tipped off to the presence of something in the discarded food category by the hopped-up activity of the area crows.

Jen Spangler would never forget the face of that victim. But the temporary amnesia that struck her in the next half-second was totally face-erasing. All it had taken was a merciful shift of her eyes to the victim's neck, her upper chest, where it bordered against the open collar—three buttons' worth—of her white cotton blouse. The openness creating an unobstructed view of the most important article of clothing the dead girl had ever worn.

From the form, it looked like a *Barely There*. But the seams of construction of the inside-out bra couldn't have been more obvious if they'd been made of form-fitted steel instead of second-skin cotton.

49

WHILE the rest of the world focused on the headless victim lying on the bed, Hewitt's attention had been drawn to the ceiling.

Getting to that point of view had been easy enough for her. As a veteran middle-of-the-night ceiling observer, she had no trouble assuming the position. Even if it was alongside the disconnected body of Mrs. Laura Pennington.

The lights of the ceiling fan had been turned on to the highest dimmer switch setting. And while revealing that the lights were in bad need of a dusting, it also gave Hewitt a revealing view of the sculpted metal housing that held the ceiling fan's motor.

Seconds earlier, she had felt the little prickle against the back of her neck and an icy quickening through her nervous system. Duly warned, she took her state-issue flashlight, used it to illuminate what she could of the inner recesses of the ceiling fan housing. As she did, she could feel her little light show attracting the attention of several sets of eyes in the bedroom. But it was the single eye she found looking back at her from the shadows of the ceiling fan that released the hummingbird inside her chest.

HORROR films. Hewitt had never had much use for them. As a teenager she'd seen her share. The chance to go to the multiplex with girlfriends—or on rarer occasions, a friend of the boy variety—

and have the living shit scared out of you. So much so that for those crazy couple of hours you could forget how horrifying it was to be a gangly adolescent in a Middle American suburb.

In her adult life, she'd pretty much abandoned the genre, the nightly news, especially when she made guest appearances, being frightening enough. But here she was now, on a Monday morning deep into the fourth decade of her life, facing the prospect of sitting down to view the kind of horror no one should ever record or be made to view.

Making the short leap that it was the kind of thing an estranged, possessive husband would do, Hewitt had sought out the kind of man-space where the image-capturing component of the minisurveillance system might be hidden.

The Chicago Bears–themed rec room had been her first clue. The drop ceiling her second—in particular the panel in the corner above the couch and end table that looked like it had been pushed in slightly from its metal frame.

One of the swimmers she'd dated at Wheaton West had also enjoyed frequent dips into a bag of pot. He had used a panel of his parents' basement ceiling to hide his stash, pipe, papers—she'd always suspected back issues of *Jugs* and *Swank* as well from the way he reacted to a real-life sighting of larger-than-average boobs.

In the rec room drop-ceiling in Glen Ellyn, Illinois, twenty years later, Hewitt wouldn't uncover any pot or porn. But as she stood on the cushion of the pseudo-leather couch, she would manage to get her hands on a wireless digital video recorder that was—thank you heaven, thank you hell—still running as she pulled it from its drop-ceiling hiding place and into the light of the Super Bowl XX table lamp.

50

HE could have killed her. He could have raped her. He could have done anything to her. Anything under the sun. Anything under a bright August sun with nothing but grasshoppers for an audience. But with all those options staring him in the face, he had chosen to focus on her shirt, her bra, and whatever happened between the time he removed both items and returned them to her body, with his backward signature as a souvenir.

She was still in the bathtub, still trying to soak away, to wash off, whatever had happened in between. Even if it had been nothing more than eye-to-skin contact.

That was where her thinking was now. The blow to the back of the head had been a temporary distraction. But now that the deep pain of that had diminished, the surface pain—a psychosomatic sunburn on her chest—had taken its place.

She hadn't been exposed long enough to have sustained any real sunburn. She'd done the self-exam. As soon as she'd returned home. Pressing the tips of her fingers into each breast, to see if they left a reverse imprint the way they always did on sunburned skin. But no. Whatever had happened had happened in less time than it would take the sun to begin to change the color of her ridiculously white skin.

But for those minutes, however many there were, she had been exposed to a kind of heat more intense than the sun could generate. And that was the white heat inside the sick head of the person who had assaulted her. A white heat that could build and explode at any minute—but which hadn't exploded, for whatever reason, on her. Not this time. Not the way it had exploded on Loreena White.

Victoria was up from her nap. In the old days—old in the sense of a life that barely covered two years—Victoria would have hung out in her crib for a while, staring at the solar system stickers on the ceiling, chirping at her "Twinkle Twinkle Little Star" mobile. The big girl bed had changed all that.

Jen heard the always surprisingly heavy rumble of little feet on the hallway floor as she sat up and reached for the liquid soap. Victoria would insist on climbing into the tub with her. Out of bubble bath, she would have to use the liquid soap, squirted liberally under the running tap, to create a little buffer between her child's body and whatever invisible aftereffects were still clinging to hers.

51

IT was as simple as plugging a VCR into a TV. For those old enough to still be referencing those things. At least that had been the implication from Zack Lathrop before he and his twenty-two-year-old body had left the little ISP screening room without explaining why. The explanation was making its way down the hallway now—in the scent of microwave popcorn.

On a normal day Hewitt would've been appalled. But there didn't appear to be any normal days left on the August calendar. And the way the case was breaking, Labor Day, maybe even Halloween, looked iffy too.

"Okay, all set," Zack Lathrop offered as he and his buttery paper bag joined her in the room.

"Had I known we'd be snacking, I would've brought Fritos," Hewitt offered back.

"They've got the honey barbecue kind in the vending machine."

Because he was actually trying to be helpful, Hewitt let it fall to the cutting room floor.

"Can we get this going, please?"

Zack Lathrop set the bag on the table, close enough to Hewitt that the smell was going to be an issue. There was a certain distance inside of which the allure of hot buttered popcorn couldn't be overridden automatically, by protocol, or revulsion.

"I brought some napkins," Zack Lathrop said at the same time the wadded parcel of them left his pocket and made the short flight to the table.

He crossed the room, turned on the TV monitor. After hitting the PLAY button on the DVR player, he dumped his body in the chair next to Hewitt, pulled the popcorn bag out of Hewitt's problem zone as the first of the recorded images wobbled onto the screen.

"We're starting at the beginning. Is that what you want?"

A familiar nun had joined them in the room. Or the actress who played her. Jesus. Julie Andrews. Again.

Let's start at the very beginning . . .

What the hell? They could fast-forward their way through all the doe-a-deer stuff. They had time. They had popcorn.

"It's the kind of recorder made for long-term surveillance," Zack Lathrop advised. "It only fires off a few frames every minute. So it'll play back kind of . . ."

He rocked his head and shoulders back and forth a couple of times as he tried to find the words.

"Herky-jerky?" Hewitt helped.

"Yeah."

For the first stretch of playback, the herky-jerkiness was confined to the changing resting positions of Laura Pennington's cat atop the bed. These images had been recorded in the daytime. From Zack Lathrop's calculations, the previous morning.

Hewitt was just fighting off an urge to take a handful of popcorn when a bizarre metamorphosis took place on Laura Pennington's bed. Because in the next jump of surveillance video time, the cat became a woman.

The surveillance time-lapse captured the woman in a series of provocative poses, wearing the same amount of clothing as her feline predecessor. If Laura Pennington had ever affected such a series of positions on that bed, it had been a long time ago. The only other possible explanation entered Hewitt's mind at the same moment a middle-aged man entered the black-and-white slide show to confirm her suspicion.

"This is gonna be gross," Zack Lathrop offered through a mouthful of popcorn.

The only saving graces of the peep show that followed were the time-lapse graininess of the video and the distance of the camera from the two participants. Hewitt didn't have an ID on the female, but she did on the male who had stepped to the edge of the bed for some good old middle-of-the-day fellatio.

Why Richard Pennington had momentarily moved back into the house he'd legally moved out of was the screaming question. As the bedside act continued, Hewitt sketched a scenario in her head. After food, shelter and reproduction, the next most powerful driving force in the human animal, at least according to her field studies, was revenge. Being unceremoniously kicked out of your house, only to return with a hide-a-key and a pay-to-play woman half your age, was one way to exact it. And, of course, with an act of revenge being so fleeting, capturing it on digital video was a way to extend the shelf life. How the experience would be relived or celebrated was another question.

Reliving it privately was one thing. Putting it in the face of your almost ex-wife—as what, punishment?—was something else.

Neither would be happening now. The twisted pathology of an estranged husband's sexcapade had been trumped by an actor with greater need and higher motivation.

"Well, that was fun. While it lasted."

Zack Lathrop celebrated the end of the sex act with that comment and a groping dip into the popcorn bag. "Is that what you were looking for?"

"Not on the drunkest, loneliest night of my life."

On the screen, the image of the bed was clear again. People-free. Richard Pennington had taken his pleasure via mouth. There had been no follow-up. Just his sudden, jump-in-time exit from the frame. There had been no bow to the camera, no end zone dance. The last animate object on-camera had been the young woman, straightening the comforter on the bed.

Hewitt and her AV assistant watched the empty frame for another couple of minutes.

"We can screen through the dead zone," Zack Lathrop volunteered.

"Have at it," Hewitt told him.

Screening the already compacted footage, Hewitt observed the way the daylight of the bedroom gave way to a thickening of gray tones until they condensed into the opaqueness of evening and held that way. When the TV screen suddenly went bright, Hewitt's nerves did their own jump in time. If Laura Pennington had turned on a table lamp, Hewitt's response wouldn't have been so dramatic. But the doomed woman had switched on the ceiling fan light. And the blast of illumination from all those bulbs had shocked the darkness away.

Hewitt knew she was looking at some of the last images of Mrs. Pennington. When her end-of-day ritual began to include changing from her out-and-about clothes into something more comfortable, Hewitt had Zack Lathrop pause the video.

"I'm going to ask you to leave the room at this point. Out of respect for the victim."

Zack Lathrop took the request in stride. A little lift of his eyebrows and push-out of his mouth were as close as he was going to get to an editorial comment. Whether he was thinking about the double standard she was invoking, Hewitt couldn't know. But she was certainly aware of it herself. Yes, she had been surprised by the earlier activity on the surveillance video. She could have requested the PAUSE button there too—out of respect for the male victim. But she had let Zack Lathrop sit in on those private moments. She was well aware he could have seen that kind of action by logging on to any of a million Internet sites.

Hewitt reached for her wallet, took out a couple of singles.

"Here, get yourself something nice from the vending machine. And get a Kit Kat for me. I'll be out to collect as soon as they roll the credits."

52

THE timing could vary significantly. But it didn't matter. Because the one thing he knew with certainty was that eventually it would work. Eventually his face would disappear.

Faces were temporary. Faces came, faces went. All of them. No exceptions. Those were the laws of the physical world.

In the world of thoughts, the world of mind, the world of memories, it wasn't quite so simple. A face could live inside that world for a very long time. A face could live inside a photograph for a long time too. But the remedy for that was much more easily realized. An Exacto blade and a little patience could take care of that. The memory face, however, the *face-in-the-head*, that was a far more delicate operation. Delicate and lengthy. As he had found out. As he continued to learn.

His own face—that was much more in his control. He is practicing his control now. Standing at the bathroom mirror. This phenomenon he'd discovered as a preadolescent. The brain-teasing phenomenon that if he stared at his face in the mirror long enough—without actually looking at it—the definition of his features would begin to blur, to fade, to erase itself. Until that moment, that perfect moment of mind and body equilibrium, when his face disappeared. Just that. Just his face. The shape, the shell of the head, would still be there. But the face would simply be gone.

The trick of it was to gradually release, to *soften*, the eyes. To pull the eyes back from their normal outward extension into the visual field.

By taming their quest for visual information, for definition, the processing of the light and the objects illuminated became less focused, less specific. Until it all kind of gave up its hold. And from there, it was only a matter of time until the desired effect was realized.

He is right there now. On the very verge of it. Feeling the tingle that always begins in his arms and hands. Moving to his shoulders, his chest. Down the back. Up the neck. To his face. Finally, to his eyes. The tingle of all that as the eyes settle back one last hair's width into the sockets.

Yes. There. It is done. The face is gone.

53

IT was odd enough when Mrs. Pennington sat down in nearly the same place on the bed as the face-for-hire had occupied earlier in the prerecorded day. And it was doubly so when she, too, stripped down to absolutely nothing in the next few swishes of video time. She sat there then, for longer than would have seemed normal if you were just going to sit there. Getting naked usually led to somewhere. But for Laura Pennington, on this occasion, wherever that was could wait.

Hewitt was still trying to put a line of reasoning against the naked coincidence when the subject of the video still life left the frame. With the remote, Hewitt screened forward, her eyes eating up the scrambled image of the bedroom, looking for any sign of life on the way to the death act.

A head flew into the TV picture. Towel-wrapped. But still attached to its body. Laura Pennington was back, fresh from a bath or shower. Some time-lapse flights around the room then, as Mrs. Pennington prepared for sleep.

Hewitt felt a tightening in the front of her neck as she watched Laura Pennington crawl into bed, leaving the light on. The paperback on the nightstand seemed the likely reason. The only other reason was obvious. Fear. A child's fear of the dark never quite grown out of. Or a gathering sense of an adult version of it, in the edges of her mind, in the corners of the room, in the folds of her down comforter.

The TV image was so grainy and unsettled that Hewitt could have easily ascribed her next observations to her imagination. But with Laura Pennington lying there on her back, Hewitt simply couldn't get past the way in which her subject was staring at the ceiling, the *direction* in which she was staring. Her eyes were looking at the ceiling fan. The center of the fixture. A slight shift of Laura Pennington's head on the pillow allowed Hewitt to believe she had positioned her eyes unwittingly into line with the surveillance Cyclops. In other words, Laura Pennington was in virtual eye contact with the woman who had come to investigate her death.

Then, as it always did for Hewitt when her mind careened outside the orange cones of reason, things got weird. Voice-inside-the-head weird. Not her own voice. But a voice she could only place inside the throat of the lonely lady on the bed.

There's a monster in my closet. He's watching me. He's been watching me all my life. He's been waiting all this time. But tonight . . . Tonight he comes for me. And there's nothing I can do, is there? There's nothing I can do to stop it.

Another slight shift of the woman's head on the pillow—a tilt to her left.

There's nothing you *can do to stop it.*

Hewitt lost track then of the time that passed in the screening room until she informed herself that a final shift of Laura Pennington's head had been caused by the letting go of her fear, the letting go of her life.

The nightstand light stayed on. And that was how she slept, how Hewitt watched her sleep. Through two hours of real time compressed into minutes by the peek-a-boo camera. Two hours were enough to put you into REM sleep, enough to dream. Hewitt could only hope her last dreams had been good.

Whatever its possible nature, the dream was rescinded at 1:19 A.M. on the video clock. That was when Laura Pennington stirred, when she sat up, when Hewitt actually brought her hand onto her own throat, greeted there by a pulse her body no longer had control of. She knew an even faster, more syncopated beat had pounded in Laura Pennington's neck.

Sleepers were sitting ducks. Supine zombies. A noise in the middle of the night got you up to see what the hell it was. But by the time your full set of rational functions returned, it was probably too late. Because the one who had planned your awakening was already on full alert, as wide awake as a human being could be.

It was just Hewitt and the empty bed now. As the minutes passed in the Pennington bedroom, as the seconds banged off in Hewitt's head.

The phantasm appeared then, bluntly, without theatrics, without a screaming soundtrack. And yet there was something cinematically familiar about the way the hunched body moved across the screen, face turned away from the camera, carrying the headless body, laying it on the bed, adjusting the comforter, the pillow.

After that, the monster left the room. Again, without theatrics, but with one moment that would be viewed over and over by his spellbound audience. Hewitt did her best to rewind to the handful of frames, succeeded, finally, at freezing the image on the fourth or fifth try.

It was the moment in the movie when the monster turned to the camera for the first shocking glimpse of its face. And shocking to Hewitt it was. And utterly, hideously demoralizing.

54

THERE were times she hated how much she looked like her father, the way her otherwise pretty face mimicked his expressions. And the thing that separated those times from the rest of the time—when she scarcely even thought of herself as Ed Spangler's biological daughter—was the presence of the thing she called *the hate*.

It wasn't when she found herself hating him. Which, of course, would happen. Although about as rarely as she imagined could happen in a father-daughter relationship. *The hate* was all about when Ed Spangler hated himself. It was those shitty, idiotic times when her father indulged himself in taking a professional failure personally. Those minutes, hours, sometimes days when the Spangler household would be transformed into a Spanglerian dungeon, from which there was no escape until the Captain's mood finally lifted.

Jen hated herself right now, hated herself more than she remembered ever hating anyone. With the exception of one human being. And that was the Motherfucker who had backed up the truck and dumped this shitload of hate right into her bedroom. But not before he'd knocked her unconscious and put her breasts out for a little sunbath.

Sitting on the bed, while Victoria played peek-a-boo with the pillows, Jen had an unobstructed view of herself in the vanity mirror. Not that she was feeling vain. Because the picture wasn't pretty. Christ, she was pathetic. Sitting here on the same princess bed she'd slept on as a ten-year-old. With the next generation of princesses looking at her from the dark seam of a pillow sandwich. And with a killer—a killer she'd stirred up—watching her from behind the two-way mirror of his imagination, waiting for her next move. Unless he got bored with that and decided to make the next move his.

"Can't find me, Mommy."

She reached out, gave the top pillow a little shake. Enough to make Victoria giggle, but not enough to be truly engaged in the game. They'd been playing this way for more than twenty minutes. And while she sat, while she stared, while she wondered *what the fuck?*, she knew she'd been doing little more than going through the motions.

"Can't find me, Mommy."

She knew she would be going through the motions in every damn thing she did until she got control of things, control of herself, control of *the hate.*

"Mommy can't find me."

She grabbed the top pillow, pulled it clear. And from the look on her daughter's face, she realized she'd put a little too much into it, a little too much *force.*

Victoria was either going to cry or laugh depending on what her mother did in the next couple of seconds. So Jen took the pillow, put it back over her, scooped up the whole works in her arms, found the first thing hanging out—Victoria's right foot—and took a mock bite of the toes.

"Mm. Yummy."

The shriek of little girl laughter didn't quite shatter the vanity mirror. But it was enough to crack the hate-mask.

"What a yummy pillow sandwich Mommy has."

Another pretend bite—this time Victoria projected the little hand for exactly that reason. More nibbles. More shrieks. Until the two pillows and the two-year-old became too much to hold. And yet the weight of that seemed infinitely lighter than the cell phone she proceeded to pick up from the princess nightstand.

The phone number was still loaded into the memory from the two times she had dialed and hung up twenty minutes earlier. She watched as her index finger approached REDIAL, lost its nerve.

Hurriedly, she entered another number, this one the day care drop-off. Victoria had been there before, knew the drill, knew how to assimilate with the other toddlers and babies. It wasn't the best solution. But it was the only one that would allow her mom to take her own next baby steps into the great big world.

55

PICTURE day was always a special day. There was always the excitement, the feeling that you were important enough for a photographer with a special camera and lights to come and take a picture of *you*. Even if you were just one of the hundreds of elementary school kids who would line up for their moment on the high stool, in the big popping lights.

And there was the whole thing with the hair. Your picture hair was never how it really was. Because they gave you a free comb while you were waiting in line. And with a free comb and time to kill, well, a kid was going to get creative.

So there was all that excitement to be dealt with. But also, there was the skin-chilling nervousness in knowing that you got only one chance with that special camera. Because film was expensive. And what the hell?—you were just another kid with a face.

The photographer was always good with the little tricks it took to get a kid to smile. But there was always one kid who—no matter what the photographer did—didn't smile. He remembered the year he was that kid.

But that was a long time ago. It is a new day now. The next day in his grown-up life.

He wonders what kind of antics it would take to make his next subjects smile for the camera. Needless to say, they'd had some fairly serious looks on their faces when they'd entered the refrigerator.

He has no desire for champagne in this moment. In fact, the thought of it produces a bitter taste in his mouth. But he knows that once the subjects are in place, when it is time for the reunion photo, his taste buds will warm to the task. The bitterness will dissolve. The taste for something overly dead and overly living will return to his mouth. As it will to theirs. And surely, with a couple of sips, he won't have to work terribly hard to get the look he wants.

He leaves his work area, crosses the room, makes his way to the kitchen. At the immaculately clean, white refrigerator door, he pauses, closes his eyes, gives a little shake of his head. He recognizes that this has happened to him before. This entering into a temporary stasis, where the two sides of his mind are competing for what is real.

Are they in there? Or has he invented them? Has he invented the whole thing? It seems so unlikely that someone would go to so much effort to bring such a thing about. He feels the energy of his confusion pooling in his hands, in the fists into which they have closed.

Breathe. Breathe.

If they are there, they are there. If they are meant to be together, they will be together. Ultimately, it is not up to him. It was never up to him. It is their choice. Their choice. A choice they will live with forever.

The focused breathing has relaxed his hands enough that he is able to raise the right one to the handle of the door. It is dark inside the box. But the light is always there. In fact, he has no evidence that the light isn't always on. He can't possibly open the door fast enough to see even a glimpse of the darkness before the light replaces it completely.

If they are there, in the darkness right now, only they know it. Only they can understand what it is like to be where they are, with what they have done.

There, yes. Better now. *He knows.* Once again, he knows. Of course, they are in there. Inside, just as he left them.

The door pulls open. The light explodes. The faces greet him with anticipation.

It is picture day.

56

SHE had video of the killer. Not only that, she had video of his freaking face. Not only that, she had a printout of the killer's face taped to the dashboard of the Mazda. Just in case, by some outlandish miracle, she saw him on the street. Just in case he decided to wear the same mask in public he'd worn in the video and the still-frame printout.

Just in case.

That was the purpose of a mask-wearer in the commission of crime. Just in case a surveillance camera caught your act. As opposed to the non-mask-wearers caught in similar fashion, whose mom, dad, siblings and cousins could say *Hey, that's Tommy on the news making a withdrawal at the bank.*

There was another possibility—that a mask could come in handy just in case one of your victims somehow managed to live through your attempt to dispatch them. As Hewitt let her traffic-negotiating eyes sneak a glance at the printout on the dashboard, she knew she wasn't dealing with either mask-wearing scenario. Because this mask wasn't one you were going to find at Masks-R-Us. This was no ski mask, no nylon stocking, no mask of a U.S. President.

This one was a custom job. Which meant, in Hewitt's mind, it had a purpose that transcended the covering of a face. It was covering something more. Something deeper. Something much uglier than a face—no matter how destroyed—could ever be.

Growing up, there'd been a children's encyclopedia set in Hewitt's home. On the cover of one of the volumes was a sculpted head of a young Caesar Augustus. Hewitt had never forgotten it.

It wasn't the details of the face of the young Augustus that had penetrated her imagination and stuck with her all those years. It was the absence of features. Oh, there was enough in the shape of the face, the style of the hair, to know it was the young Octavian. But in the soft milkiness of the marble, in the blank eyes, in the seamless contours of the nose and mouth, there was also a timeliness anonymity. As if this most powerful of the powerful could just as easily have been anyone, or no one.

The junior encyclopedia image of Caesar Augustus was the closest thing Hewitt could equate to the mask of the killer. A vague, youthful face meant to hide brilliance, madness and everything in between.

Hewitt's phone buzzed. She saw it was Captain Spangler, invited him into her Mazda version of the Roman Forum.

"I've got your warrant," he said. "You're good to go with the Boccachio residence. Paper's on its way via ISP personal valet."

"Perfect," Hewitt said. "Because I'm just pulling into his lovely neighborhood. What's your ETA on the warrant?"

"Fifteen minutes. And if that's not fast enough, you can complain to the delivery boy when I get there."

"HE'S not here."

It was intended to be a declarative statement. But coming as it had from Hewitt, there'd been way too much of a quizzical tone to make it believable. There was good reason for that. Because Hewitt was still rejecting the entire notion that Dr. Gerry Boccachio could have managed to vacate the premises while under a twenty-four-hour watch. But the proof was there. In the empty hands of the surveillance team— Detectives Schiffman and Kurkewicz. And in the empty eyes of Hewitt and Captain Spangler.

"He's not fucking here."

Hewitt's second attempt sounded better to her, in a declarative sense. But to the surveillance team, the tone wasn't that as much as it was judgmental.

Glen Kurkewicz looked the worse for the all-nighter. They both had that stale, rumpled, I've-been-in-a-fucking-van-all-night appearance. Both looked like a dip into Dr. Boccachio's pool would be the perfect remedy. Being right there at poolside on the doctor's turquoise-tiled deck, they could have all indulged themselves. Hell, they had an official backstage pass to all areas of the property.

"It was textbook watch and wait," Glen Kurkewicz added. "If he got out, it's because he really wanted to get out. According to his protocol, not ours."

"I'm not accusing anybody of anything," Hewitt said.

"It's not like we had the whole area sealed," Ed Spangler reflected. From his generally disheveled, case-from-hell look, he could have spent the night in a van of his own. "Unless he knew he was being watched, he would've used one of those nice cars all those years in medical school paid for."

"Well, obviously he didn't use one of his cars," Hewitt said.

"Maybe he saw something that tipped him off," Spangler said.

"That's virtually impossible," Kaya Schiffman countered.

"I'd take out the *virtually* from that," Glen Kurkewicz added.

Hewitt's eyes had gone ahead and indulged in a little dive into the pool. She didn't bother resurfacing before she delivered her next thought.

"Well, then, the only other possibility is that he *felt* something."

They all let Hewitt's words float there on the water.

"Or maybe he just went for a walk," Hewitt sculled. "Maybe he went out for a look at the stars. Maybe he made a wish. Maybe it came true and he found a way to make himself invisible."

57

BYRON Biffle never appreciated having his work interrupted. Especially the day before the *Mundelein Dispatch* went to press. But on this day-before-press, the world had come calling. And its representative was waiting for him on the front porch.

The feeling, the sense that it was Agent Hewitt, occurred to him three or four steps before his Minnetonka moccasins moved him into position to see her figure on the other side of the frosted window of the front door. He could only imagine what kind of news she was delivering. Or soliciting.

His brain center went to full alert—intellectual fight or flight—as he released the lock and unsealed the door. What he saw looking back at him left him breathless. So the *Yes?* he emitted came in the form of a throaty whisper.

"Mr. Biffle?"

A second *yes* confirmed that at least he still had a voice box.

"My name is Jennifer Rogers. I'm a student in the school of journalism at UIC."

He could see she was reading his face for a reaction. She offered a slight smile—mimicking, he supposed, the disarming expression she was receiving from him. But it had been such a long time since such a young woman showed him any legitimate interest, all he could do, all any man could do, was smile.

"I'm sorry to come here unannounced."

Her eyes seemed utterly sincere. There was utter sincerity spilling out of her everywhere.

"No need to apologize, Jennifer," he said—in a voice he didn't like. His professorial voice. "Any good journalist understands the advantages of the unannounced visit."

"May I have a moment of your time?"

"I believe you already have it. Would you like to step inside the palatial offices of the *Dispatch*?"

He moved sideways, made just enough space for her body to pass through the doorframe, his upturned left palm guiding her past him. She swept inside, with an aggressive kick to her heels only a young person on a mission would have.

"We can talk in my office if that suits you."

She let that be entirely his call, following him past the staircase.

"Can I get you anything to drink?"

"Only if you're having something."

"I was thinking a Diet Coke. But I believe we have root beer and ginger ale as well."

He led her into the kitchen, proceeded to the refrigerator. He paused, his fingers wrapped around the door handle as he waited for her decision.

"Diet Coke would be great."

He opened the refrigerator, dipped down behind the door as she watched, rummaged a little bit before coming up with the two cans.

They went to his office. At his palm-upturned gesture, she took a seat in the visitor's chair. He stepped behind his desk but chose to half-sit on the edge of the credenza rather than on his nice Herman Miller desk chair.

"So," he said, his smile warm but his eyes several degrees cooler, "what would you like to know about my father?"

58

IF Dr. Gerry Boccachio had, in fact, left the house through the back yard and gone for a walk the previous evening, his trek hadn't taken him to his office and the day's worth of patients who were counting on him to help them on their own journeys. Hewitt's call to the psychiatrist's office had been fielded by his receptionist, a woman who'd only been working in that capacity for a couple of months. Dealing with disappointed or pissed-off psychiatric patients that morning had taken its toll on the woman's own state of mind.

When Hewitt confirmed she *was not* calling to inform her of Dr. Boccachio's death, the receptionist seemed taken aback—as if that was the only noncrazy possibility that existed.

On a well-informed hunch, Hewitt asked the receptionist if she knew a *Mrs. Laura Pennington.*

"Well, yes. Mrs. Pennington is a patient of . . ."

Regaining her balance on the tightrope of patient confidentiality, she had suspended her information sharing right there. But Hewitt had what she needed.

At the Boccachio residence, an hour of searching by Hewitt and her two colleagues didn't turn up anything that would have attached the doctor to the physical act of murder. But Hewitt knew, intimately, that killers who were planning to be in the business for an extended period often set up shop outside their personal living space. A remote location. A staging ground. A black box theater. The worst place to leave a calling card was the place you called home. *Home* being a relative term for that brand of killer—given that they had no compunction about forcing their way into a victim's house and assuming the run of the place.

Well, she had the run of his place now. Not that she was ready to declare him the killer. But his behavior in the last several days wasn't going to win him any Mental Health Professional of the Month awards.

Hewitt was in Dr. Boccachio's study, feeling the pressure of the dark walnut walls around her, sifting through the contents of his desk one more time when something in the built-in bookcase fifteen feet away caught her eye. It was on the second shelf from the top, sandwiched between an *Ignatius Bible* and a hardcover copy of *The Grapes of Wrath*.

If she hadn't paid a visit to a bookstore and spent more time than she cared to admit with the title in question, it would have stayed in its biblical/epic saga sandwich indefinitely. But Hewitt's fingers were already beginning to wrest the book from its tight fit between the other two. And the story got even better when she opened to the title page and saw that the author had not only signed the book—she had personalized it in the most personal way possible.

59

H E never moved from his half-seated position on the credenza. Not until two Diet Cokes had been drained and his visitor had asked enough questions to establish his willingness to leave the door open to future answers. Byron Biffle hadn't left his position, his perch, behind his office desk. And yet he had managed to move all over the room.

Jen hadn't moved her car from its parked position on the street about a half-block from the *Mundelein Dispatch* offices, choosing to sit there for a few minutes to review the Byron Biffle experience. Jen was no stranger to the furtive looks of middle-aged men. It had been happening to her since she'd been a teenager. She would see it in public places, shopping malls in particular. Looking up from her browsing to catch some man staring at her with a self-conscious, apologetic look. As if he absolutely knew better but could do absolutely nothing to deter his brain and biology.

Like any attractive young woman, she had developed an armor, a return look of her own so unapologetically dismissive that she vaporized the wayward admirers without a second thought. So when Byron Biffle couldn't do anything to stop himself from exposing similar secrets with his own eyes, Jen could deal with it from a position of experience. Only she couldn't allow herself to be quite so automatically dismissive. So she'd been forced to communicate it nonverbally—that the door may have been closed but it wasn't altogether locked. And once those cat's-eyes were out of the bag, Byron Biffle had his free pass to the Fantasy Funhouse.

The interview had proceeded under those ground rules. Which had transformed a Q&A premise into a T&A pageant.

Byron Biffle's body didn't move from the credenza. But it didn't have to. Because his mind was more than happy to do the honors of judging the contestant. Which meant that while Jen was writing down his responses in her collegiate notebook, he was going down his checklist, observing her from every possible angle.

It was when he had gotten behind her with his imagination—as she sensed it—that he had caused her to remind herself that she was, in fact, armed. Because after what had happened in the grasshopper zone near Union Station, she would be armed now, either physically or psychologically, for the rest of her life.

By sneaking up on her, Byron Biffle had been able to punch out the question before she was anywhere near to asking it herself, or having it answered. "At what point would you like me to tell you what actually happened to him?"

She knew by then that a silk scarf could have been slipped around her neck and pulled tight before she even had a chance to see the face of her attacker.

"I would assume if you knew that, you would have already told someone much more important than a journalism student."

She had impressed herself with her response. And clearly, she had impressed the son of the legendary journalist.

"Well, first, don't ever discount your own importance," he'd responded. "And second, the most important person I would ever share the truth with would be myself."

Sitting in her oversized, retired police car, Jen Spangler closed her notebook at that point, saw the word COLLEGIATE pop from the rest of the words on the cover. School would be starting in another couple of weeks. *School.* Back to classes, back to commuting. Back to a structured daycare schedule for Victoria. All that, with all this. All because she had volunteered to help in the investigation. All because she was finally in a position to become the one thing she craved more than anything else—to be someone, anyone, other than *Ed Spangler's kid*.

Brutally honest, that's what the assessment was. And being brutally honest was the only way to go now. Because the real world—the world she craved—had been brutally honest in welcoming her. So here she sat now, having driven just a half-block from the offices of the *Mundelein Dispatch* before pulling over to have this little debriefing with herself.

Byron Biffle had made it very clear that he didn't know the ultimate truth behind his father's demise and that he doubted anyone ever would. They had wrapped up their meeting and finished their Diet Cokes with that on the table. But as she was exiting the front door, he had invited her to get back to him if any follow-up questions occurred to her. Which could have meant a couple of things. One, that he truly enjoyed her company—which was as clear to her as the roving eyes of a middle-aged man at Banana Republic. And two, that even if he didn't know the ultimate truth of his father's murder, there were things he did know. Things to be learned. Things to be shared. If she was willing to be a good girl and play along.

A car was pulling up to the curb behind her. She'd been so inside her own head that she hadn't noticed its approach. She looked in her mirror, saw the face of the driver at the same time the face fell apart in the sudden trembling of the reflective glass. He had hit her. Just a little bump. But contact she didn't need.

Her mirror steadied, but by then the driver was already exiting his vehicle. She powered down the window as the owner of the *Mundelein Dispatch* approached her vehicle.

"You know if you keep hanging out in this neighborhood," he smiled, "I'm going to think you're stalking me."

She sneaked a hand into her messenger bag, located what she needed.

Another smile from him, meant to disarm, but feeling more like its secret mission was to entice.

Jen's hand was out of the purse, the metal object cool against her own clammy skin.

"I had to make a couple of calls," she told him, showing him the proof in the form of the purple razor phone.

"That would have been my first guess," he said at the same time he broke into some directional hand gestures. "I drove by and saw you sitting here. I went around the block. Just wanted to make sure everything was okay."

"I'm good," Jen told him, with a smile she hoped came off as neutral. "I'll be leaving as soon as I make one more call."

Though she could see he didn't like that he couldn't be more helpful, it relieved her that he seemed to accept her explanation.

"I'm off to the bank then," he said. "It's free donut day."

His mind might have been focused on deep-fried sugar, but his eyes were on the spotlight mirror on her car door.

"Did you buy this car at a police auction?"

She smiled something well beyond neutral this time.

"If you want to know the truth, I stole it. Desperate student, you know."

This entertained him. Enough that he seemed to lose interest in the history of her vehicle.

"Well, the crullers are waiting," he said. "Let me know if you need anything else."

She told him she would. The last of his smiles seemed to hang in the air until he was back in his car, starting the engine, pulling away without waving good-bye.

60

MAYA Macy and Steve Norris had just completed a joint counseling session in a room of Big Shoulders Marriage and Family Therapies that Hewitt could only describe as *the Flower Room*. Not only was there an overabundance of the potted and freshly cut varieties, there were plastic flowers, paper flowers, flowers on the wall. And it was the wall art flowers that kept distracting Hewitt during the first few minutes in the room with the therapy team, the sexually symbolic nature of the paintings, sketches and photos.

It was like being in attendance at a floral orgy. And not as a wall-flower.

"I picked up your book," Hewitt said, making the turn from introductory chatter. She then produced the book from her bag, set it on the flower-bedecked coffee table that separated the couch where the therapists sat from the love seat Hewitt occupied.

Maya Macy seemed both flattered and embarrassed by the presence of her book, but not intimidated. That reaction had been reserved for the handsome face of her partner.

"Actually, I left my personal copy at home," Hewitt disclosed. "This one belongs to someone else."

Maya Macy knew the book's owner instantly. This time she was more embarrassed than flattered. If he was a flower, Steve Norris would have closed at that point until the next sunrise.

"You have to understand that book was written a long time ago,"

Maya Macy offered. "Written by a much different person than I am now. But as they say, it seemed like a good idea at the time."

"It's a good idea now," Hewitt told her. "I mean if that's what you're looking for. And even if you're not, it does a pretty good job of selling you up."

Steve Norris put his hand on Maya Macy's knee. But instead of taking his hand with hers and holding it, Maya Macy brushed the top of it a single time with her palm. Like a kid at a petting zoo doing everything possible not to actually pet the goat.

"If that book belongs to the person I think it does, it means you've been in his home. I can only assume on a searching mission. Which can't be good news for him. Either way."

Hewitt was struck by the *either way* of Maya Macy's statement, the presupposition. But she let it drop into the box of LATER CONJECTURE, along with the antigoat stroke.

"The news is this," Hewitt said. "Dr. Gerard Boccachio appears to have gone missing."

"What do you mean missing?"

There was an indignation to Steve Norris's question—in his voice, in the knit of the skin between his eyebrows.

"As in he didn't show up at his office for his morning appointments, and we can't locate him."

"Do you suspect foul play?" Maya Macy questioned, the slight quiver in her voice betraying the impassive set of her face.

"I guess I have to," Hewitt answered. "But there's also something that tells me it can't be as simple as that. Because nothing about this case and the people I've talked to is as discernable as it first appears."

Steve Norris didn't like the implication. So much so that he reclaimed his hand from Maya Macy's knee as he sat up and leaned his disapproval in Hewitt's direction.

"Are you implying that Maya or anyone else is withholding information?"

Hewitt knew there was additional forward-leaning aggression to be had from him. She allowed herself to settle a little deeper into the love seat.

"I'm saying I continue to be surprised by the things I find out about the people in this practice."

Maya Macy was sitting up now, reaching across the coffee table. Hewitt watched as she picked up the copy of *Learning to Love Your Inner Slut*. She thumbed to the title page, just to make sure. As if—it appeared to Hewitt—she wanted to make sure she'd actually written the words. But apparently seeing them wasn't enough.

" 'For JB,' " she read out loud. " 'Consider this your free ticket for a BJ—whenever the spirit moves you.' "

If there was any embarrassment in her reaction to these once-upon-a-time words of hers, it was completely overridden by her own amusement. A distant, quixotic look came to her eyes. Next to her, Steve Norris's hand was active again, in search of something in the knee category. This time he settled for one of his own.

"I'm not an expert in fellatio law," Hewitt said, hoping to knock this slutty version of Lady Godiva off her damn high horse and provoke her into exposing something of actual value. "But my interpretation is that there's no statute of limitations on such an offer."

"That's an uncalled-for comment," Steve Norris bristled.

"No, it's not," his significant other voiced. "I mean *that inscription* was uncalled for. I know that. You know that."

She turned to him, did something with her look, her eyes that quieted him—something Hewitt couldn't read from her angle.

"If you've been poking around in Gerry's house," Maya Macy said, without looking at Hewitt, "you must suspect him of something. Of some involvement, some connection."

"I guess I'd feel better if he was the only one I was suspicious of. I mean there seems to be a compelling series of links here. Maybe a better description would be *a web*. And for a reason known only to a select few, clients of your business and patients of Dr. Boccachio are getting caught in this web. And getting their heads removed by the spider. Or *spiders*."

Any last trace of bemusement rolled off Maya Macy's face.

"So what the hell do you think we are?" Steve Norris challenged. "Some kind of cult of mental health professionals who like to commit atrocities for kicks?"

"It wouldn't be the craziest thing that ever happened," Hewitt said.

It was two quixotic looks Hewitt encountered now. The Quixotes—Don and Donna.

"Come on, I don't think the two of you are involved in something like this. But people get sucked into things before they realize they're even being sucked."

"Once you get on a theme, you like to run with it, don't you?" Maya Macy posed.

"I'm only picking up on one of the themes that runs through your book," Hewitt countered.

"Well, as I said, that book was written by a different person, based on beliefs that person held at the time."

"And has the world changed so dramatically since?" Hewitt asked.

Maya Macy shared a look with her partner. On the walls, the erotic flora swayed in a breeze of anticipation.

"Part of it has," Maya Macy said in prelude. "*We're celibate.*"

The wall art was smiling at the joke. Hewitt scanned Maya Macy's eyes for any flicker of her own sense of humor. But her eyes and her statement held steady.

"Well, that *is* a world apart," Hewitt tendered.

"You seem disappointed," Maya Macy poked.

Now the flower art was laughing out loud.

"At the end of *The Great Gatsby*, Fitzgerald referred to something he understood as 'the orgiastic future.' I guess I've always found that romantic."

"Well, in my case, I'm afraid it's the orgiastic past."

Something in Maya Macy's eyes sealed itself away from Hewitt then. Which left Hewitt alone momentarily with Steve Norris. Only *his* gaze didn't appear to be interested in going inside as much as it was seeking Hewitt out. Something in the orgiastic future reference had hit a nerve with him, and blood was currently rushing to the site of the emergency.

61

IN the history of the city of Chicago, only two women on record had been assaulted in the vicinity of Union Station and left there with their bras turned inside out. And at that, the only records of the assaults were as far from official as they could get. For whatever reason, Jennifer Spangler had been appointed the keeper of those records. It was a custodial job she shared with one other person on the planet. A man who happened to live in Chicago. And who, on at least two occasions, had taken his sick act to the grasshopper zone.

She was back on the streets in the Crown Victoria, back on a familiar route. But unlike her previous excursion, this time she was properly outfitted. This time she had her father's heirloom revolver.

A weird thought came to her—weird in the context of the bizarre scenario she had put herself in. The first day of school was only eight days away and she still had to buy her books. That was pretty hilarious. Here she was, with the strong possibility she was creating a textbook example of *how not to* pursue a cold case, and the textbooks that would expose her as a dumbass were still waiting for her at the university bookstore.

She caught her face in the rearview, saw her dad's face in the early stages of the hate. She powered down all four windows of the Crown Victoria, let the last week of August fill her car, the wind of it knocking her hair back, and with any luck, blowing some of the hate off her face.

*   *   *

IF anything, the grasshopper population had gone up. Where the hell did they come from? Was this some kind of gathering ground? Or did they just keep hatching, developing, jumping and/or flying into full-blown, nasty adulthood?

The masses had plenty to buzz about. It wasn't every day a *victim* returned to the scene of a crime. Her disgusting insect friends weren't the only ones buzzing. Her chest, shoulders and upper back were humming as if she had her own pair of temporary wings beating like crazy back there.

And why the hell not? The last time she was here, some sick motherfucker had followed her in, watched her every move down the embankment, through the people-hole in the chain-link fence, all the way to the moment when she started pissing off the grasshoppers.

She was pissing them off again. *God dammit.* An eyebrow hit. The damn thing actually hung on to it—the hair—for a split-second. Like it sized up the length and shape of it and figured it was something to hump. She couldn't blame it, though. She was the come-and-get-it girl now.

In a way, weren't they all? Loreena White had certainly been a member of that club, with whatever she had done to set off the alarm in the mind of the man who had killed her. Maybe nothing more provocative than just showing up for life one day.

Jen made her way over to the tracks, sat down on the outside spear of the northside set, felt the heat of the August sun stored in the metal.

This was nasty business. Retracing the steps of an innocent dead girl. Retracing the steps of the not-quite-so-innocent dead girl you'd almost become. And why the fuck? Why the fuck had he spared her?

It was bizarre how she hadn't felt fully the ramifications of her good fortune until this moment. The fact that she'd been lying in the grass dead to rights, face-up to a burning sun she didn't even know was there. And it wasn't until she fully felt it that way that the ramifications of what happened to Loreena White hit her. She knew it was ridiculous to feel this way. But it was like two best high school friends being in a car accident. One would recover and return to senior year. The other would become a permanent ghost in the yearbook.

Jen Spangler had never seen tears fall on a railroad track before. If there had been a mirror there for her to look at, she would have seen the disapproval of her father-self over what she had allowed her world to come to. But there were no mirrors in the grasshopper zone. There were no pretty faces waiting to be discovered in the tall grass.

62

A *cult of mental health professionals who committed atrocities for kicks.*

It had a certain ring to it. Especially coming, as it had, from the mouth of a man who had apparently agreed never to use it to pleasure one of the area's most notorious sluts. That alone must have taken special powers of persuasion. But if it was a cult, somewhere at the top of the glassy-eyed totem pole there had to be a leader.

It was a preposterous notion. Steve Norris had served it up as such. And yet she couldn't ball it up and chuck it in the PREPOSTEROUS basket as quickly as she would have liked. As a group, there was a palpable secrecy about them. An organized evasiveness. Or was she reading between the lines with a little too much imagination? It wouldn't have been the first time in the last twenty-four hours. Some of the passages in *Learning to Love Your Inner Slut* had some pretty wide open spaces for personal reflection. The section with the subheading "69 and Counting" had given her particular pause.

Her phone went off. She knocked down the volume of the Ellington/ Coltrane duet on the car system, picked up her phone. *Brady.* The scent of the 69 thinking must've had some serious carrying power.

"I was just thinking about you—or parts of you," she said.

"I guess I'll be happy with piecework at this point," he tossed back. "I heard your numbers are up."

"As in?"

"Body count."

"I thought maybe you were referring to body temperature. As in ovulation. Or maybe I'm getting ahead of myself."

Long pause from him. Long enough to begin a pregnancy test.

"I think we have to fall back on our motto," he finally offered. "In latex we trust."

A pause from her this time as her mind pulled out of its freefall.

"If you were a cult leader, what would cause you to start killing innocent people?"

"Serious?"

She told him she was.

"Couple of things," he said, with virtually no synthesis time. "Fear that the innocent people had the power to expose me as a fraud. Or the belief that the innocent people weren't actually innocent."

It made her wet. And it wasn't just a delayed reaction to the 69 ruminations. It was the screaming fact that she was tied into a wrestler with a very serious brain.

"I love you," she heard herself say.

"What?"

"Yeah, you're right. It must be the stress of the case talking."

"I'll take it," he said, the words looped in what she knew was a sparklingly dopey smile. "I'll take as much of that as you can punch out."

63

EVENING had come, and Byron Biffle was alone with his thoughts. He knew he was in trouble. But he didn't care. There were moments in a man's life when you owed it to yourself to be beyond caring. All these years he had behaved himself. All the years since his wife's death. Out of respect for her? Or out of fear?

Yes, and yes. But especially to the latter. Fear of what? That she wasn't actually dead? Yes, again. The fear that some aspect of her had survived beyond the atheism.

So he would behave himself now, of course. If by nothing else, default. Who the hell was he kidding? Well, for a while, himself. And since there was no state statute against kidding yourself—as long as it didn't seriously hurt anyone but you—he figured he'd extend the process for at least one more day, the twenty-four hours of which would begin at 9:00 A.M. the next morning. Or if one of them was running a few minutes late, whenever they were both in the same space to start the clock.

Sitting in the bathtub for as long as he has, it has been hard for him to remain alone. So, of course, he hasn't. She has been there too. Not the entire time. Just long enough. Long enough for him to have taken care of the one physical act he needed.

It's done. And that's all that matters. It is clean now. He has washed it. With the hot water from the faucet and the soft washcloth that has been hanging from a hook in his mind.

He will go to bed thinking about it. He will wake up in proximity to the same thoughts. At 9:00 A.M. tomorrow, give or take, he will remember the feeling of washing her back.

64

SOMETHING steamy. That would work. That would keep the theme of her day going. She was standing in front of the microwave, watching the ISP mug turning on the GE carousel. The gray ISP mug that had made it into her car, into her house and never quite made it back to the dishwasher at HQ. Something steamy. Courtesy of a make-believe virgin in a blue and white dress, her pigtails bouncing in the breeze as she spread love and hot chocolate throughout the Swiss countryside.

Hewitt put her palms on the counter in front of the microwave, backed up with her legs, let her body unhinge from the hips. A modified yoga position from a class she'd taken in what felt like a past life. *The down dog.* Modified, on a tabletop. For people who were too stiff to do the real *down dog*.

Frisky bitch wants something steamy. She heard her mind-voice call that out as her body fought back against the stretch. *Breathe, doggie, breathe.* Hell, pant, if that's what it takes to get you through.

She knew there would be no fiancé to help her make it through this night. Detective Richter had been asked to pick up a second shift for a colleague whose wife had gone into labor. Hewitt's other choice for some face time, Father Brian Wilson, was at a vigil for the archbishop of the diocese who was in the end stages of congestive heart failure— or if you looked at it from the other side, in the first stages of an all-inclusive trip to paradise. Hewitt had been unable to reach Father Wilson, but his office receptionist had penciled her into his schedule for the following morning. Hewitt would take it. Anything to get a little closer to God and the hybrid psychiatrist he'd created.

The microwave was beeping. Yoga class was over.

THREE cups of Swiss Miss had helped her to create some of the steamiest sketches she'd ever rendered in her notebook.

They were all naked. No one was spared. Six naked cult members dancing around an altar, all holding hands in a prelude to a therapeutic daisy chain. The six members of Big Shoulders Marriage and Family Therapies. And seated at the altar, flanked by a couple of wedding cakes on pedestals, was the ostensible guru, Dr. Gerard Boccachio, sitting in full lotus.

She had no idea what it meant, if it meant anything. But something about it felt right, or put them in a more manageable form—the beginning of an organizational chart.

She was in the living room of the condo, in the curl-up corner of the couch. The TV was on—already several minutes into the ten o'clock news. *Her news.* The big story she was dancing nakedly around. So it came as a relief at 10:11 when the second big story of the day was finally presented. With the one camera crew WGN apparently had left, they had set up outside the Catholic hospital, the scene of the vigil for the archbishop of Chicago.

As the reverential reporter—a young guy who might've been an altar boy before journalism school—gave his on-camera update, the station cut to some clips that had been recorded earlier in the evening. One of which, for the two or three seconds it was up, included a shot of *her priest.* Just a glimpse of him. A face in the Roman-collared crowd. Father Brian Wilson, with a handful of other priests, exiting the hospital, as if their time in the vigil had been served. Father Brian Wilson, looking in that moment a little less severe than the others, taking it upon himself to add his positive vibe to the somber proceedings.

She muted the sound on the TV, cleared the airwaves for her virtual

version of "Good Vibrations." She wasted no time in identifying the
jazz artist to do the trans-genre interpretation. The search was brief.
The keyboard was the link. The theremin in the intro to The Beach
Boys' version and the Hammond organ as played by Jimmy Smith.

All through the Channel 9 weather, she imagined the piece. The big
walking bass line of Jimmy Smith's left hand. The blues-ified embellish-
ments of the right hand melody. If Jimmy Smith couldn't send a dying
archbishop into the next world a little more in touch with his soul, no
one on earth could.

It was a still chocolate-buzzed Elizabeth Taylor Hewitt taking the
vibe of all that to bed with her, while visions of naked marriage counselors cavorted in her head. Jimmy Smith played a thirty-minute solo in
the dark before Hewitt finally let him say good night.

65

THERE is no moon to be seen on this cloudy night. But it's not as if he needs visual confirmation. His eyes are closed anyway. Closed in the peace that comes to him. The peace of making things right.

The sounds of the water don't hurt either. The quiet that comes from it. Not just the quiet of sound. The quiet of liquid. The quiet of motion. The amniotic quiet.

The moon controls the ultimate amniotic pool. The oceans. But does the moon's great power also have influence over a body of water this small? Or does the smaller pool render the moon less potent?

If so, does it piss the moon off? To be less than all-powerful. Or is the moon content with the motion of the ocean? It really doesn't matter now, does it? What matters is that it is all back in sync now. It is all back in order. The moon. The earth. The stars. The movements of every damn celestial body. The motions of all oceans.

There is peace to be enjoyed here. Yes, yes, there is work to do in the house. But that can wait. For now he will sit here, with the sounds of the water, the sounds of the night. He will sit here, with his eyes closed, imagining the moon.

66

WHEN she entered the morning kitchen, she caught her dad at the coffeemaker taking his half-cup for the drive to HQ. And oddly, he reacted that way. As if he had been caught.

"I didn't know you were up," he said as another quarter-cup of the morning roast ended up on the countertop. "Dammit."

"Victoria slept through the night."

"I'm happy somebody did."

She watched him clean up the spill, folding the single sheet of Bounty into a napkin shape and blotting the spill into submission.

"How's the research going?" he asked out of the side of his mouth. "You've been quiet."

It was classic Ed Spangler, classic dad-cop. Ask a question but follow immediately with a statement to influence the response.

Jen was into the refrigerator before she answered, hunting down her grapefruit juice. "Not much to report. After a full-blown investigation like that, I'm not sure what's left for an intern to discover."

"You'd be surprised by the things even experienced people miss," he said. "Sometimes all it takes is that one thing."

It was a new bottle of grapefruit juice, and the glass she poured was almost half pulp.

"I guess most things in life come down to that one thing."

She watched his face reflect the nano-computing his mind was

doing to squeeze things down to the one thing in their lives she was al-
luding to.

"Your coffee's going to be cold before you're out of the driveway."

He smiled an uneasy peacekeeping smile.

"I'm gonna give you my New Year's Eve advice a little early this
year. Don't mix too many different drinks."

She was in mid-sip when he said it. So there was still enough pulp
in her mouth to affect her speech when she responded.

"What are you talking about?"

"That juice. On top of the piss and vinegar."

He raised his car cup slightly, as if he was about to propose a toast.
Jen's juice glass lifted mysteriously in capitulation.

"I'll bring home dinner. Thai okay?"

"Sure," she said. "Remember to ask for extra rice."

VICTORIA was up and fed and dressed. She was sitting on the
bathroom floor, playing with her bathtub set of ocean creatures
while her mother prepped in front of the mirror for her first day as a
journalism intern. Jen resisted the temptation to add some definition to
her intentionally understated makeup. Something told her innocent
would play better than precocious. If, at this point in her life, she could
pull off innocent.

When she thought of the idea, it pissed her off that she hadn't
thought of it earlier. Now it would mess up her hair. But up and over
the head it came—the Lacoste polo.

And then it was her breasts staring back at her in the mirror, as the
bra came off, before she turned it, flipped it and began to put it back
on. A little symbolic gesture. A show of solidarity with Loreena White.

On the floor, in her daughter's hands, a shark and a dolphin were
either attacking each other or trying to figure out a way to kiss. Her cell
phone was ringing in the bedroom. She pulled on her shirt, hurried to

answer. It was Hewitt, calling from her car. Just, she made clear, check-ing in.

"Nothing earth-shattering," Jen responded when asked if anything interesting had presented in the Biffle research. "The same trails. Still cold."

"Sounds a lot like my trails," Hewitt said. "The faster I go, the far-ther this one seems to get ahead of me. And I'm not sure we're even in the same woods."

The Catholic girl in Jen felt a sudden, shining impulse to confess to Hewitt what she was about to do, what she had arranged late the pre-vious day with Byron Biffle. But she overrode it, let Hewitt get on with her day, made sure she knew she appreciated the call. By the time she got back to the bathroom, the shark and the dolphin had taken their skirmish to the toilet, courtesy of the two-year-old goddess of their ocean.

67

FATHER Brian Wilson was behind closed doors with a parishioner. And whatever was being discussed was being done so in the lowest of tones. Unbeknownst to the priest, it was also being discussed outside his office, nonverbally, via the grave expressions from the middle-aged woman who was there to help with some clerical work.

As Hewitt waited on the spongy, vinyl-upholstered visitor's chair, she knew Father Brian was definitely earning his money on this Monday morning, oath of poverty or not. And whatever the volunteer worker was earning in terms of good karma or heavenly capital, she probably deserved a little bump for doing her work with such diligence and, even more so, empathy.

As the laws of physics and metaphysics dictated, you couldn't just have one empathetic human being in a room with others. Not for long. Empathy was like a bonfire on a beach, a bottle of wine in a sorority sister's bedroom. Empathy always drew a crowd. So Hewitt had joined in the eye contact and facial expression exchange with the Catholic volunteer during her mercifully short wait. Once Hewitt established the nonverbal covenant with the woman, the communications had steadily intensified. To the point that Hewitt felt the next time the woman looked up from her on-screen balance sheet, she would reveal the nature of the life-trauma being discussed in Father Wilson's office.

But it was right then that Hewitt mirrored the woman's own face-touching gesture, incidentally exposing her left hand and the gaudy ornament on her ring finger. At which point the somberness of the occasion took a momentary backseat to the promise of tomorrow. And Elizabeth Taylor Hewitt, the Lutheran antibride, was suddenly the standard bearer for the future of the world.

Yeah, me, gettin' married, gonna be great—the thoughts Hewitt knew her dopey expressions were conveying.

God threw a little mercy her way then as the door to Father Wilson's office swung open and he and his lost lamb exited the office. Neither made eye contact with Hewitt as the priest escorted a puffy-eyed but stubbornly pretty woman of no more than thirty-five from the area.

It wasn't until she had passed that Hewitt determined what was causing the woman to walk with the pronounced limp. Her left leg wasn't a real one. Although tucked in the athletic sock and running shoe and three-quarters covered by the Capri-length leggings, it was as real-looking as a prosthetic limb could be.

The good soul at the PC read what Hewitt was doing, waited until she was certain her words would be heard only by the two of them— with, Hewitt assumed, the understanding that God had the power to eavesdrop at any time.

"Bone cancer," she offered in a voice barely above a whisper.

"Is she going to be okay?" Hewitt asked, similarly softened.

"Yes and no. Yes in surviving the cancer. No in keeping her family together."

There was more. The woman seemed willing to share it. But the curtain closed on the sharing session as Father Brian Wilson returned to the outer office, his body only slightly less heavy in carriage than when he had walked through with his troubled parishioner.

"I guess that makes it your turn," he said to Hewitt.

He waited at the open door for her to enter first. When she passed him, it was close enough that she caught a whiff of the incense that had held on to him since the early morning mass.

*   *   *

S HE hadn't come to the priest's office for counseling, spiritual or otherwise. There hadn't been a passing of the torch from one visitor to the next. But the cushion on the visitor's chair was still warm when Hewitt sat down. So there was that handoff, that continuity from the previous visitor to the next one—the one with two good legs.

"One of those *life is really hard* things," the priest reflected.

"There seems to be a lot of that going around," Hewitt offered as Father Brian Wilson settled into the chair behind his mission desk.

"The Buddhists have a strategy for that I've always admired," he said. "The first tenet of their philosophy is that *life is suffering*. Once you accept that as a given, it makes what follows more understandable. So when bad things happen, when suffering occurs, you don't wander around in circles saying, 'Why did this happen to me?' Instead you say, 'Okay, this again. Suffering. How do I handle it?' "

Hewitt gave his statement a little time to breathe.

"I feel like I should make a donation for a personal homily," she said.

"My palm is always turned toward heaven," he responded.

On another day—a day when one of his deacons wasn't missing under bizarre circumstances—Hewitt knew he would have smiled in satisfaction after delivering such a remark.

"Agent Hewitt, if you've come here to tell me that he's missing, I already know. He was supposed to have helped with the mass this morning. So whatever else he's missing from, you can add us to the list."

"Dr. Boccachio has been missing since yesterday morning," Hewitt told him. "We've talked to his receptionist, looked at his calendar, made a list of places he frequents. I have a couple of teams pursuing that. One of the places he's known to frequent is St. Sebastian's. In times of trouble, it's not unusual for people to turn to the church."

Father Brian Wilson was looking at her with a visage that was part disbelief, part sorrow.

"If he had done that, it would be obvious, wouldn't it? I mean what do you think—I've given him sanctuary in the bell tower?"

Again for Hewitt, it did have a certain something to it. A cult of mental health professionals. A mad psychiatrist in the bell tower.

"One of the latest victims, Laura Pennington, was one of his patients too. And there's some evidence to suggest they may have been more than patient and client."

He spent a few moments looking at his desktop, or just above it, his eyes moving in an almost imperceptible elliptical pattern, as if, Hewitt thought, he were watching a small fish swim in a bowl.

"If he did this—and I hope to hell you're wrong—I wish he *was* in the bell tower. Because I'd go up there with you and throw him to the sidewalk. But I have to tell you, Agent Hewitt, I simply can't embrace that possibility."

"No one can ever fathom something like this," Hewitt said. "In God's universe, on his watch, how can you explain anything like this?"

She was looking into his eyes again as he formulated his response. This time the fish had stopped swimming.

"I guess you'd have to ask him yourself."

"God?"

"Yes?"

"And you believe we can actually talk to God?"

It was a question that wasn't on Hewitt's original list for the interview. But that little detail was trumped by the fact that it was a question she'd always wanted to ask, especially to someone who might actually have some clue to the answer.

Father Brian Wilson looked at her not as if she would be the latest person to whom he would give his standard response, but as the first person with whom he had ever shared the sad truth.

"When we run out of people on earth," he said, "who else do we have?"

68

"PEOPLE ask what is the job of a journalist? Is it to report the news? Is it to interpret the news? Or as we see more and more frequently today, is it to influence news?"

They were at her desk, in an office down the hall from his that had once been occupied by a legitimate employee, in the days before Byron Biffle had gone to a team of freelancers and become his own one-man band. He handled editorial duties, ad sales and oversaw production. That and managing the ghost of his famous father. On this morning, one of his ways of managing it was to play professor to her undergrad intern.

"My answer is that it is the job of a journalist to tell the story that refuses to go untold."

He was sitting in the visitor's chair. Jen was behind the big wooden desk, with its fresh lemon scent from a recent dusting, and a single legal pad with a couple of pens to complement the aging Mac monitor and keyboard that sat off to the side.

"It's not really up to us. Finding the story is a lot like waking up a person who's been asleep. Once they're awake, there's only so much you can do to influence their behavior. The best bet is usually to get out of the way and watch and listen."

"As you said, though, it seems that modern journalists are putting themselves in the story to influence the story's"—she nodded in deference to his terminology—"*behavior.*"

He didn't like something about her delivery. Jen quickly deduced it was the *modern* in *modern journalist*, as a reflection of where he stood on the evolutionary chart.

"If the journalist isn't a true part of the story, the story, ultimately, will expose that. The story will set the record straight."

His mouth curled at the corners, an upward curl that reminded her of another face, a certain bad actor who lived alone on a mountain and decided to steal Christmas from his neighbors below.

"So to me that's one definition of a journalist's job," he said. "There is, of course, another. And that's to pay your bills and pay your help. To take the high school sports scores, the details of the school board initiatives, and the names of those lovely people who—in their right mind or not—attended this year's quilting bee."

He extended the fingers of his right hand against the right side of his face, pressed them until they bent back enough to make his knuckles crack.

"So that's my little Welcome to the *Mundelein Dispatch*. And now I'm thinking you'd like to know what your first assignment might be."

Jen nodded, doing her best to smile in some anti-Grinch way. More innocent and clueless. More *Cindy Lou Who*.

"Whatever I can do to help."

"Okay then," he smiled, the upward curl retracing its pattern. "Your first assignment is me."

Cindy Lou Who lost her innocence. She felt it, saw him assessing what she was feeling.

"I want you to interview me for an upcoming edition."

"What's the angle?" Jen managed.

He did the knuckle cracking thing again, this time to the left side.

"Journalism student interviews newspaper owner as an exercise. Where it goes, where you take it from there, is up to you."

"So, in effect, I'm part of the story."

"To the degree that you make yourself part of it. To the degree that the story is amenable to your participation."

"So we're going to explore the theory right away," Jen ventured.

"Well, not immediately," Byron Biffle bounced back. "I'll give you some time to formulate an approach, come up with some questions. I have to run a couple of sorties, starting with the bank."

"Is it donut day again?"

"No, that's just Monday," he responded. "Today is Hershey's Kisses day. Today and every day. As long as my business banker keeps refilling the bowl on her desk. Would you like me to bring you some?"

69

HEWITT limped out of St. Sebastian's. Not because there was a problem with one of her legs. But empathy was a powerful force. Especially when you were walking a thin line between heaven and hell.

It surprised her that Father Brian Wilson had been willing to share the information about the woman who had hobbled from the church prior to her. But as intuition went, Father Brian seemed to be in some serious upper percentile of the earth's population—so much so that she had actually bookmarked him as someone to consider for her own pre-marriage counseling, if it ever came to that. As it was, Father Brian had known damn well that Hewitt knew just enough about the woman who had preceded her in his counsel to want to know the rest. Which meant he was all over the fact that his clerical helper wasn't much of a secret keeper.

The bone cancer had only been the beginning of the traumatic chain of events for the woman who now had a name. *Grace.* Not her real name. Father Brian, out of respect, withheld that. Grace was the name he pulled up as a substitute, something he freely admitted. And Hewitt had the strong sense it was a universal name he was in the habit of invoking to protect a true identity in matters of professional discourse.

Having lost her leg to bone cancer, Grace had also lost her husband. Or he had lost his memory of the vows he had taken in front of God and a church filled with his earthly witnesses. A certain tenet about having and holding, in sickness and in health. Father Brian hadn't assigned a universal nickname for the husband who had left Grace. But Hewitt had. *Asshole*.

Reflecting on that as she hustled the Mazda to her next drop-in—courtesy of a revelation from Father Brian—Hewitt thought of another person in her experience who had been dropped by a spouse after life had done some serious alterations to his physical body.

Detective John Davidoff. The man who'd served, protected and donated his face to the greater good in a pool of ignited gasoline at the end of a car chase. His wife hadn't been able to adjust to her husband's total makeover. But wasn't that the whole idea? Wasn't that the whole Hegelian point?

Thesis: Husband's handsome face.

Antithesis: Husband's handsome face burned off.

Synthesis: Developing the x-ray vision necessary to see beyond it.

The same with Grace and Asshole.

Thesis: Wife with two lovely legs.

Antithesis: Wife with one lovely leg.

Synthesis: Finding a way for two people to make it to the finish line on three legs.

On the dashboard, the image of the masked murderer was still on display, only now the Post-it Note from Father Wilson was obscuring the lower half of the face. Naturally, Hewitt hadn't known that Dr. Gerry Boccachio had a son, much less a son who was in his second year at UIC. A son who had hovered just off the radar to that point in Hewitt's inquiry. A son who for whatever reason wasn't positioned front and center in his father's physical world. A son who was more a rumor than a real live boy.

As she guided the Mazda into the hot zone, she found it was a 70/30 blend of weird and thrilling to be back in the student housing area of her alma mater. Not that it looked exactly like it had when she was stumbling around the campus. So much gentrification since then. But enough remained that it gave her a little shot of stored-up coed adrenaline as she parked the Mazda and got out.

One of the things gentrification couldn't change were the atmospheric conditions of a late August day. And that trigger, along with the higher concentration of college-issue pheromones from the incoming students, threw Hewitt into a sensory flashback of the audio musical variety.

Twenty years earlier, what girl hadn't wanted to be Belinda Carlisle? Especially once she'd dumped the baggage of the Go-Gos to shine a light on the virtues of feminine independence. That late summer of Hewitt's first days on the UIC campus, the airwaves had been lavish in their affection for Ms. Carlisle's first solo hit.

Hewitt was hearing it in her head now.

We'll make heaven a place on earth . . .

Her feet falling into cadence with the pop beat in her head as she walked, Hewitt did a quick review of the Carlislian philosophy in the lyrics. The notion that in heaven love came first. Obviously hard to dispute that. It got interesting with the assertion that human free will could connect the dots between heaven and earth. The idea that human beings could make earth into heaven, or at least a heaven-like place.

It was at precisely this intersection that the philosophy of Carlisle and Hegel fell happily into bed together. And as any college boy in America could have told you, *Lucky Hegel.*

She had made a visual sighting of the address Father Wilson had given her. A row house of apartments in tan brick, with silver hardware.

A pop song by Belinda Carlisle had cut to the freaking chase of the Hegelian dialectic. What was the point of building that intricate structure of thesis-antithesis-synthesis ladders? Where was all that earthly intellectual and spiritual climbing supposed to take humanity?

She was on the porch step, ringing the bell. As she waited, her mind's eye created a visual—an ascending, spiraling lattice of all that thesis-antithesis-synthesis construction. Until it turned into its recognizable form. A strand of DNA as long as the Milky Way.

The door opened. Seeing the young man, she realized she didn't need to confirm a name.

"Michael Boccachio?" she offered anyway.

Recognizing her instantly as well, his face resumed the locker room grin he'd splashed her with the only other time they'd made eye contact. The difference this time, thanks to a pair of gym shorts, was that Hewitt was able to keep her eyes on his face.

70

S HE was looking for the ghost of Loreena White. But while she was doing that, she had to come up with some questions for a very-much-alive Byron Biffle. So far, the only question she could hear herself asking was: *Mr. Biffle, if you did have information from the last case your father was investigating, where the hell would you keep it?*

After a quick look around the ground floor of the offices, she realized the answer to the Byron Biffle question was the same as the answer to her first question for Loreena White: *If you were a ghost, where in this house would you hide?*

The stairs to the basement were at the rear of the house, just off the back entrance. It was an old basement, a basement that had been left old. She could tell by the smell before she reached the halfway point of her descent down the steps. There were no modern fibers, glues or sealants down there, nothing to suggest the basement had been finished in any way.

Visual confirmation. An old basement, lit by the leaks of natural light through the two sill box windows she could see. She had tried the light switch in the back hall, but the basement lights hadn't responded. Fortunately she had brought her own light source. The miniflashlight she now pulled from her pocket.

Like most unfinished basements, the primary use for this one was storage. Not just of business-related materials, but of things totally unrelated to the business upstairs. Her flashlight introduced her to some of them. From the milk crates of record albums to the old foosball table to the antique spinning wheel to the—Jesus Christ—the old dressing mannequin, it was more like the basement of an antique shop than a community newspaper. Including the bank of antique file cabinets along the far wall.

She didn't know how long Byron Biffle would be out conducting his "sorties." But she was sure it wouldn't be long enough to go through the entire bank of cabinets with any kind of meaningful search. Her instincts told her that was a much too ordinary place for Loreena White to be hiding anyway.

If you were a man and you had to hide a secret in a basement, where would you hide it?

She heard a noise upstairs. The heavy air of the basement thinned, purified instantly as her senses went on full alert. She heard a humming through the floor. A mechanical humming. A motor. Probably the refrigerator having kicked in.

Her feet were moving over the crumbling concrete floor. In the lucid moment prompted by the upstairs noise, she had answered her own question. The flashlight previewed the way—the eight or ten steps it took to circle back around to the space beneath the basement steps, to the jigsaw puzzle of differently sized and shaped boxes that all fit together with a neatness that looked as if it had been designed that way.

The majority of the boxes had identifications written in marker—contents, initials, dates. Three of the boxes had no markings at all, at least not on the front-facing panels. Jen focused on these, stored as they were in the middle part of the configuration. Two of them were legal boxes, not terribly old. The other was an older, off-white box that had once held a case of French Colombard.

Jen paused to listen to the house again. The appliance motor continued to run. Otherwise the house was still.

Stillness was the last thing that was happening in her head as she moved the top layer of boxes so she could get at the three that interested her. She began with one of the unmarked legal boxes. Within seconds of opening it, she understood he was a chain smoker. That aspect of his life had been entombed with the files, the legal pads, the notebooks of the man who had followed Loreena White into oblivion.

After Carlton Ritz's death, it would have fallen to his son to go through his father's effects, his things, *his life*, and keep what was of value, monetarily or personally. This was one of the treasure chests. She went through the boxes, as quickly as she could manage, thumbing through the files, the volumes, looking for some glinting shard from the broken life of Loreena White.

She sensed that most of this was a prelude. Loreena White was too interesting, too good to be buried in a legal **box**. Loreena White deserved something more special.

Jen took the wine box, pulled open **the interlocked top**. Within seconds, she knew. She had found the reliquary.

71

IT was lurid being in his apartment, lurid being alone with him. And Hewitt couldn't tell who was more responsible for making it feel that way—a three-quarters-naked swimmer or her fully exposed self. It wouldn't occur to her until afterward that maybe the lurid feeling had been preexisting. This was one overly charged, priapic young man. He didn't exactly need to stick a *Glad Lurid* plug-in into the wall to create the atmosphere.

She watched him react to the news that his father had been missing for more than twenty-four hours. He didn't seem overwhelmed by it. Just confused, and only a modest expression of that.

"You haven't told me why—why you're looking for him."

"I guess I just figured you'd be able to connect the dots," Hewitt told him. "Unattractive as the picture might turn out to be."

He got up from the metal folding chair he'd insisted on taking, leaving Hewitt seated in the old padded thing he'd offered for her comfort. Old, padded and a museum for college student smells.

Crossing the room, with his back to her, he moved with the preciseness of a diver setting up on a platform. He stopped, turned around. For the first time since he'd opened the door to her, Hewitt saw the locker room look reprised. Given the reason for Hewitt's visit—which she was certain he knew—the look couldn't have been more inappropriate, ridiculous, pathetic.

"You come here to tell me—or to imply in your own special

way—that you suspect my father of being involved in this horror movie. And for that I'm supposed to sit on your knee and whisper secrets to you?"

"Look, you arrogant fucking prima donna *fish* . . ."

She stopped the line at the thought stage, made it sound a little more professional when voiced.

"If you want to have an attitude, that's fine. All I know is if *my* father didn't show for a day's worth of patient appointments and a morning mass where he'd made an appointment with his priest and his God, I might be a little concerned."

The arrogant-fucking-prima-donna-fish look hadn't completely left his face.

"Well, that's the difference between you and me," he said. "You never had the beautiful experience of living with him."

Hewitt let the air out of her lungs, put down her shield.

"Okay, Michael. I have two suggestions for you. First, come back and sit down. And we'll talk about all that. Or none of it. Whatever you want. But understand that we need information to help us find your father."

He moved toward the metal chair, stopped before he sat down.

"You said you had *two* suggestions."

"The other is that you put a shirt on."

"Is that some kind of protocol thing?"

"No, it's an I'm a woman with a pulse thing."

I T turned out Michael was just his nickname. His actual name was Michelangelo Boccachio. He didn't share with her a middle name. Although Hewitt suspected a few. *Leonardo. Raphael.* And given his swimmer persona, *Machiavelli.*

For the record, Michelangelo Boccachio didn't put on a shirt. Clearly, the woman with a pulse thing had played right into his protruding male ego—his *here I am, suck my dick* attitude. It was an attitude he hadn't needed to work terribly hard to cultivate. All he'd had to do was watch the other narcissistic male in the house he grew up in.

In any event, her tossed-together strategy had made him more interested in participating. If they had been in a bar together, Hewitt knew she would have had all the free drinks she wanted. She would have been extremely careful, however, not to leave an unfinished one on the bar when she went to use the ladies' room.

No, he couldn't think of any reason why his father would have failed to show up for patient sessions unless he was ill, or injured. The prospect of either didn't seem terribly concerning to him. On the subject of illness, he threw a little light.

"By ill, I'm not necessarily limiting it to physical."

Hewitt asked him if he considered his father to be psychologically unstable.

"Potentially," was his immediate response. "But I consider *anyone* to be potentially unstable. I mean look at what he does for a living. Seeing the worst of the worst. Hearing it every day. Taking it with you to sleep at night. I mean, shit."

Hewitt assumed that if Michael Boccachio's father was struggling psychologically, he would have likely sought refuge in some kind of place he'd used for that before. Either that, or if he was, in fact, the perp, he would have retreated permanently to his staging area now that the heat had been turned up around him. So her questions turned to any other properties Michael's father owned or had access to, aboveboard or under.

"Well, there's the lake house," he offered without further prompting. "But it's in my mother's name. They were never actually married. Which, I know, makes me a bastard. As I'm sure any of my girlfriends would be happy to verify."

"Does your father still have access to the property?"

"He always kept a key."

Hewitt asked for and received the property's location. It was when she received the name of the property's legal owner that she suddenly felt so flushed she almost took off her own shirt.

The holder of the deed on the Fox Lake retreat: Maya Fucking Macy.

72

THE trip to Fox Lake wasn't all bad. It was the last week of August. The day was plenty bright, plenty warm. But there was the feeling in the air of the summer's energy waning. And given all that, Hewitt felt it might be one of her last chances to get to the beach before the seasons turned.

It was a shame her fiancé was working. It would have been nice to throw a little picnic basket together. It would have been nice to spend a little time on Maya Macy's pier. She had the perfect musical accompaniment for water, sand and sun. A little Wes Montgomery, from his later pop period. And she had the perfect tune for him to cover. A Belinda Carlisle number. About going to a better place, and not necessarily having to give up your life to get there.

Hell yes, a lovely scenario. Lovelier still if Dr. Gerry Boccachio would greet her at the door, camera in hand, saying, "Damn, I was just about to do the honors with another couple. But now you've foiled that. Feel free to hog-tie me. Then you and your friend can enjoy the view from the pier. And if you run out of that cheap-ass Chardonnay you brought, feel free to pick out something nice from the wine cellar."

It was a calculated move to make a cold call. But to have informed Maya Macy of her intent would have allowed for any number of secret handshakes within her little therapeutic society. The best bet was to let her visit to the campus apartment of Michelangelo Boccachio's campus apartment resonate however it would.

The trip to the lake country did have its purpose. It was a place they hadn't looked. And since they were running out of those, anything that could be used as a staging ground, a personal forum, a meditation cave, was worth an hour of her time and ten bucks in gas to the taxpayers of Illinois. Besides, lake homes were interesting. They were places where you let your hair down, indulged the senses, allowed yourself—in a very controlled environment—to become just a hint more primal. Who knew? Maybe she'd find a cadre of cult members performing dance routines around a very surprised goat.

If you were going to enjoy a little getaway, why mess it up by packing your sanity?

73

THEY sat across the desk from one another, he again in the visitor's chair, she in the aging, black leather executive chair behind the desk. On the desktop, each had three silver Hershey's Kisses in a triangular arrangement he had made while she was either still downstairs or when she had sneaked back upstairs to the bathroom after hearing he had returned from his errands.

They had been talking for fifteen minutes, and still she couldn't tell if he knew she'd been down in the basement or not.

"I guess I'll have to be the one who breaks the ice on the Kisses," he said.

She watched as he picked up one of the candies and unwrapped it. He popped the chocolate into his mouth, let it sit there for several seconds before he took his leisurely time chewing it.

"You know, we don't have to cover everything today," he said, a swallow before the chocolate was completely gone from his mouth. "This is just to get you in the game. A hack writer might say *to get your feet wet.*"

"As I said, I'm here to learn," she offered as she unwrapped a Kiss of her own. The silver foil made its tiny crinkly sounds. As he watched her, she read his eyes for any similar crinkly disturbance—no matter how small—in response to her *here to learn* statement.

He revealed nothing, other than the fact that something about her having the chocolate in her mouth gave him an odd satisfaction. And as she chewed, as he watched her chew, it was as if there was something in the Hershey's Kiss that made her skin ping in a million places, that made her face flush and her armpits clammy.

If he knew, he was going to make her wonder for a while. And that was the worst possible development. Because if he was toying with her at this level, toying was part of his MO, toying was something that got him off.

But then, just as she had convinced herself she was in trouble, he did something unexplainable. Not that a man in his late forties didn't have to leave to take a piss more often than a man in his twenties. But if he was planning to fuck with her, he was giving her every opportunity to leave the scene *unfucked*.

After he excused himself, she listened as he crossed the house, his gait quickening. The refrigerator motor was off, so she had clear sound of him closing the door, locking it behind him, the struggling whir of the bathroom fan kicking in with the turning on of the light.

He was a neatnik, to the extreme. There was no doubt about that. As she glanced at the questions she'd scribbled on her legal pad, she knew they were all blown away by the only two questions that mattered anymore. One: Would he notice that his basket of magazines had been disturbed when she'd hidden the Loreena White file near the bottom of the stack? And two: If he did notice, would she have to use her daddy's gun when he came back to keep from becoming a permanent toy?

74

THERE was definitely money in madness. If the Boccachio-Macy place was a second or third home, 99 percent of the world's population would have traded in their first home for that. It was a classic trilevel log, stone and cedar shake lake home, with a massive screened porch, a huge bank of water-facing side windows, and decks on the second and third floors.

At the moment, Hewitt had the same view of the property as the next-door neighbor to the south, standing as she was just a couple of feet from the woman, Gwen Skylar, on the Skylar pier. Already determined was that the Boccachio-Macy place was currently unoccupied. Hewitt's pounding on doors and peering through first-floor windows had left her solid with that. She'd found the front and back doors were locked, as was the attached garage.

Gwen Skylar, all four feet ten, ninety pounds and eighty years of her, had confirmed Hewitt's diagnosis.

"The original owner—the doctor—I haven't seen him in some time," Gwen Skylar responded to Hewitt's question. "The current owner, Maya, now and then. Usually on weekends. It's possible there may have been someone there last night. I go to bed early. But I thought I heard a car."

"Do you ever see the son here?" Hewitt asked.

"The young man—the swimmer?"

Hewitt nodded as the woman shoed away a deerfly.

"More often than anyone. And usually with a friend."

Her eyes rolled with disapproval.

"As in girlfriend?"

"Girl-*friends*. And let's just say they're not the most bashful of people."

In Hewitt's head, Wes Montgomery was playing some big, bouncy octaves on his guitar—to accompany the big, bouncy action Hewitt assumed the woman was referring to next door.

"I mean I'm no prude. I've had my day . . ."

The octogenarian continued on her little moral diatribe. But Hewitt's focus had jumped the property line, pushing all the way to the big picture window that stood watch over the lake on the second level of the dwelling. With the brightness of the day, the window was reflecting the outer world. But Hewitt felt a sensation in the downy zones of her skin. As if, in the midst of all that reflected pine and sky, the optic nerve of the house had switched on for a squinty view of her.

Hewitt closed up the conversation with Gwen Skylar, took the woman's phone number, gave her a card. She excused herself, said she was going to spend a few minutes looking around *Maya's Place*, did exactly that. But it was a discovery she had noted earlier, on the north side of the home, that she revisited now. A ladder. A ladder built into the side of the house, hidden by a stand of pine trees.

It was a fire escape. For a trilevel building, a good idea. And it may have only been that. But with the dark part of her heart starting to pump now, Hewitt had to assume it could have been used in other ways. She decided to give it an alternative use herself.

About halfway up the ladder, the Wes Montgomery version of Belinda Carlisle ceased to pseudo-exist. She was up there now in the songbird zone. A bird was, in fact, chirping a tune in the pine tree behind her. Or was it a warning?

As she was lifting herself over the deck rail, she caught a whiff of something gone bad inside the house. The very earliest phase of it. But enough to make her heart drop two-and-a-half stories. Instantly, the beautifully appointed deck, with its lounges, tables and torches, was the ugliest place in the world.

The two high windows that flanked the French doors were canted open slightly to the screens. She pulled on a glove, tried the sliding doors. Locked. It would be a window entrance. She forced the right side window open, enough that she could get her body through, used the sharpest key on her chain to rip-cut the screen.

Reverse birth then as she lifted and wriggled herself through the window and into the house. The palms of her hands were the first part of her to make contact with the polished maple floor of the third-floor bedroom. Collecting herself, she got up, scanned what had been the master bedroom. Technically, it still was. But there were no signs of a master having used it lately. It appeared to have been co-opted by Michael Boccachio.

For the moment, the bottles of body scents on the dresser confused the air enough that the other smell wasn't as detectible. That changed when Hewitt stepped into the hallway.

It came rushing at her, the hallway, the house, alive with it. She reached inside her blazer, fingered her service revolver, left it where it was as she reached the next bedroom, as she saw the headless body sit up in the bed and scream at her, without ever moving a muscle.

75

MAYBE she was out of her mind. Sitting there, knowing the unforgiving acoustics of the house, trying her best to pee while she went through the file as quietly and efficiently as possible. Already a few things had caught her interest. One in particular. It was just a name thing. Maybe it meant something, maybe it didn't. Then again, maybe none of this meant anything. Maybe her entire supposition was wrong. It wouldn't be the first time in her life she'd done that.

The hum of the bathroom fan that went on automatically with the light switch wasn't helping her to clarify her thinking either. Like the steady drone of any white noise, it was going to have its narcotizing effect eventually. Maybe eventually was already here. She had tossed and turned the night before, in the steady drone of her confusion. The fear and guilt from the assault had been gnawing at her, burning her out from the inside since the moment she realized it had happened. Maybe she was crazy. Maybe she was exhausted from trying to force it to make sense. Maybe Byron Biffle hadn't killed Loreena White. Maybe he was nothing more than face value. Maybe he was just another overly educated person who had suffered a tragedy and was sentenced to live in its shadow. In the shadow of a larger-than-life dead father. The two being connected. The one feeding the other.

She flushed the toilet. Now it was her turn to play obsessive-compulsive as she stared into the magazine basket, assessed the positioning of the contents. For all she could tell, it appeared undisturbed.

As undisturbed as Byron Biffle had seemed, felt, when he returned from his own bathroom break.

Still, the ghost of Loreena White had been temporarily stashed down there, beneath the layers of *US News, Forbes* and the neatly folded section of *The Wall Street Journal.* Jen watched her hands and fingers as they performed the delicate art of file retrieval, taking a moment to neaten the arrangement after the file had been removed. She turned on the faucet to mask any sounds the slipping of the file into the back of her pants and under her polo and blazer might make.

She was now officially guilty of stealing personal property. But she knew if the roles had somehow been reversed, Loreena White, her backward-bra sorority sister, would have committed the same crime for her.

When she had excused herself to use the bathroom, Byron Biffle had volunteered that he would take a few minutes to return to his office and check his messages. If she could just get back to her office and slip the file into her messenger bag, she could go through it when she got home. She could spend some alone time with Loreena White—at least the Loreena White as Byron Biffle's father understood her to be.

Jen washed her hands, pulled a couple of paper towels. When she finished, she switched off the light, listened as the fan groaned to a stop. Returning to her office, she tried to make her feet less heavy against the floor, but the old wood floor of the Victorian creaked behind her anyway.

Back in her office, she breathed for the first time since she'd exited the bathroom. Besides being able to breathe again, the even better news was that Byron Biffle had, in fact, vacated her office. Quickly, quietly, she transferred the file to the messenger bag, tucking it between a couple of notebooks. She returned the messenger bag to its original position behind the desk. With the refrigerator motor still on standby, she listened for the sounds of her boss tapping the keys to answer his e-mail. Either he'd found something else to do or he hadn't received much in the way of messages.

Jen was burning for the file. If she knew for sure that Byron Biffle would be occupied in his office with other business, she would've already been looking through the contents. She decided to roll the dice, spent a couple of minutes going through the file, grabbing on to a detail here, a tripped wire there—one item, in particular that called out. By the third minute, she was forcing herself to close the file and hide it in the messenger bag. She decided to do a little fly-by of his office. Just to see. Just to find out how much time she might have to return for an additional look.

She walked into his office, realizing as she did that she should have paused to address him first.

"Mr. Biffle?" she said as she turned from his empty office to reenter the hall and continue her search.

A whirl of energy entered her peripheral line of sight on the right side. But by then, the impact of the blow to her head was already closing her eyes.

76

MAYA Macy threw a postmortem party and everyone came. The Fox Lake PD, the state crime scene techs, the media, the neighbors—including one octogenarian who was the most difficult of the unofficial people to keep off the property. But it wasn't until a living relative of the decedent arrived that the occasion found its theme.

Hewitt had directed Pete Megna to pick up Michelangelo Boccachio, leaving it to him to inform the young man that his mother had been found murdered at the lake home. With the younger Boccachio being the one who had tipped her to the Fox Lake residence, she told Megna to be careful with him, but not to treat it as an apprehension. Although, in effect, that's what it was. Nothing official, but she felt an urgent need to have him in a place where she could watch him. As she stood now in the third-floor hallway of the lake home, in the heart of the crime scene buzz, her first opportunity to observe him was coming up the stairs.

"Are you sure it's her? Are you sure it's her? *Are you sure it's her?*"

His voice cut through the buzz of official personnel, the pitch and intensity of it causing a general pause in the activity. When he reached the top of the steps and approached Hewitt, she read his eyes, saw a glazed numbness there. The natural narcotics in his brain had already begun the slow drip.

Hewitt nodded yes. "She had identification. Personal effects. I'm sorry, Michael."

She didn't tell him about the unofficial ID the victim had on her person, the same high-end perfume she'd aerated Hewitt with at Big Shoulders the day before.

Michael Boccachio's eyes became wet, but they didn't become pained. He turned his face toward the bedroom where his mother's body was still lying on the bed. The rest of him started to move in that direction. But a camera flash from the room, and another, stopped him. Hewitt reached for his arm, took it in her hands. He pulled it away laterally—until she was left with his wrist, then just his hand. This he let her have, giving it up like a little boy.

"Let's talk outside," Hewitt said.

She nodded to Megna, who had held his position at the top of the stairs. He nodded back—to the degree the cervical collar would allow. He signed off with a click of his jaw and headed down the stairs, to return to the manhunt for Michael Boccachio's father.

Hewitt led the son through the master bedroom, to the French doors, allowed him to pass her and step through the doors first, their hands losing contact. He proceeded across the deck, his body stiffening, pulling inward, but picking up speed. For a moment, Hewitt thought he might go right over the railing. Which, in effect, he did. But just the top half of him, as the emotion hit the bottom of his gut and bounced back up, bringing the contents of his stomach with it.

Hewitt felt a sympathetic revulsion in her own gut, overrode it as she crossed the deck, came up behind him and put her hand on his back, her palm pressing between his shoulder blades. She felt his muscles tense up around the contact. He lifted his head, let it fall, lifted it again.

A bird had started singing. Or maybe it had been singing all along. Not the same bird that accompanied her up the ladder. A different kind of song. More looping. More legato.

"You think one of us did this," he said, his voice constricted, higher, like it might've sounded in early high school.

"I don't know what to think, Michael," Hewitt said. "I'm just very sorry that it came down to this for all of you. But especially for your mother."

77

"I could've killed him," he said.

They were in the Mazda, Hewitt driving, Michelangelo Boccachio beside her in the passenger seat. It wasn't the ideal interrogation facility, this box on wheels. But it seemed to be working. They were barely five minutes into their trip from Fox Lake to Big Shoulders Marriage and Family Therapies, and already he was letting go of some big stuff.

"He never hit me when I was a kid. Never. But my sophomore year in high school I got a girl pregnant. An older girl. A senior. She ended up having an abortion. And my dad knew about it. He found out the same day she had it. And that night, when he came home, he beat the shit out of me."

Just that quickly the Mazda interrogation room was having to double as another venue. This time, a stage with a proscenium arch. If this was Shakespeare, it was time for the soliloquy.

"I didn't fight back. I didn't do anything. After never getting hit before, and then here he is, like he's going to kill me. But for some reason he didn't. He stopped. I was on the floor. Curled up in a ball. I heard him leave the room. A couple of minutes later he came back."

Michael Boccachio stopped talking, turned and looked—as if to see if she was still listening to him. Hewitt gestured for him to continue. This seemed to confuse him. For a moment, he just sat there, helpless. As helpless, Hewitt thought, as he'd been on the floor, curled up, waiting.

"Your father came back," she prompted. "You were on the floor and your father came back."

"He had it all figured out. He came in, took my right hand, pulled a plastic glove over it. And then . . . then he gave me the gun. He made me stand up. He got down on his knees, took my hand, the gun, put the barrel against his face. He said, 'Tell them what I did to you. Tell them I did this to myself. My fingerprints are on the gun. Just drop it next to my body, then get rid of the glove. *Kill me now*. Or someday you'll wish you had.' Then he pulled the gun into his mouth, closed his eyes."

It was just the hum of the engine then, as driver and passenger waited for the sound of a gunshot that never came. Hewitt let the quietness pass, let him feel the full impact of that silent gun.

"I just have two questions for you then, Michael. First, do you think it's reasonable for me to think that your telling me about the lake house this morning and what happened there last night are a coincidence?"

When he didn't hedge for a moment, Hewitt knew he'd either been anticipating the question, or what he was telling her was the truth.

"It was just a feeling I had. That he might be up there. Last week when I was there, I noticed a bottle of Scotch he kept there was lower than it had been a few days earlier. I thought maybe he'd been stopping in. I figured if you started watching the place, you might see him. You could do your thing. Find out. Either way."

Hewitt accepted his response, tucked it away for further consideration. "Okay, second question. When that thing went down with your father and the gun. If you had pulled the trigger at the time, do you think your mother would still be alive?"

He didn't turn to look at her when he answered, didn't look at anything. Just a gauzy stare through the windshield.

"If he did this to her, then he's already dead too."

78

THERE are things that have been done that don't seem possible. None of them more so than this.

He stands at the white door. He feels he could stand here for the rest of time and never fully embrace the possibility. But possibility is the most powerful force in the universe.

So often people speak of someone doing *the impossible*. But *impossible*, by definition, would be an absolute. There should be no degrees of impossibility. Impossibility meant something that could never happen, never be realized, never have a chance of being experienced. And yet *possibility* was a force so powerful it could, at times, transcend its absolute opposite.

With his right index finger, he traces the perfectly simple equation for this on the refrigerator door.

$P>I$.

My God. Of course. Of course. It should have all been impossible. Shouldn't it have?

He remembers picking up a science magazine from a bookstore rack, remembers opening it to a spread of images from the Hubble Telescope. He flashes the images for himself now, the gleaming white surface of the white door serving as an ideal background for the projections. He remembers one in particular, leaves that image up for a moment. A cluster of galaxies, described in a line of text as *a few million light-years away*. A cluster of galaxies, each one an unfathomable distance from the next nearest one. But in the image—as seen from a few million light-years away—all compressed into the shape, the form, the illumination of *a diamond*.

Before the universe existed, when there was nothing, such a celestial phenomenon would have been an impossibility.

All those eons later, the Hubble Telescope proved otherwise. And if something like that was possible—a diamond made of galaxies—wasn't everything else possible too?

Even this. Even what was on the other side of the white door. Who would have guessed that the universal mother would end up in such a place? A day before, it would have seemed an impossibility.

Who could have guessed? Certainly not the universal mother. Not her significant other. Such an ending would have been beyond their ability to conceive. And yet it had happened. Someone had been able to conceive it.

All it required was a little mind over matter. Or mind over antimatter. Or moon over Miami. Better yet, moon over Fox Lake.

He opens the refrigerator door, sees the confirmation of his formula, the repudiation of the impossible, staring back at him.

79

NOT even the big puffy room at *Big Shoulders* had enough padding to soften the brutal reality that one of its principals had been murdered overnight. The body count was still at one. But Hewitt's call to Eric Hubertus had confirmed her expectation that Steve Norris had been a no-show that day and, like Maya Macy, hadn't called in sick.

Hewitt had called Hubertus from the Fox Lake crime scene. He had volunteered to drive out and pick up Michael Boccachio, also volunteering to step in as a de facto guardian for the young man in the face of what was now a double tragedy—with a father missing and a mother dead. From the tone of his offer, Hewitt got the sense that Eric Hubertus and Autumn Fournier had functioned in some similar manner in Michael Boccachio's life previously.

There was no crying. That was the first thing that jumped out at Hewitt. The second was that Eric Hubertus and Autumn Fournier weren't the only ones predisposed to behaving like surrogate parents. Having called a convocation of all the surviving partners, Hewitt now had the opportunity to observe how the Fassbenders, Dennis and Lourdes, joined Hubertus/Fournier in forming a human cocoon around Michael Boccachio. They were assembled that way inside the puffy room, the four of them having taken the young man into the marshmallow chair zone for several minutes of intense consolation.

Hewitt did her best to hover patiently. Eric Hubertus was the first to emerge, to approach her. He gave Hewitt a look that indicated it was okay now for her to get on with her business.

Hewitt began by apologizing, as she always did, for her hovering. The cocoon opened up and everyone settled into a seat, with Hubertus and Fournier book-ending Michael Boccachio on the couch, and the Fassbenders on the adjacent love seat. Which left Hewitt with the big zebra chair.

"Thank you for your cooperation at such a difficult time," Hewitt began. "I know this is a time of shock and grief for all of you. So I will respect that by moving through this as efficiently as possible. Here are the facts as we know them currently. As you know, Mr. Norris did not make an appearance for his appointments today either. We suspect foul play. But to this point we have not located him or determined his whereabouts. In addition, we have been unsuccessful in locating Dr. Boccachio. He is not considered a suspect at this time. However, he remains a person of interest. Now, with the crimes having directly touched this practice, you as the principals obviously need to be aware of the possibility that you may be targets as well."

Michael Boccachio's eyes hadn't left the floor during Hewitt's briefing. But the eyes of the four therapists had been tracking closely with every word. There was no flinching, no panic or surprise coming from them at the suggestion that their lives might be in danger. There was only a collegial resignation.

"What stands out to me here," Hewitt continued, "is the way the most recent act represents a shift in the behavior of the perpetrator. Prior to this, the targets have been married couples in marital crisis. This latest act, as you know, doesn't line up with that."

Hewitt let the last of it hang out there for acknowledgment. When it didn't come right away, Hewitt became extremely interested in the reason why. So did Michael Boccachio, as he finally looked up, joined Hewitt in looking to his mother's colleagues for the reason behind the delay.

"What?" he said, directing it to Autumn Fournier first, then the rest of them. "What is it?"

"They *were*, Michael," Autumn Fournier offered. "Your mother and Steve *were* married. Last year. On their trip to Las Vegas. She was reluctant to tell you. She was *afraid* to tell you."

"She was afraid to tell me because she was afraid he'd find out."

Deep inside the zebra chair, Hewitt was getting all of it. Fear was always the first thing you found in a killer's house. Fear projected out at the outside world. And, usually with greater intensity, the same fear alive and well inside the killer.

"He never forgave her for refusing to marry him. He never forgave her for sleeping with all those other men. He never forgave her for being a fucking slut."

Hewitt felt the opening, jumped in. "Michael, when I asked you before if you thought your father killed your mother, you said, 'If he did, he's already dead too.' What did you mean by that?"

Before she had finished the question, Hewitt knew she had violated every apparent rule of therapeutic practice. She saw it in the faces, felt it from the bodies of the four licensed therapists who surrounded her. But she had to let that go. Because her focus was on Michael Boccachio. And his, with a lifting of his eyes, was on her.

"I meant that whoever he was, he can't be anymore. He can't ever be again."

80

IN the western sky, the late August sun still had the better part of three hours to burn. But already, it had begun its long, slow bow. Hewitt was in a snarl of expressway traffic, her phone buzzing against her side. It was Brady calling. Like all men dealing with a woman in crisis, he wanted to know if he could do something. Which meant, of course, he wanted to do *anything*. Men weren't good at sitting back and watching the world fall apart. Not that women were. But women had an understanding that if one world fell apart, another one would take its place. Maybe the built-in womb had something to do with that.

Brady wanted to know if he could help. Help with the case. Help *her*. Put some groceries in the fridge. Put some new washers in her leaky faucets. All of it code, of course, for the fact that he wanted to comfort her physically. When the chores were done. So she said okay. Stop the hell over. Fix the damn leaks. Beginning with her head and the way her brain fluid seemed to be doing a slow drip from her ears. The Boccachio father-son team had become so active inside her skull, something had to give.

She signed off, heard him say *I love you* before she inadvertently clicked off. She should call him back, return the volley. But she set the phone on the passenger seat, looked at herself in the mirror.

Jesus Christ. She was getting married. She had the apron on already. She was smilingly giving away 60 percent of the bed. She was giving up her right to talk to the walls at night. Her curl-up space on the couch was in danger of becoming a commons. Her libido was going to be milked like a cow.

S HE was standing in the hot zone, microwave version. Her first cup, long gone. And what was left of the second had gone late August cold. So it was inside the perimeter of the sixteen squares of ceramic tile in her kitchen that she did her damnedest to earn the money the people of the State of Illinois were paying her. She went down her mental checklist again, did her little slow dance of the mind on the ceramic dance floor.

Maya Macy and Steve Norris were actually married. Effort had been made on the part of the principals at Big Shoulders to conceal this information from Michael Boccachio and, most probably, his father. And why exactly? Who the hell was Gerard Boccachio? The Hubertus-Fournier-Fassbender brain trust had once again ducked behind the collegial firewall when Hewitt had pushed for a little enlightenment. The bigger Gerard Boccachio question was, *Where the hell was he?* She had a wide net of ISP, county and municipal law enforcement looking for him. As of five minutes earlier—if Captain Spangler's news conference had started as planned, at the top of the hour for the six o'clock news broadcasts—the local and, for all practical matters, global media would begin to join in the hunt. The person of interest she had downplayed at Big Shoulders would become a media *cause célèbre*.

She had chosen not to watch the televised proceedings. Even though it had been her idea to stay out of the spotlight this time, it still made her anxious to view those machinations from the other side of the TV screen.

Her mental checklist fell to the floor as she startled at the sound of the front door pushing in. Which was idiotic. Future husbands with their own keys could do that.

"Brady?" she called.

"Were you expecting someone else?"—the call back.

She waited until he was near enough to the kitchen that she didn't have to raise her voice again.

"It was either you or the UPS guy finally acting on his primal urge. Whoever got here first to claim full ravaging rights."

"I didn't know you considered me to be the ravaging type."

She stepped out of the thinking zone so he could get past her to the refrigerator. Mixed berry juice. Two ice cubes. In a tumbler. She watched as he fulfilled the prophecy.

"I consider you to be like any man descended from the apes. Capable of anything."

He took a couple sips of the juice, stared her down over the rim of the tumbler.

"And what superior life-form are you descended from?"

"Ladies," she said. "Lady apes."

She had delivered her response in his next mid-sip. When the mixed berry juice actually made the trip up through his sinuses and down his nostrils, she regretted the timing. But in the screen capture she made of that image of him, she wouldn't have wanted it any other way.

There he was, her raging bull, taking a beating *from her*. Taking a beating and laughing his ass off.

In the side pocket of her summer blazer, her phone was going off. *Captain Spangler.*

"It's Jen," she heard him say, his voice shaken in a way she'd never heard before. "She didn't show up at day care. She didn't pick up Victoria. She's not answering her phone."

81

VICTORIA Spangler is the last child at day care. All the other kids have been picked up. All the other kids are safely with their parents. Watching cartoons. Drinking a juice box. Having a graham cracker. Except for one little girl.

She sits at the little plastic table, in the semidark of the day care play area. This is different for her. The play area has always been brightly lit before. The little girl stops what she's doing, stops her coloring, looks up, seems to know that the lights have been turned off because no one is coming back. The big people are gone. Everyone is gone.

If she cries, no one will hear it. Except her mother, who hears it now. From the dark side of the dream, the hallucination. Her mother is the only one who can hear her crying.

It took Jen Spangler several seconds to understand that she was conscious again. And not just conscious on the other side of death. But alive in some place. Some dark, closed space that smelled of antique wood and time and loneliness.

She was tied up, her hands and feet. And she was bound, wrapped in plastic in some kind of chair. And it hit her all at once, with greater impact than whatever had knocked her out in the offices of the *Mundelein Dispatch*, that she was alive but utterly dead in her ability to communicate with her daughter. To tell her that Grandpa would be coming to get her. To tell her it was okay to be the last one there.

She hears a flutter from somewhere else in the dark space. Like a single flap of a bird's wings. She hears it again, more of it, understands it is the sound of fabric, clothing on whoever is in the dark space with her.

"You were crying," Byron Biffle says to her. "Before you woke up, you were crying like a child."

82

SHE had most of the known universe of state law enforcement looking for Dr. Gerard Boccachio. She had the four principals from Big
Shoulders and Michael Boccachio in a surveillance quarantine. A concentrated search was under way for Steve Norris, or what was left of
him. And every estranged couple in the Greater Chicago area was on
alert, and probably being more civil with one another than they'd been
in a long time.

So Hewitt had no second thoughts about turning her focus at least
temporarily to another case—technically not a Missing Persons at that
point. But by the look on Ed Spangler's face as she and Brady met him at
the front door of his Skokie home, there was no need for an official stamp.

Inside, on the kitchen table, was the chaos of a SpaghettiOs and
frozen peas dinner mixed with several days of Jen Spangler's trackable
activities. Included was Jen's Mac notebook at the head of the table
where Ed Spangler's dinner plate would have otherwise been. And
adding to the cacophony of Post-its, notepaper and a handful of re-
ceipts was the distinctive smell of curry and chicken coming from the
two white boxes on the kitchen counter.

"The daycare was trying to get ahold of me. But the news conference ran over. And then I had to get the Thai food for Jen. I told her I'd
pick up dinner."

On the floor, next to the legs of her high chair, Victoria Spangler
had been crying from the time Hewitt and Brady had arrived at the

house. But now she really ramped it up. Brady took action, got down on the floor with her.

"So what do we know?" Hewitt asked Spangler.

"Well, based on how she's been acting lately, I had the sense she was seeing somebody. Somebody she didn't want me to know about."

On the floor, Brady picked up the empty Quaker Oats box Victoria had been playing with. He set it upright on the tile floor, canted it a little and gave it a spin.

"You've checked e-mails?"

"Nothing there," Spangler said. "If Jen wanted to fly under the radar, that's the last place she would've left something."

"Browsing history?"

On the floor, Brady had succeeded in getting the oatmeal box to go from wide wobbles to smaller and smaller ones, with the accelerating spinning sound.

"Most of the recent stuff is all around the Carlton Ritz case. And the victim. The young woman."

The final spins of the oatmeal box matched the tightening that ran up Hewitt's back.

"Phone records?"

"They're running them down. Our regular line and her cell phone."

"May I have a look in her room?" Hewitt asked.

"Please," Spangler responded. "Anything."

In the dozens of times she'd been in Ed Spangler's house, she had never been inside his daughter's room. She had passed it numerous times, let her eyes poke inside. But she'd never done anything more. Seeing the bedroom for the first time like this gave her a sick but all too familiar feeling. It was the feeling she always experienced when she got her first look at a victim's personal space.

So now, in Jennifer Spangler's bedroom—still so much a little girl's bedroom—every charm bracelet, perfume bottle, handbag, magazine and stuffed animal had that look of being utterly abandoned.

Jen's father had already gleaned what he considered to be the most viable materials from the room. But he was her father. Hewitt, like it or not, was the surrogate sister. And not much of one at that. Right now, though, she was all there was.

There was a musical jewelry box on the shelf above the writing desk. Hewitt didn't have time to assess whether she was drawn to it more as a potential storage place for secrets or because she just had to touch it. Because she was already on it, her less-than-steady fingers lifting the cover, springing free the ballerina, starting the plinking of the tune—"Dance of the Sugar Plum Fairy."

As the ballerina began to pirouette, Hewitt located the little sliding drawer at the base of the box, opened it, pulled the single item it contained into the light of the desk lamp. A bracelet. But not the kind Hewitt would have ever anticipated. The size of the plastic hospital bracelet was her first clue. Victoria Spangler's baby bracelet.

The revulsion hit Hewitt's solar plexus in one direct shot. The full implication. That the human being behind this precious archive had disappeared.

She was crossing the room, the baby bracelet still in her right hand. With her left, she drew open the thin middle drawer of Jen Spangler's dresser. A jewelry drawer, a cache for keepsakes. And that's exactly what she found. A flat, miniwarehouse of accessories and trinkets—and at the very back right-hand corner, a little stash of Post-it Notes, each one folded in half, with, on one side, a phone number. Just that. No names. No initials. Keepsake numbers. Maybe archived in some way. By category. *Good first dates. Interesting potential. Guys who liked kids.*

She was sifting through them now. All Chicago area codes. The expected set of local exchanges. Then, out of the yellow deck she was assembling, a number buzzed her eyes. The exchange—566. She felt the icy rattle in her chest, her lungs, even before she opened her notebook to confirm the location in Lake County that claimed the rights to that particular exchange.

Those three numbers and the final four digits were an exact match with the business line of the *Mundelein Dispatch*.

83

"I wrote him off," Hewitt said. "Every part of my being told me this guy wasn't capable."

She had already shared the details with Brady of how Jen Spangler had been loosely assigned to research the Carlton Ritz case, at Jen's iron-clad insistence and with her father's paper-thin blessing—an assignment that now seemed to have been taken beyond what the edge could hold.

"It's possible you're still right."

Brady's words reassured her. Not so much what he said. But the fact that he was there to say it, riding shotgun in the dark as the Mazda moved through the streets of Mundelein. The fact that after the altercation at the condo, she hadn't just dismissed him right there.

"I worked through the whole scenario," Hewitt said. "A guy grows up with a famous father who covered high-profile cases. Now he's dead-center middle-aged. Running some little local newspaper. So he creates some news of his own. Buttering his bread on both sides. Living up to his father. And pacifying whatever demons have been whispering in his ear all this time. I worked through all that. And this guy just didn't have the feel."

"Sometimes you just know," Brady said.

"Sometimes you do," Hewitt responded. "But then you find out later you didn't."

As the Mazda slithered up the street and she made her first visual contact with the old Victorian, Hewitt was glad as hell that she'd insisted that Captain Spangler not accompany her on the recon. Because, seeing it now, the house didn't just feel ominous, it felt desperate. And a father seeing that, feeling that, was a lot more likely to give in to the desperation. So Spangler had stayed home, maintaining his command post there, keeping an eye on his granddaughter, while he entrusted Hewitt to chase down the Mundelein lead.

They parked a half-block from the Victorian, split off to cover the entrances, Hewitt the back door, Brady the front. Before separating, Hewitt called his cell phone, opened a line. It paid dividends right away, saving her a walk to the front of the house when she found the back door not only unlocked, but slightly ajar.

She told herself to wait until Brady joined her before moving inside. But she didn't, pushing her way into the back hall, drawing her service revolver. Brady was quietly ascending the back steps. She held the door as he stepped inside.

"You get the basement," she whispered. "I'll take the first floor."

Brady's flashlight switched on, the light bouncing down the exposed basement steps. Hewitt moved toward the inside back door, slipped inside the first level, her mind superimposing the floor plan she'd stored from her previous visits.

She swept the first three rooms as they came to her. Production area. Kitchen. The back bathroom. No one. Nothing. Then it was across the house, to the warren of individual offices. She was approaching the first one, glancing inside, when the warning scream went off—a subtle scream in the form of a scent that gave her the first bad news. She moved past the first office, followed the scent to the next open door. Something citrusy, the same something Jen Spangler had applied in her bedroom earlier that day.

This office, not as abandoned as the first one. Someone had been at the desk. Someone who owned a Vera Bradley messenger bag. Hewitt knew, before she bent down and unzipped it. Seeing Jen's notebooks, her cosmetics, Altoids, her fucking wallet, made Hewitt cold, sick, devastated. She asked herself how Jen could have just walked into his lair unprotected. Then just as quickly, she realized Jen knew damn well what kind of world she was entering. The evidence was right there in the inner pocket of the messenger bag, in the form of the dated but very functional Smith & Wesson Hewitt lifted into the light.

Hewitt forced herself to stand, felt she would vomit if she inhaled Jen's perfume one more time. But she had to abandon her, she had to abandon Jen Spangler. It was the only way she had a chance of finding the woman who'd gone missing.

In Byron Biffle's office, there was more bad news. Blood on the floor. A single spill. But enough. She could hear Brady doing his best to move quietly through the house, coming to find her. She turned, saw him standing in the doorframe, a look on his face that scared her.

"What is it?" she said.

"*You,*" he answered. "What the hell did you find?"

Hewitt told him. Asked him to stay there. She mumbled about the upstairs living quarters where Biffle had told her he sometimes spent the night. Checking it out would be her assignment. His was to secure the first floor, in case someone came back. In case she didn't come back from upstairs. They shared a brief eye contact ceremony, which she was the first to exit.

The stairway to the second-floor residence was at the back of the house. She covered the distance, began to climb the old linoleum-covered steps. At the top of the stairs she found this door unlocked as well. Not just unlocked, but as if an invitation. An Open House. Would there be cookies and cups of punch on the kitchen table? First she had to make it through the front room.

Creepy. Victorian creepy. No attempt made to modernize the furniture, the rugs, the drapes, in any recent decade. If music played, it would be on a Victrola. But the current sound of this living space was dead air. Less than nothing. Hushed.

The first two bedrooms revealed the same. Antique house. Antique air. Stepping into the third bedroom, her lungs screamed at the sight of the faces that greeted her from behind the glass case. The collected eyes catching the trembling beam of the flashlight. *Dolls*. An antique doll collection. Fucking dolls.

The kitchen wasn't as startling, but just as empty. The host hadn't gone to any trouble. Hewitt crossed the kitchen, to the walk-in pantry, switched on the light. Sparsely provisioned, but with a cache of new opportunity. Another door at the back of the alcove. A door that, when opened, revealed a short stairway to the attic.

She ascended the steps, listened outside the closed attic door, felt the cold of the old metal doorknob.

Opening the door, stepping into the dark space, the awareness of another human form in the room hit her a split second before her flashlight found it.

84

"I'M as frightened as you are."

She was bound, hands and feet, and blindfolded. So he could go on like this, play this sick game with her for as long as he liked. And the only option she had left on earth was to play the game with him. Whatever he wanted, whatever the rules.

For now the rules were to insult her, to mock her, to reflect her predicament back to her in a way she could see with horrible clarity, despite the covering over her eyes.

"My hands, my feet, they're bound together," he said—again. She had lost the sense of how many times he'd told her this already. "My head is wrapped with something. Soft cloth. Fuzzy. Like a scarf."

She had to force herself to breathe. Whenever he spoke, her chest tightened around her lungs, her heart.

"Then you know how I feel," she said. "You know how bad it feels. You know how afraid I am."

"I can't help you," he said. "I wish I could. I blame myself for this. Please, you have to believe me."

"How can I believe you if you don't do anything but mock me?"

Until this point, she had played the game according to his lead. But now she had pushed on his feelings. And she could tell from the heaviness of his silence that he didn't like it.

Again, what he said was the opposite of the truth. *Always the opposite of the truth*. It was one of the rules of the game, for him. And now, not just in words, but feelings. Antifeelings. She knew now that he was the bra-turner. He was the one who had hit her at the tracks after she strayed into his grasshopper realm. The place he had returned to—to relive the original murder. And she had wandered right into it. The whole time at his offices, he had just played along.

And now he was crying. The fucking asshole was crying—for her. But it wasn't real. It couldn't be real. Nothing he said or did could be real anymore.

"I don't know who he is. I don't know what he wants," he told her.

More fucking lies. Blaming it on someone else. Someone inside him he couldn't control.

"I don't know what he wants. He won't tell me what he wants."

It was as if he expected her to know, to explain it to him. And with no one else there, and facing the prospect of dying there in his presence, she decided to tell him.

"He wants the same thing everybody wants," she said. "He wants the truth."

If it was the wrong thing to say, it would be the last mistake of her life. She waited, listening to his uneven breathing, until it steadied, stopped.

"The truth is what we tell ourselves it is. Until the day comes when we stop believing what we've been saying. And then there is no truth. There is no logic. There is no ethos. There is no code of conduct. And then we end up here. Just voices. Just voices in the dark."

85

I T was a dressing mannequin. If she had found it in a corner with the rest of the attic clutter, it would have been perfectly acceptable. But finding it, as she had, in the center of the space, it was as disturbing a way as there was to encounter such a thing.

More disturbing still was the way it had been dressed—with just the one article of clothing. Just a bra on the female form pedestal in the middle of Byron Biffle's attic. It told her more than she was ready to absorb. Because this wasn't just some dress-up game. This was the centerpiece of a ritual. And that, coupled with the evidence downstairs, was bad news for Jen Spangler and the people looking for her.

At that point, though, the bottom line was that the place had been abandoned. They would check the garage, the rest of the property. But it was clear that Byron Biffle and Jen Spangler had taken flight. The circumstances—the manner of flight, and to where—were the questions now. Those questions, added to the pile of bodies and missing heads. So the question of why the bra had been put on the dressing mannequin inside-out would have to take a number and wait.

She took the search downstairs again, joined Brady, worked with him in going through the office where Jen had evidently spent time on the mission she had either drawn up or been drawn into.

"So you think she talked her way in here, tried to infiltrate his world, with some kind of plan?" Brady posed.

By now Hewitt was inside Jen's messenger bag again, well into the contents.

"I'm sure of it."

The only corroboration she needed was already in her hands, in the form of a file with a black Moleskine notebook filled with writing, scribbling, that wasn't Jen's, wasn't a woman's. She set the notebook on the desktop, continued looking through the pages, smelled the mustiness of it mixing with Brady's cologne as he sidled up next to her.

"It's Carlton Ritz's," Hewitt said. "Something his son thought was worth keeping—and Jen thought was worth lifting."

"It's never a good idea to take a man's personal stuff," Brady offered. "Especially if you get caught."

"But if she got caught, why is it still here? Why was it still in the bag?"

"Maybe he just caught her poking around. He got pissed, got aggressive. He acted."

Hewitt slowed her shuffling as she came to several pages that were littered with a name that jumped out at her, pages dedicated to the story of Loreena White.

"I just can't see that," Hewitt said. "This guy was too meticulous. Even if he acted, he would have spent some time in cleanup."

Hewitt stopped her paging, as her eyes jumped to four words on the lower third of the page—as if the words had been marked with a blood-red highlighter.

"What is it?" Brady said.

"Real name: Grace D'Aquisto," Hewitt answered. She pointed to the words in the jagged, jittery handwriting. "Loreena White's real name was Grace D'Aquisto."

They left the house, were getting in the car, Hewitt on the passenger's side, when her phone began to buzz. Pete Megna calling.

"Radical news," she heard his hunched voice say. "We found Boccachio. But only from the shoulders down."

86

THE darkness was no longer holding. The darkness had begun to move, to revolve around her. It had been only a few seconds since the hinges made their sound, since the door opened. But in that time, the universe had changed. The darkness was no longer still. The darkness was flying everywhere.

He was trying to fight. Jen could hear him fighting. But it was a struggle he had no chance of winning.

"Tell me what you want. Tell me what you want . . ."

The second time he said it, his voice swung past her. There was the sound of clanking metal, a squeal at floor level, wheels being forced to turn.

"It's not my fault. What happened. What he did. It's not my fault."

The voice, moving away from her now. Wheeling away.

In a maelstrom, you had virtually no chance of surviving. But in a maelstrom in the dark, your chances were zero. And Jen Spangler was spinning helplessly in this vortex of retribution she'd been pulled into. And she didn't understand, couldn't imagine why she had become a character in whatever scenario was about to play out.

The realization that there was nothing to see, nothing to know, left her totally alone for the first time in her life. She felt herself crying. Not from the inside out. Not from the feeling that she had to cry. But from the movement of her body. The inward pull of her stomach muscles, the shuddering of her chest.

Who would raise her daughter? Who would nurse her father at the end of his life? Who would pick up her list of everything she still had to do?

The farther Byron Biffle moved away from her now, the greater his protests grew. Until there was a sudden, gurgling stoppage.

It was only moments then, when he returned for *her*. Now she was the one rolling in her chair, being pushed, transported. The idea that she would die tonight had been all around, had filled the space she'd shared with Byron Biffle. But it wasn't until now that she fully realized the possibility. Now that she was animated, awake inside the terrible dream of the man who had taken her.

"Please," she heard her voice say. "I have a child."

She felt a slight hesitation in the rolling of the wheelchair. She heard a click of his jaw, the beginning of a syllable in the back of his mouth. But no words came. And when they didn't, she felt a slight pulling back of her chair, a rocking backward to produce the forward push that began to move the chair again.

"I'm sorry," Jen offered him. "I'm sorry for what happened to you. But please, I'm not the one who should pay for it. My daughter shouldn't have to suffer the rest of her life."

The wheelchair slowed, stopped. She heard him moving around her, to the front of her chair, where he faced her, his voice coming directly at her, closing the distance in a soft whisper.

"God bless you."

She felt his fingers touching her forehead, touching her blindfold. Adjusting it. Pulling it down slightly. Pulling it a second time. And with the second pull, her upturned eyes saw him, caught just a blur of his face before it grew huge, pushing toward her, his lips kissing her gently in the center of her forehead, in a way she understood, knew intimately. The way a father kissed a daughter.

87

"I think she's alive," Hewitt said. "I think she's a prop. In a bigger drama. At least I hope to God that's what it is."

She had let Brady drive so she could continue to look through the black ink scribbling on the pages of the Moleskine notebook. She had never ridden in the passenger seat of her car before. It was rare she went anywhere without driving herself or making it very clear she was available to take the wheel at any time.

"What kind of drama?"

Brady's hands looked oversized and swollen on the steering wheel when she looked up to answer the question.

"Something connected to *Grace*. Not just the name. But the state. The whole context."

"And are you planning to share your Grace theory with Spangler?"

"Let me ask you a question first," Hewitt said. "If your daughter was missing and there was a chance she was alive somewhere, what would you do to save her?"

"That's easy. Anything. Everything."

She saw his hands tighten as he processed the thinking.

"Would you be more willing to risk your own life or the life of a colleague because it was your daughter?"

"Are you saying would I be more aggressive? More likely to make an error in judgment?"

"That's what I'm asking."

"I'd like to think I wouldn't. But I couldn't guarantee it."

"That's good to know," Hewitt said.

"In case someday we have a daughter who gets in trouble?"

It was a long time before she answered. And when she did, it wasn't with words. When her left hand touched his right hand on the steering wheel, she felt the vibrations of the road, the world, passing from the bones in the top of his hand, into the softness of her palm.

"We'll do everything we have to," he said. "That I *will* guarantee."

HER feet had found a couple of viable crooks in the juniper bush in which to ground themselves. The brick of the building was painful against her skin as she lifted herself up. Not the soft facade of a therapeutic institution, but the hardened face of a fortress.

While Brady explored other areas of St. Sebastian's exterior for a way in, Hewitt concentrated on the windows. The faint glow of light coming from inside had been her first indicator. Now she was looking for the source, the people, if any, who might be illuminated by it. If the windows had been normal glass, she would have already had the information she needed. But stained glass didn't give up its secrets easily. Although this window had attracted her because of a single piece of flesh-colored vulnerability—a small section of glass broken out from the panel that formed part of Christ's front foot in one of the stations of the cross.

Hewitt was struggling with her own feet, the left one slipping from its juniper perch. Regaining her hold, she found a higher push-off point. The result was that she now had a better sight line for looking through the puncture in the glass. Not only was there light inside the church, there was activity—a movement of shadows against the light source from the front of the church. But unless there was a shift in the location of the activity, she wouldn't be able to describe it in any more detail than that. Because the small opening in Christ's foot provided a view of the middle rows of pews and nothing more.

She lifted herself, leaned in to listen through the opening. She heard movement behind her, put her right hand to the window to assist her in turning. Her left foot slipped and she felt the slice of broken glass against her palm.

Brady came at her like a big cat out of tall grass, his face wide, his voice in a throaty whisper. "There's an open screen window that'll land you in the basement bathroom. It's too narrow for me. It'll have to be you. Unless you found something better."

"The only thing I found was the broken glass in Christ's foot," she said, holding her hand out to reveal the cut that was already pooling blood in her palm.

Brady reached into his jacket, pulled out a handkerchief, took her hand, began to wrap it.

"There's somebody inside," Hewitt said as Brady tied a knot in the makeshift bandage. "Let's go hit that window."

88

SHE went feet first, worming backward on her belly. And when her hips caught, she knew Brady was right. There was no way he could get through too. No way the wrestler could make weight. Between her wriggling and Brady's pushing on her shoulders she managed her way through, her feet finding the top of the toilet tank. With her right foot, she nudged the seat cover down. The plastic slap of it caromed off the hard surfaces of the bathroom.

"I'll work my way to the back entrance and let you in," she told Brady, who was down on his hands and knees so he could see her face.

"Be careful," he said, with uncharacteristic worry in his eyes that unnerved her a little.

She stepped down to the tile floor, turned on her flashlight, saw herself in the mirror, wasn't helped by the rattled-looking face she saw looking back. But that was understandable. She was in God's house now, starting at the bottom. And in that world, redemption usually didn't come without a price.

She exited the bathroom, moved through a short hallway, entered a multipurpose space of the church basement. She could smell stored coffee coming from a kitchen area, the scent of white bread.

She moved across the floor, her flashlight finding some children's art on the wall—little stained glass facsimiles of cut paper, depicting Mary, Jesus, the Cross and one that looked like a giant eye in the sky.

At the far end of the room, she came to a hallway that led to the stairs and the upper level. She paused there to listen. Quiet. But not just the normal quiet of a building. Church quiet.

She heard her shoes against the steps, tried to make them soundless. But they made their noise. And if that was the only noise in the church at that moment, there was something terribly wrong with her premise. With her plan. With her hope of a Mother and Child Reunion for Jen and Victoria. The thought of it, of those words, the Paul Simon song, sparked the ridiculous jazz improv section of her brain.

But that's where it died, as the upstairs of the church rushed at her all at once, pinning her there momentarily in the vestibule. Still, she was close enough to the main church, close enough to make out the sound of what she could only describe to herself as *lowing* coming from inside the church proper. And certainly not the lowing of an animal at a manger. This was a human voice, rising up from the deepest level of a soul.

Brady was standing outside the main doors of the church. She could feel him waiting. But the guttural cry, almost certainly a woman's now, pulled her across the narthex and to the closed doors of the church.

Through the window of the right-side door, she could see the body lying on the floor at the base of the altar. Opening the door, stepping inside the church, she was hit by the flowing current of scents—flowers, incense, candles, polished wood, consecrated dust. Borne on that indoor breeze was the heightened volume of the crying from the body on the floor. And as Hewitt moved down the aisle, approaching the midway point, it was clear the body had either fallen or had been deposited in the precise spot a bride would occupy during a marriage ceremony—in front of the altar, on the left side.

If Hewitt had been dressed in a wedding gown, with the eyes of two hundred guests on her, she couldn't have been more lucid than she was right now, two-thirds of the way to the altar. Still no ID on the female on the floor. The body was facing the altar. And there was a covering, a purple shawl or scarf around her head.

Just a few steps from her, and still she hadn't stopped the vocalizations, hadn't turned to see who was approaching. Right there with her now. But no reaction. Hewitt knelt down, reached out to touch the victim. Her hand made contact with the part of the body closest to her. The left lower leg, the calf. But there was something badly wrong. As if the leg was in spasm. Worse than that. As if it had died and fossilized.

"Father . . ."

The body turned. An arm moved with it, a hand lifting the purple veil, drawing it away from the face.

"Oh, my God."

Having heard the muffled version of the woman's voice through the closed door of Father Brian Wilson's office previously, Hewitt was surprised it had been the same one capable of the lowing.

"I thought you were Father Brian. I thought he came back."

"Why are you lying here?" Hewitt said. "Are you hurt?"

The woman smiled weakly, tragically, through the expressionless mask her face had become.

"I lost my leg to cancer. I lost my husband to that. I wish for ten minutes I could feel like I wasn't hurt. This is the one place that helps it all go away."

She had moved herself into a semikneeling position, as best as the prosthesis would allow. Hewitt sensed it was a position the woman spent a lot of time in, here on the hard marble floor, maybe finding some grounding in the submission, the pain of the pose.

"I've been coming here so often Father Brian gave me a key—for after hours when he's not here to let me in."

"So Father Wilson isn't here?"

"No."

"Do you know where he is?"

In the pocket of her blazer, Hewitt's phone was going off. She answered, told Brady she was okay, said she'd be out in a couple of minutes, returned her focus to the parishioner on the floor.

"Why are you looking for him?" the woman questioned.

"I think he can do what he does best—help me find some answers. Please, if you know where he is, it's important that you tell me."

The woman read Hewitt's face, seemed to commiserate with her. It appeared to calm her. Enough that her eyes softened and she smiled empathetically before she spoke.

"He's at St. Paul's in Palatine. It's been shut down by the archdiocese. And Father Brian's been overseeing the closing and the dispensation."

89

SHE wanted to scream. She had never wanted to scream more in her life. But as the blindfold fell to her lap, the world to which she opened her eyes whispered in multiple voices that screaming was of little use. Screaming would only make it worse.

They were arranged on the altar, where candles or flowers would have otherwise been. These things. The missing pieces of the case Hewitt and the rest of the world had been looking for. Here they were, and she was the one who had found them.

As the first wave of shock receded, Jen began to feel the rest of the church around her, the fact that she could see again, despite the near absence of illumination in the church. Just the candles at the front of the altar display.

Bound as she was to the wheelchair, wrapped in the layers of shipping plastic, she couldn't turn her chest and shoulders enough to see the man who had brought her here, who had choreographed this scene. So she didn't try, keeping her eyes straight ahead now, trained on the façade of the altar, but not on the faces that adorned it.

She couldn't see him. But she could hear him, his footsteps moving away from her, toward the back of the church, until she couldn't hear the sound of him anymore.

Alone in the church now. Alone with the heads. Alone with God.

"I'm here, Jennifer. I'm here."

This voice next to her. Out of the dark. To her right. The groom's side. She turned her face, just enough to see what the dancing candles revealed of his.

"I'm so sorry," Byron Biffle told her. "I'm so terribly sorry. I'm the one who deserves this. You're innocent. You've done nothing. But that's why it's you he's chosen. Because of that. Because you're innocent."

"Who," Jen said. "Who is he?"

She had asked in a whisper. He responded in kind.

"I don't know. I don't know his name. But I know why. He's here to defend her. He's here to seek atonement."

A cold wave of cognition washed over Jen. "Loreena White. This is for Loreena White."

Byron Biffle said nothing. But in the far edge of her vision, she saw his head nod. On the altar, the others seemed to quietly affirm his answer.

90

"So Spangler stays in the dark."

The whine of the Mazda engine was in the upper register of its range, at an interval that harmonized with Brady's monotones.

"For now, I guess that's the unofficial plan," Hewitt answered.

Brady let out some of the tension for both of them with a smokeless cigarette sigh.

"It's like the jazz you listen to," he said. "The way you work. By feel."

"Not always," Hewitt countered. "At the beginning you follow the chart. You play the notes."

"But like any good jazzman, you live for the solo."

"I guess I do," Hewitt said, cutting a little grace note with her own sigh. "This is turning into one of those *I'm glad we had this conversation* moments."

"How so?"

"Well, it's heartening to know that the man I'm pledged to marry has a feel for the nuances."

"Interesting."

"What?"

"Well again, a nuance. But you said *pledged*. The man I'm pledged to marry. As opposed to the man I'm *going* to marry."

"Pledged, betrothed," Hewitt offered. "It's what they say. Beats the hell out of *penciled in*."

"Yeah, you're right. Pledged it is. Close enough for jazz."

Her phone was humming again. She didn't pick up. "That's him. Captain Spangler."

"How do you know?"

"It's his timing."

"And so your response is . . ."

"There's an away message that's pledged to return his call. I have every intention of honoring it."

The Mazda engine filled the interlude, dropping a third, a fifth, as she tapped the brakes twice, waiting for a chance to pass an oil-burning pickup.

"My gut just tells me this is the way to handle it," Hewitt said. "Based on the situation, the feel. And something I've interpreted as a good omen."

"That I must've missed."

"At the church," Hewitt said. "The woman at the altar. Her name was Grace."

"Another woman named Grace."

"They're all named Grace. It's some kind of placeholder. A name used to protect the true identity of the women Father Wilson counsels—when he discusses things with colleagues."

Brady seemed to get it, to accept it. Which was good. Because she wasn't sure she fully did.

S HE was down to that. A one-legged woman in the fetal position for a good omen. And a secret name she was going to stake her claim on. Well, it wasn't always the quality of the evidence. It was what you did with it. And if you could turn the occasional good omen and a secret or two into something you could actually use, then that was all to the good.

They were off the expressway, rolling into the older residential section of Palatine. The older residential section of Palatine that no longer had enough churchgoing Catholics to keep St. Paul's alive.

"You know this city is seriously outside my jurisdiction," Brady said.

Hewitt's eyes were reading the road, the horizon, for the first appearance of St. Paul's. "You want me to formalize it? Okay. You hereby have the right to save my ass in the line of duty. Unless you choose to save yours first. In which case, I'll understand perfectly."

Though it was a moonless night, the church, when it emerged, cast a rising silhouette against the Illinois night.

"If memory and scar tissue serve me, I already took one for the team. I'm reasonably sure I'd do it again."

Brady reached across the front seat, put his hand on Hewitt's leg, just above the knee. He gave it a cupped hug, the way a person would touch a child's head with encouragement.

"I've got a good feeling about this," he told her.

"Good," she said. "Then I'm gonna go with that too."

91

A flurry of robes swept out of the dark and into the glow of the altar candles, pulling the light with it, making it bend, making it break. But light was adept at reorganizing, reconstituting. And once it did, the candlelight revealed that the flurry hadn't come from a multitude of fabrics, but from a single robe that hung from a priest's shoulders, a priest who faced them with a look of unadulterated compassion.

"A reading, from First Corinthians," he said in the voice he would normally use to project to a congregation. But the reverberation of it, in the otherwise empty church, caused him to bring his tone down, to focus just on them, as he conveyed the words from memory.

" 'If I speak in the tongues of men and angels, but have not love, I have become sounding brass or a tinkling symbol. And if I have prophecy and know all mysteries and knowledge, and if I have all faith so as to remove mountains, but have not love, I am nothing.' "

His eyes lowered to the floor. The edges of his robes fluttered with the shudder that came from within. When his face rose to engage the couple before him, the compassion had been compromised by a look of fear, a look of failure, as if the *nothing* he had just referenced applied to no one more directly than him.

" 'Love is long suffering, love is kind, it is not jealous, love does not boast, it is not inflated. It is not discourteous, it is not selfish, it is not irritable, it does not enumerate the evil. It does not rejoice over the wrong, but rejoices in the truth. It covers all things, it has faith for all things, it hopes in all things, it endures in all things.' "

By now Jen Spangler had recognized the words, the passages, had placed them in a context. And the knowledge, the awareness of it sucked the air from her lungs, drained the blood from her veins. She knew Byron Biffle had made the connection as well, could tell by the strange cocking of his head, the way he turned now and looked at her as the priest went on.

" 'Love never falls in ruins; but whether prophecies, they will be abolished; or tongues, they will cease; or knowledge, it will be superseded. For we know in part and we prophecy in part. But when the perfect comes, the imperfect will be superseded.' "

On the altar, the dead faces of the witnesses seemed to change their expressions with the flickering of the candles. But Jen couldn't look at them. She could only hang on to her mind, what was left of it, by focusing on the words of the priest, the way they formed and exited from his lips.

" 'When I was an infant, I spoke as an infant, I reckoned as an infant; when I became a man, I abolished the things of the infant. For now we see through a mirror in an enigma, but then face to face. Now I know in part, but then I shall know as I was fully known. But now remains faith, hope, love, these three; but the greatest of these is love.' "

For a moment, the priest closed his eyes. When they opened, it was first to Jen, then to Byron Biffle, then to both, in a fixed gaze he had used with dozens, hundreds of couples before. The subjects of his gaze knew what he was seeing, how he was transforming them. How he was seeing beyond the wheelchairs and the plastic wrapping and the gags he had returned to their mouths. How he had transformed them into a bride and groom standing before him, before God, in all their finery, with all their expectations, their hopes, their dreams.

His eyes beheld them that way. And the two celebrants had no choice but to look back, to seek in his strangely soft eyes some sense of who he was, of how, of why he could be doing this, of where the ceremony would go next.

Behind him, beyond the white robe, the heads on the altar seemed to wait for him too. This time, Jen couldn't make her eyes go elsewhere. As she looked at them, arranged in pairs, as couples, she saw something in the configuration she hadn't recognized before. The sets of human heads had been arranged in an incomplete circle. A circle that would be closed with the addition of one final couple.

Jen's eyes moved to the priest, to the soft movement of his robe, his right arm, as he reached into the folds, to a pocket. She heard a single gasping cry from Byron Biffle as the priest withdrew his hand.

92

THE homily was written on thin sheets of stationery that amplified the tremors of the priest's right hand as he delivered the words.

"What is it that brings two people together like this?"

He looked down at them in his collective gaze. But his eyes slowly shifted to Jen's right, to Byron Biffle.

"Of course, we hope the thing that brings two people together is the greatest of these—is, in fact, love. Certainly this is what God wishes. But as we all know, sometimes God and man have different ideas."

His eyes drifted over both of them again before he returned to his written words.

"Sometimes two people come together for other reasons. Sometimes two people come together for reasons that are beyond imagination. Let us share a story of one such union."

There was a flicker of one of the candles behind him on the altar. As if somehow the head nearest it had exhaled, sighed.

"It is the story of a young woman and an older man. As often happens, the man encountered the woman by chance. But he was so taken, so struck by her that, after the one chance meeting, he decided never to leave things to chance again."

He paused, as if the next words he encountered on the page surprised him, as if he regretted having written them, regretted the obligation to say them.

"*Fuck God.*"

The silence of the church that had enveloped their gathering swirled around them in a way Jen could feel, in a way that seemed to manifest in the rattling of the pages in the priest's hand. As he began to speak again, the pages steadied, but the sound of his voice did not.

"This was what he said, this man, upon experiencing the attractiveness of the younger woman. Not, *Praise God.* Or, *Thank God.* Or, *Dear God, what did I do to deserve such a vision?*"

Jen felt movement next to her. Not outward movement. But movement inwardly expressed. As if the already sunken soul of Byron Biffle was falling even farther. Before the priest spoke his next words, the sounds of that inward collapse became audible. It sounded at first like the opening note of a hymn. But it lengthened, became less musical, became what it was. The lowest form of crying.

"The older man knew the young woman was lost, separated from her family, separated from the people on this earth who might have actually been able to help her, *to love her.*"

The crying from Byron Biffle intensified. To the point that it distracted the priest. For a moment, he appeared to have an internal conversation with himself. Then he nodded, as if he had resolved a crucial issue. He stepped away from the altar, evanescing into the darkness beyond the reach of the candlelight. A moment later he returned, returning also to the written homily.

"He professed to a love of the young woman. Professed it not to her. But to himself, in a secret agreement, a codicil, secret perhaps even from himself. Yet the agreement was made. And the love that sealed it became impure, unclean, perverted. Until the worst possible expression of it was acted out. And the older man took the young woman's life."

The priest drew a breath, looked to both his celebrants, a harder look for the groom, a softer one for the bride.

"The greatest of these *is* love. But what is love without a heart whole enough to hold it? What is love without a heart pure enough to keep it pure, to prevent the forces of darkness from stealing it away?"

Jen could feel her wheelchair vibrating in slow waves. It wasn't coming from her. It was coming from the shaking of the wheelchair beside her. The outward crying had stopped and moved inward.

"Of course, God knew of this perversion of love. God always knows. And God knew of the taking of the young woman's life. But there was one other entity in the universe who also knew. And he is here, with us, now."

At this, as the priest focused on Byron Biffle, the crying stopped and was replaced by what would have been a shouted rebuttal if the gag had been removed from his mouth.

"Every father should have the opportunity to walk his daughter to the altar one day," the priest continued. "God willing. Well, God *was* willing. But the father of this man who sits before us took it upon himself to enforce his own will. And the son of this murderer knew—and worse yet, chose to withhold this knowledge from the rest of the world."

The struggle between Byron Biffle and the gag in his mouth peaked. If he could have forced open a hole in his chest or throat through which to speak, it would have happened by then. As it was, the syllables of his protest were voicing through his sternum.

"Yet in God's eyes it is never too late to confess one's sins. As long as there is breath in the body."

Here the priest again raised his eyes from the page, appeared to spend a moment in conference with his God before he stepped down from the altar and circled behind the couple, touching Jen's left shoulder with the fingers of his left hand before he took his position behind Byron Biffle.

Jen turned her face, slid her eyes to the right as the priest's hands lifted to Byron Biffle's neck, paused there before the agile fingers began to untie the gag. As the priest continued, Byron Biffle's attempts at expression ceased. When the gag was lifted away from his mouth, the silence held.

Jen felt the fingers of the priest's hand touch her right shoulder as he reversed his steps and returned to his position at the altar. When Byron Biffle broke the silence, it wasn't with a bellow, but with a small and almost steady voice, lower, deeper than Jen had heard before.

"Yes. Yes, what you say is true. My father killed her. My father created her death. And as her father—as I assume you to be—I apologize to you from the deepest part of my heart. I apologize for his actions. And for my silence. But not for my inactions."

If there had been a congregation, it would have murmured. As it was, the priest gave a cock of his head, looked at his pages as if for a prompt at what to say to this.

"He took photographs of her," Byron Biffle continued. "This runaway drug abuser he was basing his story on. I found some of the pictures, some of his notes. I . . . I felt compassion for her. And I saw her beauty as well. I started to follow him to his meetings with her. So I could see her in person—from a distance. The third time I followed him, I saw him do it. I saw him commit the murder. After he left, I went down to the tracks where he left her. I didn't hurt her. I didn't upset her. I just needed to be with her. In my own way."

The priest lowered his head in resignation. He would not lift it again until Byron Biffle's confession was complete.

"I never said anything to my father. I couldn't. I was in shock. I avoided him. Night and day. After the story broke, he kept going back to the site—pretending to continue to investigate. I think he was just going there to relive it. To retell it to himself. And one night I finally confronted him there. He struggled with me. I got him on the ground, next to the tracks. It was the third or fourth time I drove his head against the rail that killed him—I think. But I kept going. Maybe thirty seconds more. Then I left him in the tracks. Parallel to the rails. To make it harder to see him in the dark. To make it impossible for the next train to stop."

93

THERE were two vehicles in the St. Paul's parking lot. Both vans. One a Ford Econoline, the kind of solid utility van a Catholic church might purchase—or accept in donation—for pickups, deliveries, visits, the day-to-day needs of Christian transport. But after twenty years on the job, it was a relic, and its parking space appeared to be its final resting place—until the tow truck came.

It was the van parked nearby, nearer the side entrance, that had Hewitt's full attention. The basic-issue Town & Country. The perfect vehicle for a man on a mission. Whether it was the closing of a parish. Or opening night of his latest extravaganza.

"He's here," Hewitt said as she pushed the beam of her flashlight through the darkened glass of the van's rear window.

"And you're solid it's the priest, this Grace thing?" Brady said.

"If I wasn't before, I am now."

She didn't detect any swaths of blood in the vehicle's interior. But there was clear evidence it was the vehicle of a man of the cloth, right down to the religious pamphlets, the little box of rosaries.

They found the back door of the church locked. But there were two side windows at head level, one of which had to come out. Brady got the tire iron from Hewitt's trunk, wrapped his leather jacket around it and, with several well-placed pops, knocked the window out with a minimum of noise. There were a few shards of glass remaining in the bottom of the window frame. They did their best to pull these out. Brady then doubled up the leather jacket, draped it over the frame.

"This one's mine," he said. "I'll let you in the door."

He began his climb, shimmied his way up and in with ex-wrestler efficiency. Hewitt moved to the door, listened as Brady futzed with the lock, forcing the old deadbolt open with a single squeal.

The old door swung open and Hewitt joined Brady inside. They stepped a few feet into the building, Brady following Hewitt's lead, both pausing to listen to the same silence.

From there, Hewitt led the way down the hall, following the skittish snake of her flashlight over the wood floor. The wood giving way to polished stone as they passed through an archway, the beam of her light scattering with the change of surface. They could see it now. The church proper. They could see it because of the illumination that flowed from its open doors and paneled glass windows.

The flashlight dying like a scene-change spotlight as Hewitt and Brady converged on the entrance, their hands brushing incidentally, as their eyes read the totality of the inner church in the next crushing heartbeat.

Brady felt Hewitt's body sag against him. The arm he already had around her felt her words vibrate through the bones of her ribcage.

"Well, at least they left a light on for us."

They entered, began to move down the aisle, Brady's hand still on her back. A few steps past the halfway point, they moved into the wide beam of the lone light high above the altar.

"Why didn't you say something?" Hewitt asked as she slowed, stopped, turned, like an actor in the round. "Why the hell didn't you say something?"

"What exactly would you have wanted me to say?"

"How 'bout . . . 'You know, Hewitt, you're jamming down on the accelerator so hard you just missed the DEAD END sign.' "

"Not something I'd ever say," Brady told her. "Because the rules of the road don't apply to us. There are no dead ends. Sometimes we just run out of road."

"And then we crash."

"Sometimes. But then we crawl out and start walking."

"Fuck you," Hewitt said, loud enough to slap back from the walls of the empty sanctuary.

"You'll have to tell me why I deserved that."

"I wasn't saying it to you."

"Well, in that case, I'm sure God heard you loud and clear."

94

THERE had been no response from the priest to the confession. When he had heard Byron Biffle apologize for the last time, he nodded a slight acknowledgment then proceeded to leave the altar and approach Jen's chair. This time when he moved behind her, she felt both hands on her shoulders. Briefly, but not incidentally. There was a communication there. A communication Jen could feel even through the thick coat of her fear. A communication that penetrated to mind—that said, in words she could hear inside her head. *Be not afraid.*

The words were barely expressed when she felt the hands move to her neck, her hair, as he began now to loosen her knot. As the gag fell to her lap, words flooded her head, but none came to her mouth. She couldn't die here—in this cold, empty church. She couldn't die like this. She couldn't die in a union with this man next to her, this liar, this secret-keeper, this murderer. And she couldn't die at the soft, reassuring hands of a sick priest seeking multiple retribution for the murder of his daughter.

And she couldn't die *like that*, with her head falling to the floor, to be picked up by those soft, reassuring hands. To be displayed, celebrated. Because that's where this was all going. Just as soon as the service was complete.

He was already back at the altar. And he wasn't looking at her. He wasn't looking for any words of contrition or pleas for mercy. Because he now had one sick, twisted goal in mind. And that was to hear the forced vows. She knew he even had the rings ready. That was the reason, she understood now, that their left hands had been spared the plastic wrapping.

That was where he was going. Just as soon as he finished the silent conversation he was having with God. Or himself. Or both. Just as soon as his eyes came down from their fixed, prayerful focus at something above them all.

His face relented, his prayer either answered or not. He looked down at them, his eyes lingering on Jen, sadly, apologetically, as if a greater force was at work and it was his duty to be the instrument.

"Dearly beloved . . ."

And as the words continued, from his memory this time, Jen Spangler responded to the only impulse that came to her, from her own greater force. There was one more voice that needed to be heard. A name that needed to be remembered. And the choir girl was not going to die without one last song for God.

95

IT happened at the same time. Hewitt's eyes finding the information her brain was craving—on the St. Paul's bulletin she'd pulled from the old abandoned stack of them at the side of the sanctuary. The schedule of services—the weekend versions being held in the church they were now inside. The St. Paul's *Upper Church*. Which left the weekday morning services to be conducted in the St. Paul's *Lower Church*. That brilliant flash of lucidity had come to her at the same moment a human voice began to rise from below, faint but clear, and crystally so in the lyrics that had been chosen for this one perfect moment.

Amazing grace . . . How sweet the sound . . .

Hewitt had always been an only child, until that moment in the Upper Church of St. Paul's Catholic Parish. There were a lot of ways to meet your long-lost sister. But hearing her singing for her life was the kind of thing that made walls fall.

"Keep singing, baby," Hewitt said as she grabbed Brady's hand and they started toward the back of the church. "Whatever you do, keep singing."

In the vestibule, they found the passage that would take them downstairs. As they reached the stairway, moving quickly but as soundlessly as possible, Hewitt gave thanks that the thickness of the original floor in the Upper Church had allowed them to explore without announcing their presence. But her heart fell, dropping to the basement in advance of the rest of her, as she heard Jen reach her last line.

Was blind, but now I see.

"Once more, Jen," Hewitt whispered in the stony reverb of the stairwell. "One more time."

T HE tableau that presented was a shock. Not because Hewitt couldn't have imagined it. But because Father Brian Wilson was the one who actually had. Hewitt and Brady had seconds to assimilate the vision, to accept it. This mock marriage service, with bride and groom plasticized in matching wheelchairs. Jen Spangler and Byron Biffle, the bizarre couple slated to join the display of heads on the altar. And presiding over it all, a priest to whom she had almost seen fit to confide her personal feelings, her doubts, her fears about taking her own walk down the aisle.

The betrothed detectives were positioned in the Lower Church narthex, at the left side entrance, in the heavy shadows of a plaster arch. To the glory of God, Jen knew more than one verse of "Amazing Grace." She was singing again. And Hewitt understood. Stretching the timeframe. Expanding the universe. Not ready for a welcome home kiss from God just yet.

"I can't freeze him," Hewitt whispered. "If I call out, it could push him into action. I don't know what he's got up there for hardware."

"If you green light it," Brady breathed back, "I think I can squeeze off a shot and at least knock him down."

Brady's Glock was the only part of them catching any illumination from the candle display on the altar. Dim as the reflection would be, Hewitt ushered his gun out of the illumination.

"How sure?" Hewitt said.

"Ninety. Ninety-five."

"No good. I need a hundred plus."

Hewitt had every faith that at that range Brady could hit him, could miss Jen. But something in the second half of the second verse of "Amazing Grace" had pulled Hewitt's mind off the idea and onto the only next steps she could see.

"I'm going to walk in," she said. "I'm going to walk right down the aisle. And I need you to be an altar boy one more time."

96

H E had just stared at her the whole time with an uncomprehending look. A look that said, *Who are you? Who on God's earth are you?* But as she neared the end of the third verse, that spell was suddenly broken. The uncomprehending look replaced now by a higher order of mystification, as his eyes rose from hers, shot over her head and landed somewhere at the back of the church.

There was somebody back there. Jen could tell by the way the priest's eyes formed around the movement of a human body, the movement of a body toward him. Toward all of them.

She finished the verse, heard the words leave her, hover for a moment at the altar before a new voice sounded from the back of the church. A voice that thrilled her with possibility. But because of it, because there was a chance now, it frightened her to the core of her bones in the same instant.

"Please," she heard Elizabeth Hewitt say, in a clear, unafraid voice. "I wish to petition the Lord."

The priest's mask of bewilderment gave way to one of wonder. Out of habit, surprise, or both, he nodded, poised to listen.

"I wish to offer myself in exchange for the young woman at the altar," the voice continued. "She has had a child out of wedlock. I am childless. But I am engaged to be married. Let it be me instead of her. This is my petition to the Lord."

*   *   *

HEWITT'S left hand was still raised, her palm facing her so the priest could have a chance to see the reflection of the altar light in the facets of her diamond. Waiting for his response, her own eyes did their best to perform a private scan of the side and back of the sanctuary. Looking for the altar boy. But all she saw beyond the collection of sad, shocked faces on the altar was the fixed detail of the sanctuary walls, the white marble faces of a series of statues standing out against the gold, the gilt, the hallowed haze.

Hewitt slowed, stopped walking as the priest began to shape his face for a response. But in that same moment, behind him, in the back of the sanctuary, the face of one of the statues *moved*. The surge of realization that shot up Hewitt's spine was instantly vaporized by the shock of a bullet to her body and the report of the handgun that, in its elaborate echo through the church, seemed to have sounded after the impact.

She was hit in the abdomen, low. She pulled out her service revolver, let out a cry of pain that harmonized with Jen's scream. Behind the altar, the statue was moving. Only, of course, it wasn't a statue. It was a human body, at the top of which was a featureless mask. A body moving quickly, deftly from the right side of the sanctuary toward the priest, the wedding party.

Hewitt fired at the wavy, glowing ether just ahead and beneath the bouncing mask as the body that carried it rose from the shadow and into the candlelight. Her initial thought was that she'd hit flesh. But the body continued forward, brandishing a second weapon. This one, not designed for her, but for a member of the wedding party. And as she fired a second shot, the screaming flash of a wide, flat sword swung through the candles and lifted Byron Biffle's head several inches from its neck before gravity reclaimed it and pulled it down to the marble floor.

Stationary target that the mask wearer had become, Hewitt's third shot should have killed him. But the shot never came. Because in the follow-through of the swing, the swordsman's pirouette, he had struck the priest and claimed Jen. Crouched beside her, one knee in genuflection, he positioned the blade of the sword against the back of her neck, so that neither a shot from Hewitt nor one from her invisible partner could be chanced.

97

THE sisters were in trouble. In the immediate silence of the stand-off, Hewitt had come to understand that the drops of leaking water she was hearing against the church floor were actually coming from her, from the seal that had been broken in her lower body. And little sister. Sweet little sister. A life that had started the day in a little girl bedroom had ended up here, in the hands of a masked executioner.

Hewitt felt the first shocky wave roll through her nervous system. Everything she had left went into her hold of the weapon in her hand, the words that came from her voice.

"I repeat my offer. I no longer petition the Lord. I beg the Lord."

Behind Jen, the masked face twitched twice before the voice spoke.

"It does not become you to beg. Just as it does not become me to cower."

It was his first admission of weakness. Hewitt, knowing her consciousness was draining by the second, had no choice but to confront it.

"Then let her go. Put the sword on the floor and step away from her. I promise you will not be further harmed."

"*Further harmed . . .*"

The derision in his voice was absolute.

"What do you know of harm?"

"I know the harm I feel right now in my own body," Hewitt answered. "I know of the harm to Father Brian. I know of the harm to

Byron Biffle. The men and women represented on the altar. All these I know. But your harm, Dr. Boccachio, how could I possibly know?"

"You couldn't," the mask shot back. "You don't know him. You don't know anything about him."

"You're right, I never met him," Hewitt said as another wave of shock suffused her every cell. "Is he here? Is he here in God's house?"

The mask bowed. In the silence that followed, Hewitt could hear the liquid dripping again, could hear the way her breath was outpacing Jen's.

"He is here."

Adrenaline pushed through the shock, brought Hewitt's mind into a semblance of focus.

"Does he wish to say anything? Does he wish to talk?"

She felt the first buckling of her knees. Followed by a second, worse. At the same time she saw movement in the hands, movement of the sword, movement at the back of Jen's neck, heard Jen's cry.

"Please . . ."

Hewitt saw the head lift, roll, the long hair following up and over the movement. She forced her eyes back open, rejoiced that she'd flashed the wrong picture. Jen was still there. The hair still there against her shoulders.

"It was in the mirror," a voice said inside her head. It had to be. Because it was a new voice. She felt her knees giving out, the caps of them striking the floor. The jolt of it brought her back, in time to connect with the new voice. A man's voice, but with the vestigial nuances of a boy.

"I only saw them in the mirror. But that's where everything changed. When I watched them in the mirror, I could make them go away. I could make their faces disappear."

The voice stayed with Hewitt, even when the picture of Jen and the talking mask went blank. So she also missed the flash of lightning that must have preceded the roll of thunder that started in the distance but finally, and completely, penetrated the walls of the church. Enough that she felt the vibration of it in the bones of her legs against the floor. Enough that it forced her eyes open to the end of the world.

Because God had come. God had come and struck his own altar. With such force that it was lifting and causing the heads to come loose from their stands. To change their expressions from hopeless resignation to startled joy. Until, in one great offering, they were liberated and sent forward into the air, caterwauling to the church floor, gathering at the feet of their executioner.

Her sister's scream kept Hewitt's eyes open, long enough that she could witness the transfiguration. The rising of a body from the tomb of lost souls. The strong, living human form that took hold of the arms and shoulders of the mask wearer. In one great pull, dislodging him from Jen's chair, the mask breaking free and joining the faces on the floor.

Before the vision faded for the final time, she saw Brady's face, his strong neck straining as he fought to separate Dr. Gerard Boccachio from his instrument of death.

More lightning-less thunder as the struggle hit the floor. She heard Brady's voice cry out in pain, knew he had been cut, knew nothing else beyond the edges of consciousness that finally collapsed into the void.

98

IT was a wonderful sleep, a beautiful sleep. And it angered her, truly angered her, when someone intruded upon it just as she was almost, finally, at peace.

The percussion of footsteps in her left ear, the ear that was pressed hard to the cool, hard ground. The footsteps slow, deliberate, in the final moments of a long journey.

Her eyes fluttered, but didn't open. They tried again, this time the lids unsealing to the slow drip of blood from above hitting the floor inches from her face. Her brain seized, forcing her to see the reality. The sword, poised over her own head.

She looked up to accept her death, saw the wide, bloody blade. Saw the maskless face. Saw the miracle. Saw that God had already forgiven the killer, had made his eyes compassionate, had made his face the most beautiful thing she'd ever seen.

"EMTs are on the way," Brady said in a voice that made her know he'd been wounded, too, that the blood she'd awakened to had been his.

The sword played two sharp metallic notes as he set it to the floor. Already he had taken off his shirt, wrapped his hand in it so he could push as hard as he could against the lowest part of her belly.

"Hang on, Liz," he said. "Hang on, baby girl."

99

JEN Spangler sat at Hewitt's side in the ICU for fourteen hours. Longer than anyone else, including Hewitt's fiancé, and the father she shared with Hewitt, the father she was more willing to share with her now than ever before. At that point, fourteen hours into the vigil, Jen would have signed papers granting Hewitt exclusive rights if someone could guarantee her recovery.

There was a very strong possibility the bullet Hewitt had taken had also taken away her chances of having children. That it hadn't taken her life had come down to the grace of God. Life. Death. Coming down to a couple of centimeters either way in Elizabeth Hewitt's abdomen. Jen Spangler knew all about those life-granting centimeters. Only hers were etched in permanent marker on the back of her neck.

But alive was alive. And she would take it, *they* would take it. Her father would take it. Brady Richter would take it. Not only would they take it, they would run wild in the streets celebrating it. Even if, for now, running wild meant picking up Victoria from day care on time for her father, and wandering down to the hospital snack bar for some life-sustaining coffee and a sandwich for Brady.

Captain Spangler had been keeping a dutiful watch on his fallen trooper as well, checking in every few hours in person and every thirty minutes with the ICU nurses' desk. And Brady had been the classic warrior-boyfriend. After more than fifty stitches in his right shoulder and arm, he'd shrugged that off and put the full power of his healing will into the pretty woman—tubes and all—in the ICU bed.

Of course, Captain Ed Spangler had more than suggested to his daughter that she make her visit to Hewitt, say her prayer, and get herself into the same room with a psych trauma counselor he knew. But after the first several attempts, he stood down, with the understanding that Jen would take it up later on the recovery timeline.

Her shared vigil with Brady had been brilliantly simple. Almost as if the two of them were siblings too—which, through marriage, if things held, they'd eventually almost be. It was the unstated principle that if there was something that really needed to be said, you said it. If not, there was no expectation of talking for talking's sake.

Jen considered Elizabeth Taylor Hewitt a vocal person. So when she started to come around, Jen expected some kind of vocal accompaniment. A murmur. A groan. An expletive. But there was only a butterfly-quiet ripple across her eyelids. A half-opening of the eyes. Then a three-quarters. And finally, a *Hello World—what the hell did I do to deserve that?*

"Where is he?" Hewitt whispered in a voice that was much closer to dead than asleep.

"In custody and under psychiatric evaluation," Jen answered through her smile.

"I don't mean Boccachio," Hewitt managed, in something closer to her actual voice. "Where's Brady?"

"He went down to the cafeteria."

A smile hinted at Hewitt's features. "Coffee and grilled cheese. So he's okay?"

"Took a few stitches to the shoulder."

Hewitt exhaled, relieved. But the effort made her voice even weaker. "And how are you holding up? Jesus, Jen, I think between the two of us, I got the better deal."

"People heal," Jen said, instantly aware of exactly where she'd borrowed it from.

"That's what your dad always says," Hewitt offered, her eyes rolling a little, her lids losing their fight to stay open. She fought back, enough for a new line of questioning. "Father Wilson. Why did he do it—*how* did Boccachio make him do it?"

"He had a daughter. A twenty-year-old daughter. Boccachio abducted her, stashed her at his staging place—his deceased father's house in Mount Prospect. The priest had no choice but to play along, follow the script."

Hewitt grimaced. Not in pain for herself, but for what might have happened to the priest's daughter.

"Have they recovered her?"

"Yes."

"Recovered her *how*?"

"Alive," Jen told her. "Alive and okay."

"So Boccachio's talking, he's cooperating?"

"Not just that. According to my dad, he's concerned about the priest's daughter. He wants reassurance she's okay from the ordeal."

"Jesus," Hewitt said. And it was as if the peace of that name made her drift off. But only momentarily. When she drifted back, she had already moved to the next item of semiconscious business. "When Brady gets back, tell him to rub my feet. Even if I'm asleep."

"Okay, I'll tell him."

"One more thing," Hewitt's face said, the lips barely moving. "Tell him I like it when he calls me Liz."

"I'll tell him," Jen said.

Hewitt was out again. Except for that one last part of her that would always refuse to go quietly. "You found Grace in his notebook, too, didn't you?"

Jen nodded, smiled a sisterly smile. "That's why I sang it. I thought it might make him think. Shift his brain waves. Buy some time."

"Who would have guessed," Hewitt whispered, her eyes closing, her face finally letting go, "that Grace would be the key to everything?"

100

PEOPLE heal. Two weeks of that mystical human process had been enough to put Hewitt back in her safe place on the couch. She was able to move from room to room in the condo on her own. Movement she described to herself as a cross between an old lady and a ladybug.

She was sketching in her notebook again. Whether that activity was helping her to heal, she didn't know. But it *was* helping her to see. On these particular pages, it was helping her to visualize some of the details from the baseline report she'd received from Phillip Baker, the forensic psychiatrist who had the first crack at the exposed brain of Dr. Gerard Boccachio.

On the left-hand page were two wedding albums that had played holy hell with the subject's mind since he was a boy. The first album Hewitt sketched was the one the preadolescent Gerry Boccachio had destroyed by using an Exacto to cut out the heads of his parents in every photo in which they appeared. The second album Hewitt sketched was the one that had ultimately destroyed the man the boy grew into—the album he'd found less than a year earlier, in the attic of his boyhood home, a week after his widower father had died. It was a duplicate of the album he had destroyed, re-created in meticulous detail—as if, in the prisoner/patient's words, "*It wasn't just a copy. It was a reincarnation.*"

Hewitt thumbed back a couple of pages to the sketches she'd made of the train tracks near Union Station, her depictions of the original crime scene. The murder of Grace D'Aquisto, the name Loreena White had been known by until, less than a year into her life, she'd been given up for adoption. This action, unbeknownst to the biological father, because in his younger, bang-anything-that-moved life, a medical school student named Gerry Boccachio had knocked up a prostitute named Angela D'Aquisto.

Upon learning of the pregnancy, the young Boccachio had taken out a twenty-thousand-dollar student loan—a drop in the bucket for a future psychiatrist—and told his pregnant acquaintance to have a nice life. But life is a pretty resilient force. And the life of this abandoned daughter eventually washed up on the beaches of Chicago. Or rather, the tall grass near Union Station—where runaways had been known to make camp, and a heroine-dazed teen named Loreena White was on a muddled mission to find her estranged but well-to-do father. Only to have that mission cut short.

The body of Loreena White had gone unclaimed until Dr. Gerard Boccachio came across the stories by Carlton Ritz and pieced the puzzle together—at which point he had made an anonymous donation for a county burial. Later, when he heard through the psychiatric grapevine of a local newspaper owner who had shared an allegorical tale in his therapist's office of a terrible, though unnamed act committed by his father, it was only a matter of time until the festival of retribution began—the little photographic gifts serving as a shot across the bow for the hell to pay that would follow.

Hewitt reached out to the coffee table, took her mug, the silky chocolate still warm to her lips twenty minutes after she'd removed it from the microwave. She flipped the pages to her freshest sketches. These, of a married couple in bed, in the procreative act. Behind them, a long vanity-dresser, with the long mirror to match. How better to reflect the passionate activities of the participants? But with an unintended consequence that wouldn't bear its poison fruit for decades to come.

Hewitt had one last figure to add to the sketch. The smallest so far.

That was the thing with adolescent boys. They were still little, still fragile. But their keen eye to the world would never see things in more vivid detail.

Little Gerry B. Eleven years old. She drew him now. In the hallway position the grown-up version of him had described all these years later to a forensic psychiatrist. The place he'd observed from. Night after night. When the sounds had awakened him. Standing on a cedar chest in the hall, at an angle so he could see, through the always partially open door, not his parents, but the reflection of them in the mirror.

The repetition, the recycling of these pictures—the twisted, introverted, overwhelming shame—had driven him to destroy the wedding album. To remove the faces, the heads. Just as years later, he would remove the face of the witness to the acts by donning the featureless mask.

Gerard Boccachio had years to bake and decorate his own version of the wedding cake. All of it building to the two ghosts, in black tux and white dress, who would ultimately stand at the top. The bride, his lost daughter. The groom, an odd newspaper owner who had made the unforgivable mistake of censoring the story.

Dr. Boccachio hadn't been nearly as forthcoming in describing his relationship with the members of Big Shoulders Marriage and Family Therapies, the surviving number of whom had been officially reduced to four with the discovery of Steve Norris's disembodied head on the floor of St. Paul's. The body had been unwittingly discovered in the parking lot outside Dr. Gerard Boccachio's office, mocked up as the doctor himself, with the appropriate Brooks Brothers suit, Ralph Lauren wallet and all the proper identification. Without a head, of course, it was easier to disguise a body.

Hewitt had spent considerable time contemplating Boccachio's last move. The masquerade. It wasn't as if he would have gotten away with the switch. It would have been only a matter of time until Steve Norris's body was properly identified. So there was no grand illusion. No great escape. There was only, to Hewitt's mind, the advantage of throwing his pursuers off track, to buy the time he needed to execute his grand finale.

Regarding the Big Shoulders connection, the quartet of Gerard Boccachio, Maya Macy, Autumn Fournier and Dennis Fassbender had first hooked up in their University of Illinois Urbana-Champaign, days. How the cult of personality had cultivated itself from there Hewitt had yet to ascertain. Whatever had compelled the three marriage counselors to refer some of their clients to Boccachio years later was open to theories too. On the subject of referrals, one element the postinvestigation had clarified was that Naomi Nelson had, in fact, been a patient of Boccachio but had opted to keep the relationship under the radar—and outside the social stigma—by paying in cash and keeping her name off the records.

As for the therapists, whatever it was that had allowed them to either miss or elect to avoid the possibility that their esteemed colleague was a habitual killer was the big mystery for now. Who knew? Maybe it all started with a group therapy session in college with a little too much LSD in the punchbowl. Maybe a few sessions like that would have been enough to fit Gerry Boccachio with some sort of invisible crown, some kind of lifelong, Manson-like immunity from rational judgment. When she had the energy, Hewitt would probably poke into that one day. For her own peace of mind, if nothing else.

There was a knock on the front door of the condo. By that point, Hewitt had sketched everything of the young Gerry Boccachio but the facial features. For now she would leave it. Maybe she'd finish it later. Maybe it was already done.

She closed the sketchbook, set it on the couch beside the flowers and the handwritten letter she'd composed for her next visitor.

101

"NICE roses. From Detective Richter?" Captain Spangler said from the straight-back chair closest to Hewitt's couch spot. He caught the business tone of his "*Detective Richter*," amended it to "*Your fiancé.*"

"Actually, they're from Father Wilson."

"He ought to send you flowers every week for the rest of his life."

"Maybe he will. This is the second delivery already."

"How's he doing?"

"People heal," Hewitt said. "I believe that's one of the entries in the *Spangler Book of Quotes*. The good news for him was that the flat side of a sword doesn't cut like the blade."

"He can thank God for that."

Hewitt took a sip of her hot chocolate. Still just a hint of warmth at the back end of the sip.

"Actually I think he can thank his former deacon. The guy was pretty adept with that thing. If he'd wanted to take out Father Wilson, he would have. But he had no reason to. Father Wilson was just performing a role in the play."

"So Boccachio abducts the priest's daughter, stashes her, gets the priest to agree to anything and everything."

Hewitt took another sip. Definitely the last one before room temperature.

"And Jen," Spangler continued. "Exponentially wrong place, wrong time."

"Phil Baker, the FP who's been talking to him, says Boccachio revised his plans when he found Biffle and Jen together. He was just going to do Biffle. But when he found both of them, he saw opportunity, got creative."

Until then, Captain Spangler had been the perfect visitor to a recovering gunshot victim. Upbeat. Engaging. Nudging the envelope of humor. But all that left him now.

"Jen. Jesus, I can't believe how close . . . I can't believe I missed it."

"You didn't," Hewitt said. "She just decided to make herself missable. Hell, Ed, your daughter cracked the Carlton Ritz case."

He gave Hewitt a long look, tried to smile, managed only to raise his brow. "That's what scares me. Well, that's half of it."

"And the other half?"

"That Jen Spangler is a mini-you."

"Despite the fact she's at least an inch taller."

Now the corners of Spangler's mouth joined the brow in lifting, instantly taking ten years off his face. She hoped what she had for him next wouldn't put them right back on. She picked up the handwritten letter from the table, stood up, handed it to him.

"Leave of absence or resignation?" he said as he took it.

"I'm not sure. But definitely more than a leave."

"And for income—beyond the injury settlement?"

"There's a couple of people out west—more than a couple, actually—who for some insane reason, are interested in my story."

Now the captain's smile turned into a little laugh.

"Who plays me?"

"The young you, Brad Pitt. The more mature you, Brad Pitt with a little gray dye in his hair."

He was on his feet, hugging the hell out of her, the letter held in such a position that it would be safe from any tears.

102

PEOPLE heal. In the medical community, healing was often measured by the degree to which a patient had returned to normal activities. Swinging on a swing set wasn't a normal activity for a woman in her late thirties. Although if she had been feeling a little closer to normal three weeks after the shooting, she would have joined Father Brian Wilson on the playground swings at St. Sebastian's.

The walk from the church to the playground had been her idea. Walking was good. Walking helped the healing process. Walking was normal.

Hewitt sat down on the step-up platform of the monkey bars, a couple of giant steps from the swing Father Wilson occupied. It had been quiet for most of the walk over. It remained quiet for a while longer.

"How's your daughter?" Hewitt finally asked.

The priest's body slumped a little in the swing before he raised his face to her. "Thankfully, she seems to be doing okay. He never hurt her. She told me he didn't abduct her as much as he facilitated her movement to the basement of his father's house. *Father* in terms of his familial father. Not God."

"I got that," Hewitt said, feeling the look of kindness spreading over her face. She knew it wasn't all just to keep him talking.

"He was actually *gentle* with her," he offered in a voice that mirrored the gentleness of the claim.

"If you call giving someone an injection to sedate them and tying them up with no forwarding address *gentle*," Hewitt countered.

"She told me he assured her that after he took care of matters, he would come back and release her."

"What if he'd been killed?"

"I'm quite certain that never entered his plans. And as it turns out, it wasn't God's plan either."

"That's your area of expertise," Hewitt said. "I'll take your word for it."

To that point, the only movement of the swing had come from the kinetic effect of the priest's breathing. But now he pushed off a little with his feet, swung back and forth a couple of times before he stopped himself.

"He's not an—"

An gave it away. Hewitt supplied the rest.

"He's not an evil person?"

"No. No one can say that, can they? Especially me."

"You'd have a difficult time making the case."

"Which begs the question I know you came here to ask. If he was an evil person, how did I not know? How did I allow myself not to believe it?"

"Well posed," Hewitt responded. "As I'm sure your response will be."

"I'm not sure it will," he told her. "Because this is where it gets personal. Intensely personal. My daughter—my daughter was sexually abused as a child. She was only eight when her mother died. When I made my decision to enter the seminary, she went to live with my parents. A neighbor, the father of a girl her age who she was friends with, abused her during a camping trip. She never said anything to my parents. Or to me. But in the last couple of years, she came out with it. And Gerry was counseling her. Through that. Through the loss of her mother at such a young age. Through the betrayals, the loss of innocence no child should ever have to endure. Gerry was helping her. I feel he was *saving* her."

"So obviously she trusted him," Hewitt said. "She trusted him right down into that basement."

"She's alive," Father Wilson said. "And where there's life, there's hope. Isn't that the kind of thing I'm supposed to say?"

He stood up from the swing, his black oxfords moving against the wood chips. When he reached the monkey bars, he grabbed on to the nearest rung with his left hand.

"You could also say *where there's grace, there's hope*," Hewitt said. "Which brings me to my other question for you."

"Yes, I understand," he said as he pulled on the metal bar, as if to steady himself.

"Did you know her? Did you know *of* her?"

"I didn't," the priest answered. "But I wish to God I had. Because if he had ever told me about it, we would have had that in common. Maybe I could have helped. How much, I don't know. Enough to have kept this from happening?"

Hewitt felt her eyes brighten for him. "That's the thing about cases like this. There are some things we can determine. Other things we'll never know. But in this case, we do know Grace was the key."

He relinquished his hold on the metal bar, stepped back, his feet sinking into the wood chips. " ' 'Tis Grace that brought me safe thus far. And Grace will lead me home.' "

He hadn't sung it, but the effect was the same as if he had. Hewitt gave the last of the lyrics a respectful moment to fade.

"The lady who lost her leg—you called her Grace. If you hadn't, I would never have made the connection."

"That was something I picked up from him. From Gerry. Ethically, he couldn't refer to patients by their real names in discussing a case. He used Grace as a proxy. Obviously we understand why now. I liked the sound of it. What priest wouldn't like *Grace*? So I started using it, too, when there was a need to protect the innocent in a discussion, a homily, whatever."

Hewitt used one of the support rails to lift herself up, took a couple of steps toward the priest. For a moment, they stood there facing each other, like two people who were either going to fight or embrace.

"I'll tell you what," Hewitt said. "I thank God you did."

103

BY the end of September, she was a month into the healing process, a month into her new life as a person who wasn't handcuffed to one madman or another. And she was doing her damnedest to work things through via the sanest man she had ever met. Although in choosing her to be his future wife, his final sanity score had yet to be determined.

It was an early Saturday evening, and the coming hours held the promise of pizza, white wine and a purple-orange sunset. They'd been seeing a lot of those—when the atmosphere cooperated. Lately, it had been cooperating a lot, giving them the perfect backdrop, or perfect enough, for the evening walks that had become a habit when Brady visited for the night.

Which was a little weird for her. All those years she had walked that same route—*her route*—and now here was this guy with whom she was willing to share all of it. Not just the asphalt. But every wildflower along the path. Every bird. Every cloud. Every kiss of wind against their faces.

What the hell was happening to her? This bizarre, but strangely wonderful feeling that came over her with increasing frequency. Could it actually be relaxation? Could she dare to think it could be something as outlandish as letting go?

It was only a little past five thirty and Brady had a movie on in the condo living room. He'd come across the original *Godfather* on cable. Which meant, of course, they were going to watch at least a decent chunk of it. Brady had asked if it would be okay if he watched *just a couple scenes*. Which was a little like an alcoholic coming home to tell his wife he stopped for only a couple of cocktails.

She let him have his little indulgence. There were worse habits. And hell, there were probably no more than a hundred direct-hit gunshots in the Sonny Corleone execution scene. But on that evening, it seemed like a reasonable posttraumatic price to pay for relational harmony.

Well, that lovely sequence had come and gone. And unlike Sonny, Hewitt had survived. She'd survived a lot worse. She could survive worse again if she had to. But not now. Not for a while. And for the first time it played in her mind, maybe never.

On the TV, it was the scene where Vito Corleone and his men bring Sonny's body to the nervous undertaker, fulfilling a service contract the Don had prophesized in the beginning of the movie, at his daughter's wedding.

Hewitt closed her eyes, listened for Brady to say the line along with Marlon Brando.

"Look how they massacred my boy."

When she opened her eyes, it was to Brady's face, turned toward her, his eyes reflecting the tragic look in Brando's. And he wasn't kidding. Hewitt nodded reassuringly, let him know she empathized—with him, and the Don, the whole damn world.

T HE walk opened her lungs, her mind. And her thoughts began to coalesce around another massacred boy. One who hadn't been left dead in the causeway. One who was still very much alive. Michelangelo Boccachio. She was a little surprised, and more than a little relieved, that he hadn't attempted to contact her. Maybe his team of surrogate parents at Big Shoulders had counseled him as such. She was pretty sure she'd hear from him eventually. And they'd have their talk, she and the swimmer. And she would be okay with it. As long as the talk was held on dry land, with a warmed-up wrestler in the immediate vicinity.

The song was in her head now. The song that had been knocking on the door for a while—only she'd been a little too embarrassed to answer.

Like the others that had been playing in her mind during the whole crazy episode, it was a pop song. But a pop song that had come before the word *pop* meant something other than a dad or a soft drink.

The refrain was coming, and this time she let it play.

Going to the chapel and I'm gonna get ma-a-a-ried.

Well, wasn't that sweet? Wasn't that ideal? Walking down the road with the man who was willing to make that happen. Her walking partner, doing his best not to pull away from her. Of course, she still wasn't 100 percent, and he wanted to get his heart rate up at least a little. But for now, the speeding and slowing would just have to do.

For a moment, in the open field, she saw the vision again. Chopin playing. Poe composing. A Samurai ghost performing his art. And above them all, the omniscient, omnipotent offspring of the mother of God. She knew she could never again in her life interface with such manifest madness. And so she'd resolved that she wouldn't. She would simplify her life. She would simplify the world, if that's what it took. And the conduit to her passing into that world would be the simplest, most pleasurable things she could conjure. On this evening, it would consist of baked dough, tomato sauce, mozzarella cheese, mystery meat, and the nectar of fermented grapes.

Pizza and wine. There, that was a better vision. A lovely vision. Looking ahead, the purple-orange sunset was contributing to the projection. Earth. In all its glory. It was amazing the things you saw at the end of the world and the beginning of another. Especially when you lived to tell about it.

They were inside a quarter-mile now—not of where the world ended, but where the asphalt did, coming as it did to a stop at the edge of the woods, with the appropriate yellow and black signs to give drivers a heads-up.

"You're pretty quiet tonight," Brady said as he decelerated for her benefit once again.

"Just on the outside," she responded. "On the inside I'm trying to figure out who the best player would be for a jazz version of 'Chapel of Love.' "

He looked at her with a little smile, happy to have her there, happy to have her at all.

"And how's the search going?"

"Done," she said. "There's only one possibility. Mr. Miles Dewey Davis."

"Well, I'm glad that's resolved," he said as he pulled out his phone. "To celebrate, let's order a pizza."

"How about if we wait till we get back?" Hewitt said.

He hesitated, wanted to say something pizza-related, but didn't. By the time he put his cell phone back in his pocket, they were within a hundred yards of the turnaround.

"Since you brought up the chapel thing, I've got a question," he said. "As far as *I love you*, do you like to hear it a lot, a little? We never really discussed it."

"I guess I didn't know it was a potential topic," Hewitt said. "But since it's come up, let's say skewing to *a lot*. How about you—from me?"

"Oh, I'd be happy with once a day. With feeling."

"You got it."

They were both decelerating now. But instead of beginning the gradual swing back around, Hewitt kept going, leading them ahead until the road ended, where they both stopped.

"Well," Brady said.

"Well."

"Isn't this where we always turn around?"

Hewitt started moving again, her cross-trainers leaving the asphalt, negotiating the gravel and the little slide of ground that led down and then up again to where the grass gave way to thatch, then pine needles. She could hear Brady covering the same terrain behind her.

"Maybe it's time for a little adventure," she said as her hands began to make contact with the first wave of wildflowers.

"What did you have in mind?"

"I don't know. Something I've never done before. Or maybe *everything*."